UNBIDDEN HUNGER

OTHER BOOKS BY ANNA DURAND

Unbidden Hunger

Undercover Elementals, Book Five

Anna Durand

JACOBSVILLE BOOKS JB MARIETTA, OHIO

UNBIDDEN HUNGER

ISBN:978-1-949406-68-9 (paperback)
ISBN:978-1-949406-69-6 (ebook)
ISBN: 978-1-949406-70-2 (audiobook)

Manufactured in the United States.

Jacobsville Books
www.JacobsvilleBooks.com

Publisher's Cataloging-in-Publication Data
provided by Five Rainbows Cataloging Services

Names: Durand, Anna.
Title: Unbidden hunger / Anna Durand.
Description: Marietta, OH : Jacobsville Books, 2021. | Series: Undercover elementals, bk. 5.
Identifiers: ISBN 978-1-949406-68-9 (paperback) | ISBN: 978-1-949406-69-6 (ebook) | ISBN 978-1-949406-70-2 (audiobook)
Subjects: LCSH: Shapeshifting--Fiction. | Magic--Fiction. | Gods--Fiction. | Redemption--Fiction. | Romance fiction. | BISAC: FICTION / Romance / Paranormal / Shifters. | FICTION / Romance / Fantasy. | FICTION / Romance / Suspense. | GSAFD: Love stories. | Occult fiction. | Fantasy fiction. | Suspense fiction.
Classification: LCC PS3604.U724 U53 2021 (print) | LCC PS3604.U724 (ebook) | DDC 813/.6--dc23.

PROLOGUE

THERE IS A WORLD, PARALLEL TO THE ONE MOST HUMANS KNOW, THAT houses myriad species of supernatural beings. The world is called the Unseen realm, for it hides just beyond the comprehension of all but a few mortals. The elemental creatures of the Unseen once ran rampant in both worlds, abusing mortals for their own pleasure and caring not a whit for the damage they wrought. The Great Bargain ended the chaos these beings had caused, but even the elders of the elemental races could not have foreseen what the gods would do.

Mortals know them by name and belief, though not by their true nature. These are the beings memorialized in myths and legends, the supposedly fictional characters invented by humans to explain aspects of their own world that they could not understand. But mortals did not invent the gods of the Unseen realm. Their ancient ancestors wrote down the names of their deities, the all-too-real beings who visited them for the sole purpose of harvesting their devotion by magical means.

Why do they do this? Because the reverence of humans feeds them untold strength and utter dominion over all living things in either world. For millennia, these beings have stayed in their little kingdoms in the Unseen, satisfied with harvesting energy from their cadre of devotees. But now, the gods of the Unseen are no longer distant memories. They have gone too far, and the balancing powers must act. The Four Winds alone wield the authority to command the gods.

So today, we gather in our temple in the clouds to debate an issue that will decide the balance of power in the multiverse.

"The matter before us now is of the gravest importance," I say to the three beings convened with me here. "I urge you to consider the issue with the utmost gravity, for we risk more than our existence. We risk everything and everyone in the Unseen and the mortal realm, not to mention every corner of the multiverse."

"We all know what must be done," says Javren, his tone placid though faint wrinkles have formed around his eyes. "What other course is feasible? None. The being in question has flouted every tenet of the Great Bargain."

"But do we have the right to reshape any being's future?"

"That is our role as guardians, Miriella," Zerith says. He raises his chin, the way he often does when expressing his considered opinion. "We maintain order, and the being in question has threatened that order."

"Yes, and yet other gods have done the same. How can we punish one but not the others?"

"Zerith, I agree," Lartellon says, her voice as soft as a spring breeze, "but perhaps there is another way."

"None exists. We have sought advice from all the oracles, with each one providing the same prophecy."

Javren nods solemnly. "Yes, there appears to be no other option to prevent a catastrophe. Unless we will consider destruction."

I glance at each of my companions in turn. "We have discussed that option already. Even with our combined powers, the Four Winds cannot destroy a member of the primordial echelon without the participation of other gods and the most powerful elementals. It is a dangerous course to take."

"Which leaves us with one option," Lartellon says. "We must enact the plan before it is too late, before this one has gone too far."

"Javren and Lartellon are correct," Zerith says. "Hearing their words, I know them to be true. Are you yet in accord with us, Miriella? We all know of your fondness for mortals. You must see the necessity of this plan."

"As you know, I have love for all living things. But yes, I have become rather fond of the mortal world and its denizens."

I gaze up at the high ceiling of the temple and the swirling clouds that ever hang there, swirling and yet unmoving. Destruction is a violent act, and though the being we consider today has behaved abominably, I remain unconvinced that scattering of the god's essence is the best course. The plan presented by my companions offers the only compassionate course, and yet, they have included provisions that would leave a former god defenseless in a world that can be harsh and unforgiving. What else can we do? I've seen glimpses of humanity in the god, which gives me hope that salvation can be attained.

Humanity is more than a condition of slowly approaching death. It is…the heart and soul of every good being, the thing all must strive for if we are to save our worlds.

I face my companions, my voice imbued with all the gravity of the situation. "Let it be done."

Javren waves a hand, summoning the one who must enact the plan. The figure materializes within the circle formed by our gathering.

The god Janus looks to each of us in turn. "Why have you summoned me?"

"The problem we discussed with you has been decided," I say. "We require you to enact the solution."

"You shall destroy the one in question?"

"No." I shut my eyes briefly, then meet Janus's shimmering golden gaze. "We speak of the alternate plan. After much deliberation, we have agreed this is the only humane solution that will cause as little upheaval as possible in the mortal and Unseen realms."

"Is this not too severe a punishment? And what if the being proves incapable of reformation?"

"That is the risk we must take. Two worlds lie in the balance." I lean toward Janus, infusing my voice with the power and certainty of what must be done. "You know we do not make such a decision lightly. We urge you to do as we ask."

"You wish me to adhere to the parameters declared when first we discussed the issue."

"Precisely."

Janus bows his head, silent and unmoving for a long moment. Then he looks up and nods once. "Your will shall be done."

He vanishes—and the gears of time and space begin to crank.

I shut my eyes. "Oversoul, I beg you to protect us all. For we have done what we swore never to attempt, and the consequences may yet prove too dire for anyone to survive."

For the gods who once feared the one we are punishing will now see an opening and seize it. Perhaps my companions cannot foresee what will come, since they are not oracles, but I need no magically empowered foresight to understand. Power abhors a vacuum.

And we have just ripped a hole in the fabric of two worlds.

CHAPTER ONE

Travis

CLOSE YOUR EYES, INHALE DEEPLY, AND LET THE SWEET, SENSUAL AROMAS all around you penetrate your senses. Imagine a bed with scarlet silk sheets and the softest cushioning you've ever felt, and picture me dragging that silk across your skin while I taste every part of your body. Sink into the fantasy, and soon, I will make it real for you."

The blonde girl in my arms arches her back, grazing her torso against me, her lips falling open just enough that I could steal a taste of her if I wanted. She slides her tongue across her lower lip, moaning and tipping her head back to expose the slender column of her throat. The back of her head meets the brick wall behind her, and she writhes her hips as if she's desperate for me to give her what I promised.

Yes, I'll give it to her. In a minute or two. First, I need to get her so worked up that her lust will permeate her entire body.

I drag my tongue up her throat, groaning at the flavor of her skin. But it's the scent of her that drives me wild. She will taste incredible, I know that for sure, but I won't be eating her flesh. No, I plan to devour every iota of her sexual energy. That's what an incubus does, after all. I can't survive without that energy. How do I get it? By stripping this girl naked and giving her more pleasure than she could ever hope to receive from a mortal man. Oh yes, I love being a salamander, aka an incubus. When I'd been a mortal man, I did well enough with the ladies, but as a salamander… Oh yeah, I rock the bedroom. And anywhere else a girl wants me to take her—in both senses of the word. I could whisk this tasty morsel away to another world, literally, and show her my private lair in the Unseen realm, if I had a lair. I'm still shopping for the right one.

This girl won't want to say goodbye once she's had a taste of me.

Okay, I might've gone a little overboard there. But I honestly do love what I am. Most of the time.

"Yes," the blonde breathes. "Please, yes, I want all of that."

"And you'll get it—soon." I nibble on her earlobe, shuddering when a blast of hunger fires out of her into me, giving me a delicious appetizer. The taste of it intoxicates me. "Damn, you're hotter than the Texas sun in July. I ain't going to stop until you're too weak to move from all the pleasure I'm fixing to give you."

The girl's brows knit together. Her lips tighten, and she peels her lids open, fluttering them as if she's dazed. "What did you say?"

"I'm going to pleasure you for days, that's what I said." Not in those exact words, but that was the gist of it.

"No, the other thing." She pulls her head away from the wall. "Fixing to? Ain't? Pretty sure that's what you said."

Oh no, I did speak those words. I've spent months trying to shake off my old self, but sometimes it creeps back into my speech. Maybe I'm not one hundred percent committed to talking like a British person. The Unseen did arbitrarily decide to change my accent, without my permission. I was born a Texan and died a Texan, then I became a salamander. Nobody asked how I felt about that.

"Sorry," I tell the girl. "Forget what I just said. Let me show you—"

"Hold on." She bites one side of her bottom lip. "Why do you talk like a Texas cowboy when you have a British accent?"

Dammit all. Why do I keep slipping up?

"Never mind that," I say, tugging her closer. "I want to—"

She wriggles out of my arms. "Sorry, but the way you talk is creeping me out. I mean, make up your mind, huh? Are you British or are you a cowboy?"

"I can be both, you know." Now I sound annoyed. Perfect. That will convince this girl to let me seduce her for sure. Taking two slow breaths, I try to relax and recover from my blunder. "Let's start over. We were hitting it off a minute ago."

With more effort than I've needed to use in a long time, I amp up all the supernaturally enhanced pheromones I have inside me. I'd given her a low dose earlier, but now I release a large enough surge to make her swoon.

And she does just that. Her knees buckle, and I catch her.

I probably shouldn't have tried to seduce her in an alley, twenty feet away from a dumpster. But I need privacy for this.

Movement to my right catches my attention. I rotate my gaze in that direction without turning my head.

A woman is standing on the other side of the dumpster, staring at me with wide eyes.

Who in tarnation is that?

"Go away," I shout to her. "We're having a private moment, in case you hadn't noticed."

The woman just stares at me.

"Fine, watch us if that's how you roll." Since I plan to whisk this girl away soon, the pretty little spy won't see much. I turn my attention back to my quarry. "You want me, don't you?"

"Yes, oh God, yes."

A feminine snort of derision comes from the other side of the dumpster.

I don't want to look at the pretty voyeur, but I can't help it. The noise she made, full of condescension, spurs me to glance in her direction. No longer wide-eyed, she has her mouth twisted into a disgusted expression.

"Get your ass out of here," I shout. "Or I'll go over there and make you leave."

"Please," she says like she's the queen of the world and expects everyone to bow down to her. "Can't you get a girlfriend without drugging her senseless?"

The girl in my arms abruptly snaps out of her trance, probably because my annoyance with that obnoxious woman over there has doused all my pheromones. Dammit all to hell.

"I can't do this," the girl I've been trying to seduce announces. She shakes her head, biting her lip so hard it turns white. "Don't know what I was think-ing. I mean... No, this isn't right."

She scurries down the alley in the opposite direction from the giant trash receptacle.

And I stalk over to the woman who ruined my chances of feeding tonight. Once I round the corner of the dumpster, I get my first good look at her.

The woman is wearing what looks like a maid's uniform with a skirt and top as well as god-awful sensible shoes, but even her drab clothing can't de-tract from her sensual appeal. She has the kind of body any man, from any world, would love to enjoy all night—sensual curves, alabaster skin, raven hair tied into a ponytail that hangs down her back, and breasts that seem just the right size to fit in my palms. But it's her eyes that seize my attention. Their pale, greenish-gold color reminds me of a cat's eyes.

Yes, she is stunning. But the stupid girl wrecked my evening meal.

I tower over her, though she's of average height for a woman. Leaning in just enough to project menace, I hope, I speak in a growling tone. "What are you doing in an alley at night, alone? Do you want to be eaten by a monster?"

"Monster?" she says with a slight laugh. "Please. You aren't as terrifying as you think. I've seen much worse creatures than you."

"Then maybe you shouldn't hang out in dark alleys."

"Not my choice." She points toward the dumpster. "Trash goes in there."

I finally realize she has a large black plastic bag slumped on the ground behind her. "Why are you dumping your garbage here?"

The better question is why am I asking. The answer doesn't matter at all.

She rolls her eyes and huffs. "Because I work here. In this fleabag motel."

"Motel?"

"Are you mentally incompetent?" She points over her shoulder at the building behind her. "That's the motel."

"Oh. I see." That fact had escaped my attention because I had teleported my quarry straight into this alley and there's no sign back here announcing what the building is. "Well, go back to work, then."

She eyes me up and down, licking her lips. "Let's have sex."

"What?" Two seconds ago, she hated me. Now she wants to screw me? She's obnoxious and insane.

The woman gives me another oh-please look. "Are you deaf as well as blind? I said let's have sex. You were trying to get it on with that silly girl. Now I'm offering you the chance to enjoy sex with a real woman."

"No thanks. You stink of disinfectant and garbage." Mostly, though, I don't want to get it on with her because she's so damn annoying. But her body… Oh yeah, I'd love to explore that for days and days.

Her posture wilts. Her head hangs down, and she moans pitifully.

That is not fair. Why does she have to look so sad? I've never been able to tell a pitiful woman to go to hell. I should walk away right now. Find a less…complicated girl to seduce. Something about this one makes me uneasy, though I can't quite figure out the reason why. Mortals who aren't my friends find me intimidating, usually. This woman doesn't.

Time to exit this conversation.

I march down the alley until I'm sure the woman can't see me anymore, then I zip myself away to the place where I've taken up temporary residence, not far outside of town. No idea why I chose Phoenix as my new hunting ground, but I've just moved here, and I refuse to leave the area because of one rude woman. Since she seems to like hanging out in the run-down part of town, I can easily avoid her.

Whoever that woman was, I will never see her again.

Chapter Two

Larissa

I FLIP UP THE TOILET LID AND SHOVE THE CLEANING BRUSH INTO THE filthy water, scrubbing furiously in the vain hope I can make this hellhole they call a motel seem less like the bowels of a demon. Why can't people flush the toilet? Why can't men aim better when they urinate? And why oh why do people try to flush away unflushable objects?

Those are the questions I often ask myself, but they are not the most vital ones. I will never find the answers I truly need, not until *someone* decides to share them with me.

I breathe through my nostrils to avoid inhaling the stench and keep scrubbing. Never in a million years would I have volunteered to become the cleaning woman at a vile motel where people come to screw each other, for money or for free, staying only a few hours at most. I've learned they call this kind of place a "seedy" motel. I think "slimy, wretched garbage heap" sounds more appropriate.

And what do seeds have to do with anything?

Ugh. I don't want to know. It might involve "seed" of the sexual kind, and I do not need to endure the image of that type of fluid while I'm sanitizing a receptacle for…things I don't want to imagine.

No need to imagine. I've seen everything. Yes, *everything*.

I trudge out of the room, heading for the next one while lugging all my cleaning paraphernalia. Yeah, the motel owner is too cheap to buy the kind of cart any other place like this would have. I stop at the next door and knock, announcing, "Housekeeping. May I come in?"

Silence. That's my tacit permission to go in and clean up somebody else's bodily secretions.

But movement catches my eye, and I glance down the walkway.

A little girl huddles beside the door to a room three units down, her knees drawn up and her arms locked around them. Dark hair falls over her face because she has her head down. But I know she has beautiful brown eyes.

Setting down my stuff, I walk to where the girl sits. Then I kneel in front of her. "Mommy's busy with a friend again, hey?"

The girl raises her head, nodding while she bites her lip.

I know her name is Dani, and she's a sweet six-year-old who loves coloring books and daisies. That's all I know about her, since she rarely says much. But I've deduced the rest. Having seen her mother's "friends" coming and going from the room she rents by the month, it's obvious the woman is a prostitute. I don't look down on women like her. She's doing what she feels she has to do to survive, but my heart hurts for Dani. The little girl deserves better than getting locked outside while her mother takes care of business. In this neighborhood, it's not safe for a child as young as Dani to be out here alone.

At least her mother doesn't entertain "friends" every day.

"Want to come with me on my rounds again?" I ask.

Dani nods, her lips ticking up at the corners the tiniest bit.

I rise, and she gets up too. "How about we stop in the office to get some snacks first?"

"Chocolate?" she says in a soft, hesitant voice.

"Absolutely. Let's pig out."

She slips her little hand into mine while we head for the lobby, where the snack machines are. Then we eat chocolate-covered peanuts while we walk back to the room I'd been about to clean before I saw her. She helps carry my stuff into the room, and I turn on the TV so she can watch cartoons while I work.

By the time I finish cleaning all eighteen rooms, I feel achy all over and nauseous from the smell of disinfectant. Dani's mom has said goodbye to her "friend," so I drop the girl off there, then put my cleaning supplies back in the closet in the lobby.

I rub my aching back. God, I'd love a massage. Maybe that man I'd met in the alley would rub me down.

No, no, no. I might understand more than he thinks I do, but I am not stupid enough to beg a stranger to touch me. Except I had done that in the alley. Living a life of lonely desperation has made me, well, desperate for attention. Plus, I haven't been touched or kissed or screwed in ages. I miss physical intimacy, and I mean more than sex. For too long, I'd been spoiled by always having someone around to cater to my needs, and I'd never wanted for a companion who would massage me from head to toe and love doing that.

But is that true intimacy? I don't know anymore.

I can't resist envisioning his body, from his wild, glistening black hair that I would love to knot my fingers in, to his insanely muscular body and the jaw-dropping bulge in his pants. Though he'd glamoured to make himself appear essentially human, I know his true skin must be tanned with a hint of a coppery sheen. That's what all salamanders look like.

Now that I'm released from my daily servitude, I head home. Or I try to. Never had I lived in a city of any sort, much less a large one like this, before my circumstances were altered by means beyond my control. Once, I'd lived in the lap of luxury. Now, I need to stand on the curb waving my arms and shouting at every cab that drives by, praying one will stop to grant me the privilege of paying for a ride home.

After ten minutes of trying, I give up. Nobody wants to pick up a maid with disheveled hair and weird-colored stains on her skirt. So yet again, I'll need to walk home down a street as seedy as the place where I work.

I've gone one block when I see him.

Yes, *him*. The insolent jerk who thinks I don't understand anything. I'm used to others, especially male others, underestimating me. I'm not statuesque like all those models in magazines, which are apparently the gold standard for what a woman should look like. What complete nonsense. Men used to love my body. Women too. Everyone admired me and aspired to become like me.

Now I can't get a fucking taxi to pick me up.

When I see that obnoxious male, I stop walking and consider going down an alley to avoid him. But alleys make me anxious. Dark, smelly places inhabited by rats, and human vermin too. For a minute or two, I weigh my options. Risk the alley, or encounter *him*. Stinky vermin, or rude male. Stinky, rude. Stinky, rude.

The decision is made for me when *he* turns this way.

And of course, the jerk walks toward me, sauntering in a distinctly male way that always makes me feel warm. I never even try to quash my desire for anyone, even if that someone happens to be a complete asshole. Desire is the nectar of life. And damn, the scent of it wafts off him in steamy, delectable waves.

Oh no. I can't be falling for that old trick. I have never, never succumbed to it, and I refuse to do so now. *Turn off your crummy pheromones, incubus, before I turn them off for you.*

Not that I have a snowball's chance of doing that.

He stops ten feet away and smirks at me. "You again? Come back to beg me to—"

"Shut up, you caveman, and move your ass. You are in my way."

A chuckle rumbles out of him. "Damn, you are sassy. That's okay. Doesn't matter if you're a prissy prude who's got a stick up her ass. I'll fuck you anyway."

I huff. "Does that kind of crude talk actually work for you?"

He moves closer, narrowing the gap between us to an arm's length—my arm's length, not his. The man is huge. His voice becomes a sultry purr. "Since you heard me talking to that other girl, you know I can sweet-talk like no-body's business."

A tingle rushes over my skin, but it is not desire or anticipation. Absolutely not. I will never have sex with such a rude man, even if it has been far too long since I've enjoyed the company of…anyone. So what if I begged him for it earlier? That was one moment of insanity.

"Come on, sugar," he says, inching closer still. "Let me show you what I've got."

"Oh please. I know very well what you've got." I cross my arms. "Maybe you were doing an adequate job of sweet-talking that silly child, but you ruined it when you started talking like a cowboy in a cheesy B-western."

His lips tighten, and his eyes narrow.

It feels so good to knock him down a peg or two, since I haven't had the power to do that to anyone in such a long time. Maybe I enjoy it a little too much, because I can't stop my mouth from generating more caustic words. "No wonder that silly child ran away. Talking like an ignorant lout is not sexy. You might have big muscles, but you are—"

He rushes forward, grasping my upper arms, and pulls me into his body. Oh holy heaven, he feels good, all heat and hardness and male deliciousness. I haven't been this close to a man since—I swallow hard. Not since the night when another, much less polite man tried to stand in my way. I gave him a piece of my mind, and a piece of metal whacked into his skull.

The scent of this man envelops me in waves of spicy, seductive maleness. It's pheromones, I know that. But my body wants me to sag into him and tip my head back for a kiss.

No, no, positively no.

"Let go of me," I snarl.

"Why? You want me." He dips his head to sniff my neck, then groans. "Damn, you smell good. Can't wait to taste you."

"You wanted that stupid girl too. I don't like men who are so indiscriminate." Of course I like that kind. I love sex, period, and never used to care how I got it. Maybe I was kind of a slut, but I've changed my ways. Okay, maybe I was given no choice but to change. That's irrelevant right now.

"Don't pitch a hissy fit," he says in his British accent, which makes the words sound ludicrous. Then he drags his tongue up my throat while another, stronger wave of pheromones inundates my senses.

Oh my word, I want to beg him to take me. But I do not beg. Never.

"I can smell how much you want me," he says in that deeply erotic rumble.

"You're cheating. I only want you because you're an incubus." *Oh shit.* Why did I blurt that out? Now he knows I know, and that is never a safe situation to be in.

He lifts his head, squinting at me. "I'm a what?"

Since I've already jammed my filth-covered shoe in my mouth, I might as well keep going. "You are an incubus. That means you have supernatural pheromones that make it easy for a bumbling idiot like you to seduce women."

"Bumbling idiot?" He takes one large step backward. "I could've had you in five seconds flat. But I don't like stuck-up wannabe princesses who aren't as hot as they think and who stink like they've been swimming in a sewer."

Oh no. Do I actually stink? Damn that "seedy" motel.

I snap my spine straight and lift my chin. "Get out of my way. I have—well, things to do that are none of your business."

Microwave a frozen dinner, that's what I have to do. Those meals are almost as vile as the excrement I scrubbed out of toilets for eight hours today.

"What's your name, Your Highness?" he asks. "Just so I'll know what name to snarl the next time I bump into you."

"There will be no more bumping. Stay away from this area. It's mine." I don't want it, but yes, this grimy part of town has become my domain. No one else who inhabits this area would even know my name, much less agree that this neighborhood belongs to me. But I think of it as mine. When I gaze upon the giant asshole again, I can't stop myself from saying, "In fact, get out of Phoenix altogether. Go haunt another city where the women are much stupider."

He raises one brow and smirks. "It's yours? Sorry, Your Highness, but this is a free country. That means I can go wherever I want."

"Well, go someplace else."

"Maybe I will." He tips his head to the side, sliding his gaze down my body and back up again. "If you let me give you the most intense pleasure you will ever experience."

"All you care about is devouring sexual energy."

"Yeah, but I only get that if I make you come so hard your eyes roll back in your head."

That sounds wonderful. I want it, but I can't let him touch me. But oh, I need it.

"All right," I say, having no clue why I speak those words.

His brows hike up. "You're saying yes? The prissy princess wants me to fuck her the dirty way all night long?"

Oh yes, please do that to me.

Despite my lustful thoughts, I shrug. "You seem desperate for sex."

"Gee, thanks, Your Highness. I'm honored you would deign to do the nasty with me." He screws up his mouth and shakes his head. "Forget it. I can find a much nicer girl to seduce."

He turns to walk away.

I grab his arm. When he squints at me over his shoulder, I clear my throat. "Who are you, anyway?"

"Why do you care?"

"So I know whose name to add to the sex offender registry."

"You are one stone-cold piece of work." He twists his torso to haul me into his body with one arm lashed around my waist. "Travis Blackwell."

"Travis? That's a terrible name. And since when does an incubus have a surname?"

He shoves me away. "What's your perfect, high-and-mighty name, princess?"

"Larissa Robustelli."

"And you think my name is stupid," he says with a laugh. "Go on, scurry home to your castle, Larry."

"My name is Larissa, not Larry." That might not be my original name, but he doesn't need to know that. "Why don't you scurry home to your lair, caveman?"

He smacks my bottom. "You'll miss me. Go on, admit it."

"Ugh." I push past him, then whirl around to knee him in the groin. "Good riddance."

I stalk away from him.

Maybe I should've mentioned that I recognized his name. I've heard it more times than I can count, but I'd never met the man until today. It's hard to believe he is the same creature who helped save two worlds, twice. Or was it three times? Who cares.

But damn him, I stay awake half the night remembering how good that odious man smells.

Chapter Three

Travis

EVERYONE KNOWS WHAT CURIOSITY DOES TO A CAT, BUT FOR A SALA-mander, it can be both hot and dangerous. I was a cop in my previous life—a police officer in Texas, then the sheriff of Mandan County, Michigan—so I should know better than to stalk a woman. But that curiosity bug has bitten me, and I find myself shifting into my alternate form as a small red lizard and following Larissa Robustelli home.

Right, I believe that's her name. If she's an Italian porn star.

Something about the dark-haired beauty intrigues me and activates my law enforcement instincts. The woman is obnoxious, but I need to know who she really is. Any mortal who knows about the Unseen pings my radar and rouses the dormant cop in me. And no, I don't care that I'm mixing metaphors or similes or whatever the crap it is.

I skitter along behind Larissa, because skittering is all a salamander can do. Though it's hard to glamour when I'm this tiny, I manage to do that and make myself look like a rat instead of a cute red lizard so nobody will try to pick me up and take me home. I don't think I'm cute like this. Women do. My friends Harper and Lindsey sometimes beg me to shift into this form so they can pet my "itty-bitty cutie-pie head." Both women are married, but their husbands don't view me as a threat, despite the fact I'm a pheromone-laden incubus who needs lots and lots of sex. Maybe I should be offended that they don't worry I might seduce their wives. But all I can think about right now is the annoying woman with a silly name who knows too much about the Unseen.

Besides, I haven't seen my friends in five months—by choice.

Larissa has pulled further ahead of me, so I speed up my skittering to catch her. I do love watching her ass while she walks, but I love it even more when I get close enough that I can peek up her skirt. That woman has fantastic legs. She doesn't have any underwear on, so I can tell she has a fantastic ass too.

I know I shouldn't peek up her skirt, but I can't help it. Besides, if she doesn't want anyone to admire her butt from below, she ought to buy some underwear and make sure no salamanders are following her. That's right, it's her fault I'm licking my lizard lips while I imagine sinking my tiny teeth into one of those luscious cheeks.

What? She would only feel a pinch if I did that. My salamander teeth aren't all that sharp, and they're minuscule. Elemental girls I've gotten dirty with loved for me to shift into this form and nibble on them.

I bet Larissa is a dirty girl too.

She's walking an awfully long ways to get home. I watch her trying to hail a taxi, but nobody stops for her. What kind of morons are these guys? A hot girl flags them down, and they refuse to help her. If I turn back into a manlike incubus, I could sweep her up in my arms and teleport us both to my current hideout. I've got a bed so soft she'll moan when she lies down on it.

No, I don't want to take that obnoxious woman home. If I fuck her, I'll do that somewhere else. I bet she'd love it if I took her in an alley, despite the way she wrinkled her perfect little nose at the idea when I was trying to seduce the blonde.

Up ahead, an elderly woman drops her two bags of groceries, and every passerby sidesteps her.

Larissa kneels to help the woman.

What in the world? She's rude and prissy. I never would've thought she'd be a good Samaritan. But Larissa carries the woman's groceries until they reach the next corner, then the woman thanks her and gets on a bus. Larissa keeps walking, and I keep following her.

She veers into a building that looks like no one has painted it in about a thousand years. Things only get worse inside the lobby. My salamander feet stick to the floor, and I can smell things I wish I didn't smell and hear things I don't want to hear, like the unmistakable sound of someone retching nearby, though I can't see whoever it is. There's no elevator, so Larissa trudges up the stairs. I don't want to admire her ass now, because I'm starting to worry about how sanitary and secure this apartment building is, not to mention whether it might blow down if a large man farts outside the front doors.

No one should live in this place. It's awful. Maybe I ought to report it to the health department or the mayor's office or...something.

Larissa reaches her apartment and digs her keys out of her purse, then tries to unlock the door. She looks exhausted, and she drops the keys. I want to shift back into humanoid form, pick up those keys, and carry her into the apartment, but then she'll know I've been following her. Suddenly, I don't want to intrude on her dreary life, or maybe I don't want her to find out I've spied on her, possibly both. I still have questions I want answered, but this might not be the best way to find out what I need to know.

She snatches up her keys, unlocks the door, and shuffles inside.

I scamper along behind her, taking in the floor-level view of her apartment. It's clean but stark, with no carpeting, just worn linoleum. At least it doesn't stink in here. The faint scent of something flowery mingles with the aroma of vanilla, though it's a light scent too. The only decoration on the walls is a wrinkled map of ancient Egypt with all the big monuments noted on the legend and drawings of kings and queens along one side. It looks like the map came out of a magazine.

She's into history, I guess. But I don't see any books on the subject, or any other posters.

Now that we're inside her apartment, I stop glamouring to look like a rat.

Larissa takes off her shoes and carries them into the bedroom, which is separated from the rest of the apartment by a large sheet that's strung up using push pins. The bed has linens with a flower print pattern and a fuzzy blue blanket. They both look like she might've bought them in a thrift shop. A door on the other side of the makeshift room leads into a cramped bathroom with a cramped shower stall that I can see in the mirror above the sink. When she starts to unbutton her shirt, I know I should leave—the room, if not the apartment. But I can't move. The aroma of vanilla that permeates this tiny home is making me horny. Or maybe that happens because she's just tossed her shirt on the bed and is currently shimmying out of her skirt.

She's naked. Buck naked.

What is wrong with me? I squeeze my eyes shut because I should not be watching this woman undress. Surveillance is one thing, but this has become voyeurism. I'm not that kind of man. Or incubus. Or small red lizard.

I hear her moving around, then I hear the soft click of a door shutting.

She must've gone into the bathroom. Soon, I get confirmation of that fact when I hear the sensual sound of water running. She's taking a shower. Naked Larissa. Water sluicing down her alabaster skin. I crack my lids open, strictly to make sure she really is in the bathroom. I'm not hoping she's still standing naked in front of me or that she left the bathroom door open a crack so I could peek in there to see her showering. No, that would make me a pervert. But I am an incubus, which means I have strong sexual urges, more powerful than anything a human male could ever hope to feel, and those impulses can be overpowering at times. I've gotten much better at controlling the lust, but I don't think any salamander can ever completely master it.

That's no excuse. I shouldn't have watched her undress, even if I only saw her nude backside.

But now that Larissa is otherwise occupied, I have free rein to investigate her apartment and possibly find out how she knows about salamanders and exactly how deep her knowledge of the Unseen is. I shift back into human form and search the place. My task doesn't take more than a few minutes, and I find nothing at all to explain her knowledge of another world that few mortals take notice of, much less talk about with strangers.

The bathroom door clicks open.

I shift back into salamander form, shrinking out of view just in time since I'd been standing six feet from the bathroom when the door opened. I'd rooted around in her nightstand drawer a minute ago, but my search netted me exactly squat.

Larissa emerges from the bathroom wearing only a towel and carrying a blow dryer. She wanders into the kitchen, plugs in the appliance, and starts waving it around those wet, raven locks.

Time for me to skedaddle.

I hightail it for the front door—and freeze inches away. The space under the door is too narrow for me to squeeze through, even if I exhale all the air in my lungs and suck in my little red belly. *Dadgummit.* How can I get out of here without exposing my presence? I can't jump out the window since it's closed, and I'd noticed during my search that it's nailed shut.

Larissa shuts off the hair dryer and pads into her depressingly small makeshift bedroom.

I can't see her with the sheet blocking my view. Just as well. I don't need more temptation. No way in hell can I seduce a woman who knows too dang much about the world that made me what I am. Maybe I should hang out here until dawn, strictly to keep an eye on her so I'll know if she does anything…unusual. Anything that might give me a clue about how she knows about the Unseen.

No, I'm not sticking around because she's beautiful and sexy. And it's definitely not because I worry about her being alone in this crummy apartment complex, in a neighborhood that even a burglar wouldn't visit. This is still surveillance only.

I crawl under a table and curl up to sleep. With my supernatural salamander senses, I'll wake up the instant there's even the faintest sound.

Noises wake me sometime later. Sounds like gasping and soft but sharp cries of distress.

I scurry over to the bedroom, climb up the blanket at the foot, and skitter up Larissa's body until I can see her face. Her eyes dart behind the lids. She's dreaming. The noises she makes are part of whatever fantasy or nightmare her mind has created for her. Larissa is not dying or injured.

Relief makes me relax so abruptly that I sink onto my belly on the blanket and sigh.

Larissa's eyes flutter open. She glances down at me, and her lips gradually curve into the sexiest smile I've ever seen.

I perk up, raising onto my hind legs to smile back at her. Does she know it's me? If she does, then she must not mind that I'm lying on her chest, right between those perfect tits.

Her smile disintegrates. She flattens her lips, narrows her eyes, and hisses a breath out through her nostrils. "You slimy, disgusting, spying bastard. Get off me."

Suddenly, I can't move. No idea why. But I'm frozen here, gaping at her with my black salamander eyes and wondering who she thought I was before she decided it's me.

Larissa grasps my tail and leaps out of bed, hurrying toward the front door while I dangle upside-down from her fingers. With her other hand, she flings the door open. "I can believe you're so hard up for sex that you have to stalk women and sneak into their beds. But you are the most pathetic excuse for a salamander I have ever seen. Go away and leave me alone, or next time I'll cut your tail off with scissors, then move on to an even smaller part of your anatomy." She makes a scissor motion over the spot where my tiny salamander dick lies. "Stay away from me, Travis."

She tosses me out into the hall and slams the door.

Okay, I deserved that. But honestly, I wasn't spying when she caught me. I'd been checking to make sure she wasn't having a stroke or choking on her own saliva. She could be slightly grateful for that.

But I will respect her wishes and stay as far away from her as is reasonably possible.

Can't stand her, anyway, so that's no hardship. *Goodbye, Larissa with the completely fake-sounding stupid last name.*

I shift into my normal humanoid form and zip away.

Surveillance? Really? I've become that kind of ass, the type of guy who stalks a woman and then convinces himself he's doing a good deed. I've lost my mind, no doubt about it. Oh yeah, I'm the stupidest dadgum idiot on the planet.

And I'm thinking like a Texan again. *Shit.*

Chapter Four

Larissa

I TOSS AND TURN ALL NIGHT, LITERALLY, AND WAKE UP TANGLED IN THE sheets with the blanket wrapped around my ankles. My pillow has wound up on the floor. My nightie got pushed up under my breasts and twisted to the side, so I'm seriously stuck. I rub my eyes with the heels of my hands and yawn, then extricate myself from the mess caused by that stupid salamander. Why is Travis stalking me? If he doesn't want to have sex, then there's no reason for him to steal into my home in the dead of night.

How did he get in here? The door was locked.

Well, he's a supernatural being with magical powers. It wouldn't be that hard for him.

Great. I've got a supernatural stalker.

As I pull on my work uniform and head into the bathroom to wash my face and brush my teeth, my thoughts keep traveling back to last night. When I'd woken up to find a salamander on my chest, I'd experienced a ridiculous surge of excitement and happiness. My sleepy mind convinced me the creature watching me was the incubus I wanted to see, not the peeping salamander who calls me "princess" and tells me my alias is stupid. A man who talks like a Texas hick while speaking with a British accent shouldn't complain about my chosen name. At least my accent matches my slang. I sound and talk like an American.

But I'd been so happy when I thought the salamander in my bed was… the one I wanted to see. I can't ever see him again, though. After the things I'd done to that man, I wouldn't blame him for cursing my name and shouting to the world about what a rotten cow I am. Maybe I had been slightly obsessed with him and did my best to drag him back into my world again and again. I've outgrown that nonsense. I've changed.

Still, I cannot ever see him again. The thought makes me sad, but I know it's for the best.

On my way out of the apartment, I stop to gaze at the map of ancient Egypt pinned to the wall. When I'd first landed in this city, I hadn't known up from down and had no idea how to survive. My dreams of Egypt had kept me going. Dreams of things I'd done, things I wished I had done, and things I never could do. Having power over others doesn't mean a person has no limitations. I don't think anyone who knew me before understood that. They assumed I had all the answers, all the power, everything I could need or want. But now I realize I never had the most important thing of all.

I never knew love.

Whether I'm capable of love, I don't know. But I've never received it. I'm sure of that. Even now, I don't know if I ever truly loved the man I nearly destroyed. He will never forgive me, and I've accepted that, though I doubt I will ever move past what I'd done to drive him away. I don't deserve to get over it.

I run a finger along the map, following the path of the Nile from its origins deep inside the Two Kingdoms and along the twisting track to the delta. My life has been like that. Too long, too twisting, too uncertain. Like the Nile floods, my life has been an unending series of highs and lows.

Mostly lows.

Why did the powers that be do this to me? I know why in the specific sense, but not in the general one. Maybe I deserve to be cleaning toilets and struggling to eke out a meager living, with just enough money to keep from starving.

I leave the apartment and head to work, then I spend eight grueling hours cleaning up after people who think filth is a fashion statement. By the time I'm done for the day, everything aches—muscles, bones, even my hair hurts. I didn't see Dani today, but that probably means her mom took a day off and they're hanging out in their room. I've only spoken to Dani's mom twice, and she wasn't particularly pleasant to me. She found me talking to her daughter and seemed to think I'd infringed on her territory. At least the woman seems to feed her daughter, but leaving the girl alone outside whenever she's servicing her clients is not good parenting.

It's none of my business. I've considered calling social services, but I can't get involved with any kind of authorities. They'll want to know my personal details, like my age and where I'm from, and they'd probably want to see my driver's license. I have one of those, but it's not the, um, legally obtained variety. So no, I can't report Dani's mom to the authorities. I don't know the woman's name, and anyway, a foster home might not be a better place for the child.

I hate all the ambiguities in this world. Most of all, I hate that I can't fix the bad things.

That night, I lie in bed for hours while struggling to sleep. I doze off now and then, but it's not enough to refresh me. I need to relax, but my brain and body think I should stay awake and think about that horrid salamander, Travis. I despise him, but he is an incubus. That means he gives off wickedly erotic pheromones and has a body to match his biological hotness. Even though he's vile and a stalker, I wouldn't say no if he poofed into my bed and offered to get it on with me for hours. That would relax me, for sure.

Okay, yes, I'm pathetic. Two years without sex will do that to a girl.

Maybe I haven't had sex in that long, but it's been a lot longer than two years since I enjoyed sex. Way too long. I have no idea if Travis can give me real, scorching pleasure or if he's an impotent incubus. It wouldn't surprise me. I mean, the odious man can't even speak properly.

Since I don't have access to a living, breathing, pheromone-powered sex machine, I decide to take matters into my own hands. It probably won't alleviate my sleeping problem, but it's worth a shot. So what if I have never been able to give myself an orgasm? Apparently, I'm not only an evil cow but a frigid one too. It's been so damn long since I reveled in sex, but I don't think I've ever experienced a real, earth-shattering orgasm. Or even a halfway decent one.

I slip a hand under my nightie and begin to stroke myself while imagining an incubus is licking my flesh while his intoxicating pheromones intoxicate me. At first, the face I see is generic. Then it becomes the image of the salamander who had once been my closest friend, the one I'd hurt so badly he will never speak to me again. Finally, as I rub myself harder and faster, the face mutates into another salamander.

Travis.

My arousal intensifies while I picture him, that body, and imagine how it would feel to have him inside me, thrusting faster and harder every second. Oh God, I'm almost there. So close. I imagine Travis flipping me over and taking me from behind while he clamps one hand over my breast and shoves the other between my thighs to pinch my taut nub.

"Oh yes, yes, yes," I moan while my back arches.

So damn close. Any second. I'm—almost—

The orgasm I'd been so close to having that I swear I could taste it…fizzles out. I stroke myself some more but can't get it back. Why am I incapable of experiencing sexual pleasure? I suppose I'd gone without it for so long that I'll need more than a fantasy to push me over the edge. I need someone to fuck me. Honestly, why is it so hard to find a man who can handle me? I thought guys wanted sex anytime, anywhere, with any woman. But every man I've tried to seduce turned me down.

Maybe there is something horribly wrong with me.

Duh, of course there is. You're a horrible person.

Am I still the bitch I used to be? Everything I had then has been torn away from me, and I don't feel like that woman anymore.

Doesn't matter how I feel or what I want. The powers that be will determine my fate. And apparently, they want me to suffer eternal frustration of the sexual variety while being tormented by the sexiest salamander in the multiverse.

The next day is Friday, which means I have the weekend to throw myself into the kind of behavior I used to love and try to seduce a man who doesn't turn his nose up at me or act like I'm too annoying to live. Maybe I should try a nightclub, where people go to hook up with anonymous strangers for a quick roll in the hay. Anonymity might be my only hope. I probably shouldn't speak either, or make any facial expressions. That stuff always gets me into trouble.

I used to be powerful. Now I scrub toilets. So yeah, sometimes I get a little uppity, but only when someone goads me into it.

Change is hard. So goddamn hard.

After work, I hurry home to shower, dry my hair, put on some makeup, and apply temporary color foam to add purple streaks to my raven hair. I need to look mysterious and tempting. I also change into a sexy outfit that's appropriate for a nightclub, then I grab a taxi. Yes, I have a much easier time getting those jerks to stop for me when I'm dressed in a skimpy outfit and don't smell like a backed-up toilet. I arrive at my destination ten minutes later and, after paying the cover charge, I sashay into the club. Naturally, I'm sashaying on purpose to make myself more alluring to the men in this place.

I've baited the hook. *So please, please, somebody grab onto it.*

Don't think I can survive another round of rejections.

CHAPTER FIVE

Travis

FOR PRECISELY FORTY-FIVE HOURS AND EIGHTEEN MINUTES, I STAY AWAY from Phoenix, Arizona. I can go anywhere I want, whenever I want, just by thinking about whatever place is it. So I zip around the world from city to city and even into remote oases in the deserts of various continents, planning to seduce as many women as possible. Not that I'm starving. Unlike my mentor, Max, I have never let my energy levels deplete to the point of starvation. I have no trouble finding bedmates.

But I don't seduce anyone.

Why? Because I keep thinking about the annoying woman I met in Phoenix, the one who ruined my chances of getting laid. I don't want that obnoxious girl, the one with raven hair and beautiful eyes. No, I don't want her. I'm just…not in the mood for sex.

Right. An incubus doesn't want sex.

Maybe I should talk to Max about my sudden lack of desire. He's my mentor, and he was responsible for turning me into a salamander when I was on the verge of death. But I can't talk to him. For the better part of five months, I've stayed away from everyone I know, both humans and elementals. I don't want to see anyone. Why? Because I finally realized I need to break free of my past and find a way to forge a new path for myself.

I haven't exactly done a bang-up job of that. But I can do it. I have to.

Breaking free of the past isn't as easy as it sounds.

So, after forty-five hours and eighteen minutes of trying my damnedest not to go back to Phoenix, I do it anyway. The city is big enough that I can troll the clubs for a lover without running into that obnoxious girl. Besides, she'll be busy cleaning sewers or whatever she does for a living that makes her smell that way.

I teleport onto the top of a tall building and sniff the air, searching for a den of iniquity, aka a nightclub. There, I've caught the scent. Clubs are full of desperate people indulging in every kind of naughty behavior, but I ignore all of it except for the distinctive aroma of lust. One club in particular smells of it more than the others, which means I've found my hunting ground for tonight.

Zipping myself straight into the club, I saunter down the darkened entryway and into the main area where music blares loud enough that a deaf person would wince. I notice other patrons of this club all have the same stamp on their hands—to show they paid for entry, no doubt, unlike me. I glamour the stamp onto my hand so no one will realize I've crashed the party. At the edge of the dance floor, I stop to survey the options. Men and women gather in pairs and groups, writhing and thrusting their hips, waving their arms, bumping into each other on purpose in the most bizarre sort of mating ritual. Even as a human, I'd never understood clubs. They're noisy and dark, but with blinding flashes of light too, and the floors are always sticky.

Does nobody know how to use a frigging mop?

My gaze lands on a woman who stands slightly apart from the throng, at the periphery of the dance floor. Her dark hair has streaks of deep purple in it, and the wavy locks bounce in time with the swaying of her body as she tips her head from side to side in a sensual rhythm. Her short skirt clings to her thighs while the short top she wears exposes her midsection. I watch her hips, the way they rock and gyrate, and I can't help imagining what it would feel like to grip those hips and drive into her from behind. The scent of her desire rolls off her in sensuous waves, so powerful that I suck in a sharp breath and let the intoxicating scent penetrate my senses.

A man approaches her, mimicking her dance moves like he wants to join in.

Oh no, that cockroach is not horning in on my score.

I saunter up behind the woman. She doesn't seem to have noticed me yet, but the cockroach has. I give him a scorching glare—literally, since my eyes flare with molten shades of copper and blood red.

He blanches, then turns and scurries away like the insect he is.

And I move closer to the woman, who still hasn't noticed me. Maybe she's so entranced by the music that she doesn't see anything. I let my pheromones envelop her as I clasp my hands around her hips and tug her backward into me, sliding my palms over her belly.

She leans that sexy body into me.

I still can't see her face, but she feels incredible, so I dip my head to whisper in her ear. "What is a woman like you doing all alone in a club?"

All right, maybe that isn't the most seductive opening line. But my pheromones are inundating her senses, which means I don't need to be on my A-game to get her naked.

The girl freezes.

Not the response I was hoping for, but maybe I just need to dose her a little more with my secret weapon. Pheromones always do the trick.

She wriggles free of me and whirls around. Her eyes go wide. "Ugh, not you again."

My jaw drops. It's her, the high-and-mighty princess of the sewer. "How—What are you doing here?"

"Same as you, Casanova. Trying to get laid."

"At least you don't stink tonight."

Larissa bars her arms over her chest. "No wonder you can't get any action if that's how you talk to a lady."

"I talk to ladies just fine. It's stuck-up little goody-goodies I can't stomach."

She waves a hand in a regally dismissive gesture. "Leave me, you oaf."

Bending closer, I grind words out through my clenched teeth. "You leave. This is my turf, princess."

She lifts her chin. "Make me."

Oh, she really shouldn't have said that.

I pick her up and throw the stuck-up girl over my shoulder, then I whisk us away to the alley where I'd first seen the little witch. I dump her on the ground, where she lands in a very unladylike pose. Her skirt has ridden up so high that I can tell she doesn't have any underwear on.

And fuck, I can smell her lust.

She lies there in a jumble of legs and arms, her hair stuck to her face, and blows out a breath that flutters those black-and-purple locks but doesn't quite dislodge them. "Are you going to help me up or not?"

"Help yourself. You are the queen of the sewers, after all, and I wouldn't deign to touch a goddess like you."

She goes stone-still, seeming not to even breathe. Through the veil of her hair, I can tell she's gaping at me wide-eyed.

What did I say? All right, maybe I shouldn't have called her queen of the sewers. And yes, I guess I've been kind of a dick to her, but she hasn't been very nice to me either.

What, now I'm twelve years old again? Next, I'll stick my tongue out at her and say "nah-nah-nah-nah-nahhhh-nah."

Shit. I bend to offer her my hands.

Larissa lifts her chin, but then sighs and takes my hands.

I heft her off the grimy asphalt and brush the hair away from her face. "Sorry. I shouldn't have dumped you on the ground like garbage."

"Why not? I'm the queen of the sewers."

Since her lips curved up a touch when she said that, I start to wonder if she's teasing me. Well, she is hot as sin. Maybe I should seduce her. Then I'll be able to stop fantasizing about her and move on.

I remember what she was doing when I first saw her in the club, and I start to wonder again, though not about whether she was teasing me a minute ago. "Why were you alone in that club, dancing by yourself?"

"You scared away my only prospect, you big oaf."

"Only prospect? But you're a beautiful, sexy woman. Why can't you get anyone to dance with you?"

She stares at her feet and mumbles something I can't make out.

"What was that?" I ask.

"Forget it."

I hook a finger under her chin and lift until our gazes align. "Tell me."

She puckers her lips, glaring at me, then throws her arms up and huffs. "I'm sure you'll just love hearing this. But what the hell? My life can't suck any worse." She straightens, rolling her shoulders back, and affects an air of haughty indifference that's clearly an act. "No one in this world understands me. I've tried to seduce men, but they lose interest the second I start talking. One jerk even told me I'd be the perfect woman if he just duct-taped my mouth shut."

"Duct tape, huh? Never thought of that."

"Men hate me. That's why I can't get laid."

Well, I can see why men would have trouble getting past her worthier-than-thou attitude, but I can't believe no man on earth will sleep with her. We're not that picky. If a woman wants us, we go for it.

"Come on," I say. "You must get lucky once in a while."

She bows her head. "I haven't had sex in two years."

"Oh." I'd gone more years than that without sex back when I'd been human, but only because I'd convinced myself I was in love with a woman who thought of me as only a friend. "Well, maybe you should try women."

Larissa raises her head just enough to peek up at me with her hair falling around her face. Her bottom lip juts out in a half-hearted pout, and tears pool in her eyes. "I did try that. No one wants me."

Christ, I have no idea how to respond to that.

She bursts into tears.

Aw, come on. Why did she have to do that? I've never been able to watch a woman cry without at least trying to console her. So that's what I try to do. First, I pat her upper arms and say, "Don't worry. Things will get better."

She sniffles. "A two-year dry spell won't get better, not when everyone thinks I'm obnoxious."

"Well, ah..." What should I say? I've never been great at this kind of thing. Never been a hugger either. "Cheer up, nothing lasts forever."

Her head jerks up, her lips pucker, and she narrows her gaze on me. "That is so not true. Only a clueless jackass would barf up such an idiotic platitude."

Perfect. The haughty bitch is back. Now at least I don't need to feel bad for her.

"Good luck, princess," I say. "Hope you find the right clueless jackass who will screw you despite your insufferable attitude."

I turn away, intending to march off down the alley, strictly for dramatic effect, since I can whisk myself away whenever I want.

Three beings materialize in front of me. Three sylphs. All brandishing gleaming silver swords. The sylph in the middle raises his blade and sneers at me.

"Out of our way, salamander," he snarls.

I fold my arms over my chest. "Sorry, this filthy, stinking alley is mine. Go find your own."

What on earth are they doing here? Sylphs don't haunt the gutters in the mortal world. They rarely leave the Unseen realm.

The sylph who'd spoken takes one step toward me. "If you have come for the bounty, give up now. We outnumber you, puny creature." He sniffs the air near my face. "You stink of humanity. Why does every incubus roll in the muck with mortals? It is revolting."

"Your former king married a mortal."

"And we are grateful a gnome destroyed him."

So, the sylphs have no love for Nevan. I'm crushed. Nev and I are such awesomely good buddies. Well, at least he's finally stopped threatening to toss me over a boundary to "watch the fireworks."

"Who is your king these days?" I ask.

"Silence, you filthy gutter-dweller," my new pal hisses. "Give us the woman."

Woman? The only female in this alley is Larissa. Do they want her? I've sensed no magic in her and nothing like the strange scent of Janusite magics that Nevan had detected from Lindsey when they first met.

"Obey us," the sylph says.

"No, I don't think I will." A good fight sounds very appealing right now.

"As you wish." The sylph nods to his companions, who raise their swords. "Get her!"

I conjure my sword and shout to Larissa, "Run!"

She takes off down the alley.

The middle sylph attacks first, swinging his blade at my chest, but I duck sideways out of its path. His comrade lunges at me next, but I whack the flat side of my sword into his skull, knocking him off balance and probably making his head swim. The two sylphs keep slashing their swords at my body, but I duck and dance and jab at them, scoring several more blows, including a few that draw blood.

But the third sylph vanishes.

Where the hell did he go?

I risk glancing back, just in time to see the sylph pop in right in front of Larissa. She yelps and stumbles to a halt. Just as the bastard reaches for her, she kicks him in the groin. He howls while she whirls around and sprints toward me.

No time to think. I plunge my blade straight into the chest of the sylph who'd spoken to me. Without an endued weapon, I can't kill these bastards, but I can wound them enough that they'll have to run home to recharge. The other sylph raises his sword and lets out a nasty bellow as he swings the weapon's tip down toward my chest.

I sidestep, and his blade smacks into the asphalt. While he yanks it free, I thrust my sword into his side, then pull it out. Blood drips from the blade.

Both wounded sylphs bare their clenched teeth and glower at me.

Then they vanish. Running home with their tails tucked firmly between their legs, I reckon.

Larissa screams.

I barrel down the alley toward her, where the third sylph has locked his arms around her torso. She flails her legs but can't get in a position to kick him, even if that would help. It won't, not with an elemental. Her feet dangle above the ground, and her head is tucked under the sylph's chin. When she thrashes her head, I hear the crack of his jaw slamming shut. The sylph growls and bares his teeth.

Just as I reach her, I shout, "Duck!"

Larissa bows her head as far as she can.

It's enough. I swing my blade sideways toward the sylph's head, driving the sharp edge deep into his neck. Blood pours from the wound.

He releases her, stumbles backward a few steps, and vanishes.

Larissa tumbles to the ground.

I send my sword back to my lair and offer her my hands.

She grasps them, letting me help her get off the ground, then she gazes up at me with an almost dazed expression. Her lips fall open, and her mouth curves into a surprised little smile. "You saved me."

"Uh, yeah, I guess I did."

"No one has ever protected me before. Thank you."

"You don't need to—"

She throws her arms around my neck and mashes her lips to mine.

I can't stand this annoying woman, but I am an incubus. Saying no isn't in my nature. So I lash my arms around Larissa, tug her into my body, and kiss her back.

CHAPTER SIX

Larissa

OH GOD, IT'S BEEN FAR TOO LONG SINCE ANYONE KISSED ME. AGES ago, I used to love the feel of a man's lips on mine, his tongue teasing me, his warm body pressed against mine. But too many bad experiences had left me numb to pleasure of any kind. Now, with this irritating salamander, I finally feel something again. His body is more than warm. It scorches with the heat of an elemental male, the fire penetrating my skin and sinking deep inside to the core of my sex. Despite his heat, my nipples stiffen. I'd almost forgotten that could happen for any reason other than being cold. When he slides one hand down to cup my bottom, I can't help moaning into his mouth. He glides his tongue around mine, flicks it over the roof of my mouth, and gently nibbles on my lips. I sag into him, tunneling my fingers into his silky hair, and let the kiss envelop me.

Between our bodies, his dick stiffens and swells.

The heady but indefinable scent of his pheromones drowns my senses, and I rub myself against his erection, though I can't rub it where I most want to feel that hardness—between my thighs, where I'm so wet and hot that I almost can't stand it.

He grasps my ass with both hands.

Cradled in his palms, I hoist one leg to hook it around his hip, then do the same with the other leg. Oh yes, now I can get what I want. With a bit of wriggling, I nestle his hard cock right where I need it and thrust my hips, shamelessly rubbing my body on his.

He groans, the sound so deep and feral that a sizzling shiver tingles over my skin from head to toe.

My skirt has ridden up above my hips. Since I never wear panties, the sensation of his arousal rasping against my cleft makes me whimper and thrust my hips faster, though his jeans keep me from getting what I crave from him with a hunger that throbs inside me. Why doesn't he fuck me? Honestly, that's what an incubus lives for—literally. Since he won't do it, I scrape my flesh along his cock and let the rough texture of the denim intensify my arousal until I'm panting into his mouth and fumbling with the button on his jeans. He groans, the sound so rough and deep that it vibrates through my whole body.

I free the button, yank down the zipper, and clasp his cock in my hand.

He rushes forward until my back hits the wall of the building.

Don't care that I'm making sharp, frantic grunting sounds. I frisk my palm up and down his length, then start to tug it free of his jeans.

Suddenly, he breaks the kiss and peels my legs away from his body. Then he sets me on my feet, tucks his dick back into his jeans, and zips up.

"Why did you stop?" I ask. "It was just getting good."

He grasps my upper arms, holding me at arm's length, and bends his knees until our gazes align. "Why are sylphs after you?"

I don't appreciate the way he's squinting at me and his mouth has become a hard line, but I won't tell him that. Not yet. If he keeps doing that, I might give him a piece of my mind—despite my sex throbbing and my heart pounding. Right now, silence feels like my best option. I can't tell him the truth, that's for sure. I lift my chin and stare right back at him with what I hope looks like a haughty glare.

"Give it up, princess," he hisses. "I used to be a cop, which means a prissy little girl like you can't intimidate me. I just took on three sylphs for you, so I expect some answers. Now."

Oh, I've had enough of his interrogation. I might've been ready to fuck him, but he just blew any chance of getting lucky with me by acting like an arrogant ass. But wow, did he ever take care of those sylphs. It was the sexiest thing I'd ever seen. Never in my life has anyone protected me. But Travis did, despite the fact he thinks I'm a prissy princess. Well, I think he's an overly muscled testosterone addict with no manners whatsoever. We're even.

I lift my chin a little higher to stare down my nose at him. Well, up my nose with my eyes almost rolling back in my head so I can see his face. Why are all elemental males ridiculously tall? I wish so badly that I had a throne on a dais I could sit on while I aim my best haughty look down at the salamander.

Travis grabs my wrists and gives me a hard shake. "Answers, princess. Now."

Okay, silence didn't work. I have no choice now. I must lie.

With a careless shrug, I say, "How should I know why sylphs do anything?"

His gaze sharpens on me again, and he leans in until his nose almost brushes mine. His breaths bluster over my face, making my hair flutter. "Bullshit. Why are sylphs hunting you?"

"Try saying 'bollocks' instead of 'bullshit.' It goes better with your accent."

"Don't need advice on how to speak from a girl who just tried to mount me like a wild animal."

I huff and pucker my lips.

"Answers, Your Highness, or I'll take you to the dankest, darkest cave in the Unseen and leave you there for a few months."

He wouldn't do that. Would he?

Well, I can't give him what he wants, anyway. The honest answer is that I have no idea why three sylph soldiers came after me. Will Travis believe that? Doubtful. Once upon a time, no one would've dared threaten me or abduct me or so much as lay a finger on my arm. Now, I'm a weak, pathetic shell of my former self. Should I confess everything? To an incubus? One who annoys me so much that I want to shove his head into a toilet no one has flushed in six months.

No, I can't confess. He will never understand. No one could.

I shut my eyes, clamp my lips together, and take one deep breath, exhaling it in a rush. Then I look at Travis. "I swear to you I don't know why those sylphs want me."

He keeps studying me with narrowed eyes for several seconds. Releasing my wrists, he sighs and crosses his arms over his chest. "I believe you."

Thank the stars.

Wait. Why do I care if he believes me? I stifle a groan. *Why* do I care? Because three elemental soldiers just tried to abduct me and I'm about as battle-ready as a bunny rabbit. I need a protector, as much as it galls me to even think those words. I've never needed to defend myself, so I have no clue how to do that. I'm no woman warrior.

"I believe you about the sylphs," Travis says. "But I still have plenty of questions. Like how you know about elementals. You recognized I'm an incubus on sight, even though I was glamouring to look human. You recognized those sylphs too, but no mortal should know what they are."

"Maybe I'm not your average mortal."

"Cut the crap, Larissa. You need my help, and I want answers." He squints at me *again*. "Let's start with your real name."

"I am Larissa Robustelli."

"And I'm Leonardo da Vinci." He leans in, though not as close as before. "The truth, Larry. Now. Or I'll walk away and leave you to fend off the next sylph attack on your own."

He wouldn't really do that. I think. I hate needing help, especially from him, but I am dismayingly helpless. I managed to slow down one sylph, but I can't battle an army alone.

I can't tell Travis who I really am either. It would not go well.

Maybe I can satisfy his curiosity with a few strategic confessions.

I chew on my lip for a moment, then forge ahead. "You are not the first elemental I've met. I, uh, had a longstanding, um, acquaintance with a salamander who sort of…knows you."

Travis's whole face cinches up, carving lines across his forehead. "He knows me?"

"Yes." I chew on my lip again. *Suck it up, girl, and tell him.* "I know—or rather, I knew Maximus."

His eyes widen, then go squinty again. "You know Max? Good, let's head on over to the Unseen so he can verify your claim."

"I can't. Please."

"Why can't you?"

No way am I telling him the real reason. But I suddenly remember one salient fact about the other world. "If a mortal doesn't have a touch of the Unseen in them, they'll die if they try to cross the veil. Do you have the ability to sense whether a mortal has that?"

He screws up his mouth, blows a breath out through his nostrils, and clenches his jaw.

I snort. "Yeah, that's what I thought."

"Maybe I can't take you there, but I can go talk to Max and describe you to him. If you guys were such good buddies, he'll remember you."

"What about the sylphs? They might come back."

He snarls words under his breath that I can't quite understand, but from his tone, I'm pretty sure the incubus is cursing a blue streak.

"I'll take you somewhere…else."

"That's your great plan? Go somewhere else. Wow, I'm so impressed with your cop skills."

"Unless you've got a better idea, keep your trap shut."

I roll my eyes heavenward and shake my head. "Ugh. Why can't you talk like Max? All your down-home Southernisms don't mesh with your British accent. You sound ridiculous."

Travis throws his hands up and lets out a loud growl. "Is it my fault the Unseen decided to make me sound British like Max? I hate it. This is not my voice. I never wanted to sound this way."

I study him for a moment, trying to understand his determination not to speak like Max, who uses all the British words. "You can't fight it forever, Travis. If the Unseen wants you to change, you will change. Your accent was the first phase, but the longer you struggle against it, the more miserable you'll make yourself."

"How do you know what the Unseen does?" He holds up a finger when I start to speak. "Uh-uh, princess. I don't buy that Max told you all about the Unseen. My cop nose smells a rat."

"Now I'm a rat? For pity's sake, just help me hide from the sylphs."

"All right," he says slowly. "But only if you agree to do whatever I say."

"That's an outrageous demand."

"Get over yourself, sister, or I'm gone."

I know what I've done to deserve this punishment. But how long must I suffer for my past sins? Isn't two years long enough?

Letting out a long sigh, my shoulders collapsing, I nod. "Fine. I'll do what you say."

"Good." He slings an arm around me and tugs my body snug against his. "Ready?"

"Wait. I need to get my things from my apartment."

"No time for that."

I slap his chest. "You can't expect me to wear this outfit all the time?"

He glances down at my body, at my crop top and short skirt, and he smirks. "Looks fine to me."

"You can't be serious. This is a nightclub outfit, not everyday clothes."

A sigh groans out of him. "Where is your apartment, Larry?"

I want to chastise him for calling me Larry again, but that seems ill-advised. Instead, I recite the address of my apartment building. He spirits us away, straight into my living room. Which is three feet from the bedroom. Which is really just a corner of the room partitioned off with a sheet.

Yeah, my life sucks.

"Better get a move on," he says. "Those sylphs wanted you real bad. Can't reckon why since you're prissy as all git-out."

Although I desperately want to tell him again how ridiculous he sounds talking like a Texan when he has a British accent, I have something more important to do. I rush into the bedroom and gather up as many clothes as I can carry.

Travis follows me, watching with an amused expression while he leans against the bathroom doorjamb. "Don't you have a suitcase?"

"No. I never really needed one." That's sort of the truth.

"Are you saying you've always lived in this shitty apartment?"

"No, but—It's none of your business."

Still leaning against the jamb, he shakes his head at me. "You can't carry all that."

I drop the pile of clothes on the bed. "Conjure it to your lair."

He rakes his simmering gaze over my entire body, his tongue slipping out to wet his lips. "I might could do that, if you'd say pretty please."

The deep, sensual tone of his voice suggests he wants me to do more than say please.

"If you wanna get down on your knees and beg," he says, "that'll work too. I know you're dying to get my cock in your mouth."

"No, I wanted it inside me. I do not do...that other thing. Not ever."

"Because you're a stuck-up wannabe princess. And you wonder why I didn't fuck you in that alley."

I scoop up my bundle of clothes and hug them to my chest. "I'll hold my stuff. You just take us to wherever."

"Used to ordering people around, aren't you?" He pushes away from the jamb, ambling toward me, though he halts at the foot of the bed an arm's length away. "But you work in a seedy motel. Doesn't really jibe with your high-and-mighty attitude."

"Shut up and teleport us already."

He flourishes his hand, and a set of luggage appears at the foot of the bed. "Cram your crap into these bags. Might lose some of your girlie junk in transit if it's not secured."

"You're that inept at teleporting?"

"No. You've got too damn much stuff, that's all."

Oh, I really, really dislike him. And I'm pretty sure I don't want to know where he got the luggage. Travis doesn't seem adept enough at being an elemental to know where he gets things from when he conjures. Even Max doesn't know. Only the most ancient beings in the Unseen truly understand.

"Shoo," I say, waving him away. "Go back to the living room. I need to change clothes."

He flashes me a smirk, then saunters away.

I ditch my nightclub clothes and choose something more practical for my escape to…who knows where. Jeans, a T-shirt, and hiking boots seem like the best choices. Not that I've ever hiked anywhere. I like these boots because they're both sturdy and cute. They are pink, after all. I rinse the purple color out of my hair since I don't care to stand out in a crowd right now. Though I hadn't worn underwear with my crop top and skirt, I put some on when I changed. The last thing I need is my boobs flapping around while I'm running for my life from an army of sylphs.

Maybe I do have some idea of why they might be after me. But why wait two years to do it?

After packing as much stuff into the conjured luggage as I can, I pull on a denim jacket and shout for Travis.

He ambles up to the sheet, my makeshift wall, and peers around it at me. "Did you need something, Your Highness?"

"I'm ready to go."

The insolent man rakes his gaze over me from head to toe again, making it a leisurely appraisal this time, and his lips kick up at the corners. "Nice outfit. You dress exactly the way I imagined a spoiled ditz would."

Ditz? He must be implying my clothes are too girlie. What's wrong with my outfit? Blue jeans, a pink T-shirt with a rainbow on it, and my pink boots. My socks are pink too. So are my bra and panties, but I will not show him that. My denim jacket has pink flowers embroidered on it.

I suppose an ex-cop thinks this is a silly outfit. *Screw you, salamander.*

He picks up the luggage. "Better hold on to me for the ride."

The living-room window explodes. Shards of glass spew across the room and even under the sheet to pepper the bedroom floor. Something whumps down out there, then the sheet is ripped away.

A harpy hunches before us, hissing as she lands smack on her feet an arm's length from me. Her white hair flares out around her head, though there is no wind, and she clacks her long black talons.

Harpies are such show-offs.

I glance down at the floor and the glass shards littered there, then I realize some of the glass has gotten on my pretty pink boots. I glower at the harpy. "Why couldn't you just teleport like everyone else?"

She extends one bony finger, her razor-sharp talon almost touching my nose. "Did you think you could conceal yourself here forever? The bounty has been set, and I will be the one to bring you in."

Her voice sounds like a harsh wind.

And she leaps at me, cinching her birdlike, taloned fingers around my wrist. The creature spins me around and clamps her other hand around my throat. Her talons scrape my skin.

God, I hate harpies. My heart is pounding, and a cold sweat breaks out on my brow and in my palms, making them clammy.

Travis drops the luggage and grits his teeth. "Get your filthy hands off her, you rotten hag."

Wow, he is awfully hot when he's angry.

Before the harpy can whisk me away with her, Travis wrenches her talons away from my throat with such force that I hear bones cracking. The harpy shrieks in agony, stumbling backward away from me, her hand no longer gripping my wrist.

Travis grabs me and spirits us away.

Chapter Seven

Travis

I take us to the only place I can think of, though I've never brought anyone here before. I have no choice. Sylphs and a harpy have tried to abduct Larissa, and I want to know why. But I won't get any answers from Her Highness if bounty hunters get their hands on her. Why is a mortal so coveted by elementals? It makes no sense, unless she has hidden powers that only a chosen few can detect.

We emerge inside my lair. My temporary lair. I'm kind of a squatter here, which doesn't sound cool at all, so I'm hoping Larissa won't notice that fact. Not that I care what she thinks of me or my lair. I just don't want to listen to her whining and her stuck-up complaints.

I release her, though not quite at the instant we materialize. Maybe I take a moment to enjoy the feel of her warm, soft body pressed against me. But only for a few seconds. Okay, maybe thirty seconds. Not a minute, that's for damn sure. Then I step away from her.

She glances around, wrinkling her perfect little nose. "What is this place?"

"My lair. For the moment."

One side of her mouth twists downward. "You can't be serious. A salamander's lair is supposed to have smoky lighting and furniture with lush padding, not to mention the scent of vanilla and spices in the air. I mean, this place looks…unfinished and sterile. It's not sexy."

Did she just call my temporary home sterile? And not sexy? I resist the urge to fist my hands, because she would just love it if I got angry. Then she could spew even more haughty insults at me while hoisting her perfect little nose in the air.

"This is a hotel room," I say, working very hard not to snarl at her. Can't swear that I succeed. "A room in a luxury hotel, actually. There's a bed—with silk sheets, in case you were wondering, and down pillows. There's also a dresser, a table, and a small sofa."

"It's a love seat."

"Which is a kind of sofa."

She huffs and rolls her eyes. "You're squatting in this hotel, aren't you? I get that it's not open yet, which explains how you can claim this as your 'lair.' But I suppose it will do, for now."

Of course she had to say the word "lair" like this place is not suitable for someone as high-and-mighty as Queen Larissa of the Sewers. But I'm letting her distract me from what's important right now. Answers. I need them, and she will give them, or else I'll...do nothing. Yeah, she probably realizes that, which explains why I can't make her tell me anything.

She's not getting off that easy anymore.

I bar my arms over my chest. "Why are elemental bounty hunters after you?"

"How should I know? I'm not telepathic."

"Stop sidestepping. I want the truth. Now."

"Truth is relative."

I give her my cop stare, the one I haven't used in a long time, not since I became something other than human. "Sylphs and harpies don't come after mortals without a damn good reason. What have you done?"

She sniffs and rolls her eyes again.

Time to step up my game. I stalk up to her, glaring down at the prissy princess while leaning in just enough that I loom over her. "Why do bounty—"

"Like I should know." She throws her hands up. "What about 'I'm not telepathic' did you not understand? Should I use smaller words?"

She really won't explain herself, will she? Well, I've got other tactics I can use.

"Fine," I say. "I'll check out the scene to see if your friends left any clues behind."

"The scene? What on earth does that mean?"

I bend my head even closer to hers. "The crime scene, that's what it means. I used to be a cop, and I know how to assess a scene. Maybe I'll learn something about you while I'm doing that."

She raises her chin and turns her head away. "I will not go back to that horrid alley or my apartment."

"No, you will stay here."

I grasp her shoulders, lift her off the floor, and toss her onto the bed. Her legs dangle off the edge.

She bounces and yelps, then glares at me. "You big, stupid oaf. How dare you—"

"Quiet." I say it sharply enough that she stops talking. It's a miracle. "I doubt the hunters can track you to this place, unless they have some kind of supernatural GPS chip on you."

Her brows draw together, and she pushes up into a sitting position. "What is GPS?"

Everyone knows what that is. Don't they? Well, I guess nomads who live in the middle of the Gobi Desert probably don't. But Larissa lives in Phoenix, Arizona, and I have a hard time believing she's never heard of GPS.

"I'm going back to the scene," I say. "Stay here. This shouldn't take too long."

"Please. With you, it'll probably take days."

Though I'm pretty sure she's insulting me, I decide to be the bigger person and let it go. This time. I straighten, muscles taut, and think about where I want to go.

Larissa jumps off the bed and smacks my chest. Hard. "You can't leave me here alone. What if a bounty hunter finds me? I have no way to defend myself."

"You need to take a self-defense class."

She stares at me. "Does somebody really teach that?"

For a moment, I assume she's being sarcastic. Then I realize she is genuinely confused.

I study her, but I can't figure out what's going on behind those striking eyes. "Are you an elemental? Or were you one sometime in the past?"

Larissa bites her lip, veering her gaze away from mine. "No, I have never been an elemental."

Why does she seem wary about saying that? If it's true, she shouldn't care. But she seems anxious.

"Are you any kind of non-human being?" I ask.

"Not that I'm aware of."

"Which isn't a denial. How can you not be aware of what you are?"

She flashes me a scowl. "How can you keep behaving like a mortal cop when you're an elemental incubus?"

I won't get answers from her, not yet. Might as well go assess the two crime scenes. I don't have a lot of hope I'll find clues, not when elementals are involved, but I have to try.

Larissa does have a point, about me behaving like a mortal, but I won't admit that to her. She would just love that, wouldn't she?

"When I get back," I say, "you and I are going to have a nice long talk."

"You can't leave me here. What if that harpy finds me? Am I supposed to beat her to death with a down pillow?"

I rub my jaw while I think about her complaint. Maybe she does need a way to protect herself. I doubt she could handle my sword, since it's large and very heavy. But I do have something else that might help. I conjure the weapon that had kept me safe for years, before I ever became an incubus. I hold it out to her.

Larissa eyes the weapon with her lips puckered. "A firearm? I've never touched one of those."

"Time to take the gloves off, princess." I grasp her wrist, turn it so her palm faces up, and set the gun in her hand. "This is a .40-caliber Sig Sauer semiauto."

"A what? You're speaking gibberish."

"The term .40 caliber tells you the size of the rounds—the bullets this gun uses. Sig Sauer is the brand name. And semiauto means it's not fully automatic, like a machine gun is."

"Oh." She gazes down at the weapon. "Is it hard to use?"

"Turn off the safety and pull the trigger. That's all you need to do." I point to the safety. "Just flick that little switch, and you're good to go. All right?"

She nods, grasping the gun in her hand, aimed at the floor.

"Only shoot if you absolutely have to," I say. "The Sig isn't endued, but if you shoot an elemental in the right place, it will slow them down. Hopefully, that'll give you time to run."

"Run where?"

"Out the door. Find a place to hide."

She sits down on the bed, setting the gun beside her. "Okay, go. Explore the scene."

I suddenly feel like I shouldn't leave her, but I can't imagine how the hunters could find her in this place. Right, because elementals never use magic. I don't feel protective of her. That's not the reason I'm hesitating. I would feel bad about leaving anyone under these circumstances.

So I teleport to the alley.

Walking the scene doesn't take long, since the sylphs had materialized close to me and Larissa. She had run down the alley, though. I follow the track of our movements as I remember them, but I don't see anything of use. A bit of blood here and there. I conjure a razor blade and a sheet of paper, then scrape some of the blood off the asphalt and place it on the paper, then fold that into the shape of an envelope. Stuffing the sample in my pocket, I continue my analysis of the scene. Scuff marks show where the third sylph had grabbed Larissa, but I don't find anything useful there.

Next, I go to her digs.

I see shattered glass everywhere in the tiny, one-room apartment, but that's no surprise. The harpy had blasted through the window to get to Larissa. As I carefully walk through the room, avoiding the glass as much as possible, I notice a strange shape on the floor. Something long and thin and black. I kneel to get a closer look.

A harpy's talon.

That's what the object is. It must've been torn off the creature's finger when I ripped her talons away from Larissa's throat. I conjure a plastic bag and tweezers, then use those to collect the specimen. Not sure what use I'll get out of blood scrapings and a talon, but I was a cop for long enough to realize the importance of collecting evidence, even if it seems unhelpful at the time.

Should I take the samples to someone who can analyze them the elemental way? I doubt a mortal forensics lab would know what to make of blood from a sylph and a talon from a harpy. I can't leave Larissa alone for too long, though, since I have no idea how the hunters found her before. Maybe I can take her with me when I go to Ennea, the fae witch.

I return to the hotel.

Larissa yelps and swings the Sig up, aiming it at my chest. When she realizes it's me, she sets the gun down and rubs her forehead. "Could you please knock or something before you appear out of thin air?"

Of course she's on edge. Two attacks within minutes of each other will do that to a person.

"Next time, I'll try to knock or something." I kneel in front of her, settling my hands on her knees. "I found some clues, but we need to go into the Unseen realm to have the samples analyzed."

She gapes at me like I've suggested I'll cut her head off so I can stuff it into an evidence bag. "I can't go there."

"Why not? I'll be with you the whole time."

"Ugh. We've been through this already. If I don't have a touch of the Unseen in me—"

"Right, yes, I remember." *Dadgummit.* But I really need to have Ennea analyze the evidence for me. "Uh, maybe I could get one of my elemental friends to stay with you while I'm gone."

"What friends? I thought you were a loner."

"You know I'm friends with Max. He could protect you from another attack. Max used to be a Roman soldier, a long time ago, so he knows how to fight." I squint at her. "But you already know Max, don't you?"

"Kind of," she says carefully. "He's not the right person to be my bodyguard."

"Why not?" I'm getting more suspicious every time she refuses to explain herself.

"Because—Well, it's just not a good idea."

"Give me a concrete reason why, or I'm getting Max. He can tell me what your problem is."

She crushes her lips together, clenching handfuls of the bedspread.

"Come on, Larissa," I say, "or whatever your name really is. You can't fool a cop for long. I know you're hiding something, and it's time to come clean."

"You won't understand."

"That's a risk you'll have to take. Otherwise, I'm out of here—and I won't come back."

She squeezes her eyes shut, sucking in a breath through her nostrils. Then she blows it out and looks me in the eye. "Larissa Robustelli is not my original name."

"No shit."

Though I can tell she wants to scowl at me, to her credit, she doesn't do it.

Instead, she stares down at the carpet while gripping her knees. "I told you the truth when I said I've never been an elemental. I don't know what I've become, but apparently, I'm human. Or some approximation of human. Honestly, I have no idea what I am anymore."

"Maybe we can figure that out together. Start by telling me your real name."

"I don't know if it's my real name, but it's the one I've always had." She drops her elbows to her thighs and covers her face with her raised hands. Then she mumbles something.

"Sorry, I didn't catch that."

With a pitiful moan, she sits up and shuts her eyes. "Hathor."

Chapter Eight

Larissa

MY HANDS HAVE TURNED CLAMMY, AND I FEEL LIKE I MIGHT THROW UP any second. My pulse beats so fast it's almost fluttering, like a hummingbird's wings, and I can't make myself move a muscle. I certainly can't look at Travis. Not after what I just told him. Why did I do that? No one in the multiverse could possibly feel anything other than hatred for me. But I want Travis to like me. It's pathetic, I know. Yes, he drives me crazy with that "princess" and "Larry" nonsense, and I'd convinced myself I don't like him. Maybe that was fear talking. He is only the person who has ever been kind to me or tried to protect me without being ensorcelled so they had no choice.

When I finally force myself to look at him, his expression is blank.

"You can go now," I say. "The bounty hunters are my problem, not yours. I deserve to be hunted like an animal."

He blinks slowly, twice, then scrunches his eyebrows. "You're Hathor? The goddess?"

"Are you deaf? Yes, that's what I said." Maybe I shouldn't get testy with him, but it's a defense mechanism. I think. According to the TV talk shows I've watched, that must be what I'm doing.

His mouth opens, but he doesn't speak for several seconds. "You can't be Hathor. She's an evil bitch."

The nausea roiling in my gut shoots acid high up into my throat. I swallow it and try to stay calm, but really, I don't have much hope of accomplishing that. My life is at stake here, quite literally. If I am human, which seems to be the case, then Travis could snap my neck with two fingers.

Maybe I deserve that.

He springs up and starts pacing the room while rubbing the back of his neck.

I pick up the gun and hold it in my palm. "Here. At least shoot me and make it a quick death."

Travis freezes, rotating his head to stare at me. "What?"

"You can probably claim the bounty."

"Claim the—No, I don't want to do that."

I stand, walk straight up to him, and offer him the gun. "You'll be the greatest hero the Unseen has ever known. The salamander who killed Hathor, the evil bitch who destroyed more lives than anyone in the history of the multiverse." I thrust my palm toward him. "Here. Take the gun. Go on, you know I deserve to die. Max must've told you about all the horrific things I did to him and all my thralls. You know, the people I enslaved with magic so they would adore me and do my bidding, do anything to make me happy."

He shakes his head slowly.

"I deserve it!" I screech. My entire body is trembling, and the gun might slip off my palm any second. Tears well in my eyes, then spill over my lids to stream down my cheeks. Sobs hiccup out of me. "Please, just do it. I can't live like this anymore, and I can't go back to what I was. Even if the Four Winds would let me, I can't be that person again. Please, kill me."

Travis watches me for a moment like he's trying to gauge my sincerity. Or maybe he's calculating the best trajectory to shoot me squarely between the eyes. Finally, his body relaxes as he exhales a long sigh. Then he snatches the gun from my hand, making it disappear back to wherever he keeps his belongings.

He pulls me into his arms. "I'm not going to kill you. Don't suggest that ever again."

"But I—"

"You do not deserve to die." He leads me to the bed, where we both sit down. "You haven't been in the mortal world for long, but you sure seem comfortable here."

Not long? Where did he get that idea? "I've been here for two years, cleaning toilets at that revolting motel and trying not to get in anyone's way."

"Two years?" he says with shock in his voice. "No, it's only been six months since you disappeared."

"Six months? I wish."

He leans in, lowering his face to within a hair's breadth of mine. "Right after Harper came back from the dead, you disappeared. Even oracles couldn't find you. Everyone gave up."

"And they threw a party to celebrate."

"I'm sure some did, but two people did everything they could to find you."

"Yeah, bounty hunters."

He shakes his head. "Max and Harper."

I gape at him, unable to believe what he says. Or maybe I'm unwilling to believe it. This makes no sense. I had been one of the most depraved beings in the Unseen, possibly the most depraved, and I used magic to force other beings into kowtowing to my every whim. Worse, I had made them enjoy it. How could I have done that? Maybe I've forgotten the reasons why, burying them deep inside myself so I never need to deal with them.

Travis is watching me, waiting for my response.

I swallow, but the tightness in my throat won't ease up. "I—I don't understand. Why did they care what happened to me?"

"Because they're good people."

"Yes, but I am a horrible creature."

He lays a hand over mine. "Max told me how you helped him rescue Harper from the obsidian fae. You risked your own immortal life to do it."

"As if that makes up for everything I've done."

"No, it doesn't." He clasps my hand in both of his. "But it's a start. I didn't know you before, but if you were a monster then, you sure aren't one now."

"You hate me. I'm a prissy princess with a stick up her ass."

"Well, maybe I've seen other sides of you recently." He twists his mouth into an expression I swear reveals a touch of shame. "You know I sneaked into your apartment the other night."

"Uh-huh."

"I also…followed you home before that. Saw you being nice to an old lady." He brushes a hair away from my cheek. "Why don't you ride the bus to get home? It would be a lot easier."

"No bus stop anywhere near my apartment. So no, it wouldn't save me time." I focus on our hands, the way he's still holding mine. "Maybe I'm putting on an act to trick you. I might ensorcell you any minute."

"If you had that kind of power, you would've used it on me already." He moves his thumb in slow circles on the back of my hand, the sensation more soothing than seems rational. "I don't know what you are now, or how you wound up in this world, but we can find out together."

"Why are you being so nice all of a sudden?"

"Look, we don't really know each other. But you're in trouble, and it used to be my job to help people. I can't just walk away and leave you to the wolves."

I start to feel tingly the more he rubs his thumb on my skin. Maybe it's only incubus pheromones affecting me, but I might sort of have decided I don't totally despise him. "Thank you. I'm not used to needing help, so it's possible I acted like a spoiled bitch because I'm feeling…powerless."

"From omnipotent to vulnerable. Yeah, that must be a tough transition."

He's not being sarcastic, as far as I can tell. But I still can't understand why he's being nice to me. I burst into tears and begged him to kill me, so that might have some bearing on the situation.

Still holding my hand, he eyes me sideways. "What did you mean when you said even if the Four Winds would let you do it?"

"Do you know who the Four Winds are?"

"Powerful beings in the Unseen. They have a big-ass temple in the clouds, and they're the ones who released Janus from his imprisonment."

"Yes, but they're more than that. They are the balancing powers in the Unseen, the four cardinal points that keep everything in check." I try to wriggle my hand free of his, but I can't do it. Maybe I don't actually want to do it. Never before has anyone treated me with any measure of kindness. "Apparently, I am the worst being in the multiverse, and I had to be stopped. The Four Winds locked me up in their prison—not the same place where Janus was held, since he had been nothing but an essence with no physical form. The Winds kept me there while they decided how to deal with me."

"They sent you here? To the mortal world?"

"Yes. They didn't explain their purpose in doing that. They didn't explain anything. After who-knows-how-long, Janus came into my cell and informed me I was being given one last chance to redeem myself. If I fail, a coalition of gods and the most powerful elementals will use their combined powers to destroy me."

Travis gazes down at our hands, turning mine over so he can rub my palm.

Oh, that feels wonderful. I try to keep hold of my wits, but his touch is distracting. I need several seconds before I can speak again. "I was…transported into the mortal realm, naked and apparently human. I have no powers. I can't sense portals to the Unseen, though I tried over and over to find one. After a month, I gave up. In the meantime, I had to take any awful job I could find to keep from starving."

"Thought you were afraid to go back to the Unseen."

"Not at first. I was confused and desperate to get home." I shut my eyes and sigh. "Then I realized going back would be deadly for me. Anyone who saw me would kill me."

"A helpless mortal? I didn't realize the Unseen was that brutal."

"Then you have led a sheltered existence since becoming an incubus."

"I've kind of kept to myself, except for visiting Max and Harper, and a few others. But for the past five months, I haven't even visited my friends."

"Seriously?" I shake my head. "You're as bad as I am, hiding out from both worlds."

He turns his head slightly toward me and smirks. "Don't get any ideas. I still can't stand you."

"Likewise." The fact we both spoke in huskier voices lessens the impact of our statements. Do I hate him? Well, maybe "hate" is too strong a word. I don't understand him, that's for sure.

"Tell you what," he says. "I'm going to help you figure out what's happened to you and how these hunters keep finding you, not to mention who put a bounty on your head."

"Why would you do that?"

"Once a cop, always a cop. The forging didn't erase that part of me."

He's helping me because he feels a civic responsibility to do it. Well, I guess that's better than nothing.

"We need to visit my friend Lindsey," he says. "She and her husband, Nevan, can help us get in touch with the right people. We need to know what you are now."

"Okay." The hesitance in my voice is dismaying. I used to be powerful, unstoppable, untouchable. Now I need a salamander to protect me and tell me what to do.

He clears his throat. "We also need to find out how you could've been here for two years, but everyone else thinks it's been six months."

"Magic is how." I can't help the haughty tone in my voice. "Honestly, an elemental being ought to know magic is the root of everything in the Unseen. It is the very fabric of reality."

"But it sounds like you were sent back in time. Only one being can do that."

"Janus despises using his temporal powers. I can't imagine what the Four Winds could've said that would convince him to alter the flow of time simply to punish me."

"We will find out." He squeezes my hand. "Together."

I think he genuinely means that. After the way I've behaved, I still can't comprehend why he's determined to sort out the mystery—with me. But I need help, and if I'm lucky, at least I can get some mind-blowing sex in the process. Yeah, I'm getting horny right now. Probably because I'm sitting inches away from an incubus who is still holding and caressing my hand. He can't help giving off pheromones like humans give off body odor.

Do I stink? No matter how much I scrub myself in the shower, I feel like I never get rid of the filth.

Travis gets up, then gestures for me to do the same. "Better get started on our investigation. I've got the evidence. All we need is an elemental forensics specialist to analyze it."

"Are you calling me evidence?"

"No, I wasn't. But I guess you are evidence too."

"Thank you so much. Would you like to stuff me into a little plastic bag now?"

He throws an arm around me, pinning me to his body. "Shut up, Larry."

Before I can speak, he whisks us away.

CHAPTER NINE

Travis

I TAKE US TO THE ONLY PLACE WHERE I KNOW I CAN GET HELP WITHOUT needing to cross the veil and risk getting Larissa ripped apart at the molecular level. Larissa. Should I still call her that? Her original name was Hathor, and until two years ago, she'd been a goddess. That's…bizarre. Now an invincible immortal needs my help because she can't take care of herself.

That's even more bizarre.

Since I don't want to terrify the tourists, I drop us off in the garden behind the rock shop, amid the concrete statues of unicorns and fairies and other creatures I used to think were myths. Nope. They are real. Freaky, annoying, insane, and virtually impossible to kill—but real. I've become one of those creatures. Are unicorns real? I haven't seen one, so I can't swear to that. As for fairies… Well, I had once called Nevan a "jungle fairy" to piss him off. The fae are the closest thing to what mortals call fairies, though I haven't met any of them who have wings.

"Are you awake?" Larissa says in her haughty voice, the one that reminds me she is not a normal woman. It's the voice of a goddess who's used to everyone bowing down to her.

No way in hell will I ever do that.

She slaps my face. "Wake up."

I grasp her wrist just as she tries to pull her hand away. "Enough."

The former goddess gives me a peevish look, lifts her chin, and turns her face away. She probably wants to cross her arms over her chest, but she's pinned against me too tightly to manage it.

Since I can't bring myself to call her Hathor, I decide to stick with Larissa. She might have chosen the dumbest, most obviously fake alias in history, but whatever. I don't have time to worry about that. Her first name is growing on me, but Robustelli... No, I'll never get why she picked that last name.

"Where have you taken me?" she asks.

"Someplace where I'm hoping we can get some help. Friends of mine own this shop and the surrounding land." I glamour myself into something close to the way I'd looked as a human and head out of the rock garden toward the rear door of the shop. When I glance back, Larissa hasn't moved. She's standing there hugging herself, biting her lip while she warily eyes her surroundings. What is her problem now? I wave my arm. "Come on, Your Highness. Giddyup."

She scowls and shakes her head.

With a groan, I march back to her. "Are you planning to stand in the rock garden all day?"

"No, I—" She rubs her arms again, hunching her shoulders. "I know this place, and trust me, I will not be welcome here."

"You've been to the shop before?"

"Not exactly." She spoke the words with deliberate carefulness, like she's trying not to lie but doesn't want to tell the truth either. In the thankfully brief time I've known her, she's done that a lot.

My mind insists on forcing me to replay our conversation back in the hotel suite. For reasons I can't explain, I had empathized with her. Which is nuts. She's annoying and arrogant, and the only reason I'm helping her is because that's what I do. Or what I did. When I was a cop in Texas and then the sheriff of Mandan County, Michigan—the county in which we now stand. Maybe I still can't wrap my head around the idea Larissa is Hathor, but that doesn't explain why I...comforted her. She started crying and begged me to kill her. Then I hugged her and tried to make her feel better.

I'm insane. That's the only explanation.

"What is your problem with the rock shop?" I ask. "We need to go in there so I can talk to Lindsey and—"

"Lindsey?" Her face goes blank, then her eyes go wide as she glances at the barn-red, corrugated-metal building that houses the rock shop. "No, no, I can't go in there."

"Why not? Lindsey has never met you. I know because she told me so."

"But, uh..." Larissa scrunches up her face. "She's married to Nevan."

"Yeah, I know."

She bites down on her bottom lip and veers her gaze away from me. "He won't be happy to see me."

I start to speak, then stop. Why would she think... Oh, of course.

"You ensorcelled him," I say. "Didn't you?"

Larissa bows her head and nods.

Perfect. If she treated Nevan anything like the way she treated Max, the former king of the sylphs will probably snap her neck on sight. No, Nevan wouldn't do that. He might glower and squint at her, but he won't hurt her. Besides, I have nowhere else to go for help.

I grasp her hand. "Lindsey and Nevan are my friends. And you'll have to face up to your past sooner or later. Might as well rip the Band-Aid off."

She raises her head. "I tried that once. Don't know why mortals think ripping an adhesive strip off their skin is somehow cathartic. It just hurts. A lot."

"It's a metaphor, princess." I tug her hand. "Let's go."

Though she twists her mouth into an irritable expression, she lets me lead her to the shop's door. I push it open and hold it for her while she shuffles inside. As she passes me, she gets an odd look on her face.

"What's wrong now?" I ask.

"You opened the door for me. Without being ensorcelled to do it."

"I might not always be a gentleman, but my mother taught me to open doors for ladies—I mean women." Larissa isn't quite a lady, not in the sense of being elegant and refined and polite.

The door shuts behind us, and I head for the waist-high counter where a familiar figure waits for us. Lindsey is on the phone, probably talking to a customer. I don't see Nevan, but I'm sure he's around. Lindsey has one of those baby slings hanging across her body at a diagonal, and I can just make out the chestnut hair on baby Liam's head. Lindsey manages to cradle her son with one arm while talking on the phone.

She's just ended her call when Larissa and I reach the counter. When she sees me, a bright smile lights up her face. "Travis, where have you been? Haven't heard from you in months."

"I know. Sorry. I've been…busy."

Her brows hike up. "Max told us you were 'finding your way,' whatever that means."

Max was being diplomatic, I guess, though I've never known him to do that before. Maybe he feels sorry for me because I'm such a useless elemental. Can't even speak the right way anymore.

Lindsey glances at Larissa, then raises her brows again—at me. "Who's your friend?"

"She's not my friend. We just met and—Never mind." I hesitate, trying to figure out how to ask for Lindsey's help without spilling the beans about the fact the woman standing beside me is Hathor. "This is Larissa."

No, I can't make myself use her whole alias because Larissa Robustelli still sounds to me like the stage name of a frigging Italian porn star.

Lindsey smiles at my, uh, companion. "Nice to meet you, Larissa. I'm glad Travis got a girlfriend. He's been lonely for a long time."

What is she talking about? I haven't been lonely. I seduce women all the time.

But I don't have conversations with them. Bang-and-run has been my style lately, though I can't say I really enjoy being that kind of man. Then again, I'm not a man anymore, so it doesn't matter.

I'm fine. One hundred percent fine.

"She's not my girlfriend," I say. "Larissa is in trouble—the elemental kind—and I'm trying to help her, but I can't do it alone."

"You know we're always here for you," Lindsey says. Then she extricates Liam from that baby-sling whatsit and thrusts him at me. "Here, hold Liam for me. I need to get Nevan, but he's in the storage room. Don't like to take my little pumpkin in there. It's dusty."

Little pumpkin? When did she start calling her son that? Well, I have been gone for five months. I suppose a lot has changed since the last time I was here.

I take the baby, cradling him in my arms the way I've seen women do. "You guys need an intercom system. Then you wouldn't need to track your husband down in the storage room."

"Oh, I've tried suggesting that. Nevan thinks it's ooky to hear someone talking through a speaker where he can't see them." She laughs. "My hubby is still adjusting to the mortal world."

I can't imagine Nevan used the word ooky, but I can believe he'd be wary of technology. The man had been a warrior in ancient Ireland, then he died in battle and became a sylph, living in a world that doesn't need tech.

Lindsey walks through an open doorway into the back room.

While I cradle Liam and rock him gently, I glance at Larissa.

Her eyes have gone wide, her lips are parted, and she stares at the space behind the counter as if she's expecting evil spirits to leap out of the cash register and assault her.

"Are you worried about seeing Nevan?" I ask. "I might not be best buddies with him, but I've gotten to know Nevan enough that I can promise you he won't do anything to hurt you."

She swerves her terrified gaze to me. "But I—The things I did—He—"

The man himself saunters out of the storage room doorway, approaching the counter.

Larissa sidles behind me.

Nevan nods at me. "Lindsey tells me you need a hand. How may I assist you?"

His Irish accent always annoys me, but that might have more to do with the fact I sort of tried to steal Lindsey away from him, and he hurled me into a massive tree with a flick of his hand. That happened ages ago. Maybe he's forgotten about it.

I clear my throat. "Uh, well… Where's Lindsey? I thought she'd come back with you."

He sighs. "The phone rang, and my wife can't stand not to answer it. Might be vitally important nonsense. She'll be out in a minute."

"I didn't hear the phone ringing."

"Her cell phone. You know how she is about that. Lindsey must have that device on her body at all times." He leans his hip against the counter and eyes me up and down. "What's the problem?"

"Maybe we should wait for Lindsey." Because maybe Nevan won't get quite as angry when he sees Hathor aka Larissa if his wife is here to act as a buffer.

And of course, Larissa is cowering behind me.

Well, I can't say I blame her. Reuniting with a man she ensorcelled must be nerve-racking.

Lindsey finally emerges from the storage room and joins her husband at the counter. Nevan slips an arm around her waist.

"Do you want the baby back?" I ask her.

"If you want to cuddle with him a little longer, I'm cool with that."

"Uh, thanks, but I'm good." I pass her the baby, careful not to move too much or else Nevan might see Larissa. Once Lindsey has Liam nestled in that sling contraption again, I dive in. "Listen, the friend I've brought kind of, ah, knows Nevan. He might not be happy to see her, and I don't want this to get nasty. But Larissa is in serious trouble." I look at Nevan. "So please give her a chance."

"You think I know her, but I've never met any Larissa."

"That's her current alias. You knew her by another name." I glance over my shoulder, and Larissa squeezes her eyes shut, but then nods. I face Lindsey and Nevan. "It's time to show you."

I step aside, revealing Larissa.

Lindsey has already met her, so she doesn't react at all except to gaze up at her husband's face.

Nevan's brows pull together over his nose. He tips his head from side to side like he's examining Larissa and trying to decide who she is.

I had never met her when she was Hathor, so I have no idea how different she looks now.

"She does seem familiar," Nevan says. He rubs his chin, still scrutinizing Larissa. "But I can't quite place her."

"Oh for Ra's sake," Larissa huffs. She marches up to the counter and raises onto her tiptoes to stare straight into Nevan's eyes. "It's me, you fool. It's Hathor."

Nevan stares blankly at her for a moment, then he grins and laughs. "So it is. You look different now."

"That's because I'm human or…something." She takes a step back, eying him with suspicion. "Aren't you enraged by my presence? Don't you want to murder me for what I did to you?"

"Murder?" Nevan says with a laugh. "Why would I do that? The months I spent in your temple were the most fun I ever had—until I met Lindsey, of course."

His wife rolls her eyes at him. "Nice save, honey."

Larissa gapes at him. "Fun? I ensorcelled you. Made you my slave, bound to do my bidding and fulfill my every desire."

Nevan shrugs one shoulder. "Ensorcellment never bothered me, not when you were the one bespelling me."

Is he serious? Max makes magical enslavement sound like the worst kind of torture imaginable. But Nevan thinks it's... What? A carnival ride?

"You liked it?" I ask. "Being forced to screw Hathor whenever she wanted and do any depraved things she asked of you?"

"I only had sex with Hathor once, but I had months to enjoy the company of every female thrall in the temple. Many of them still remember me fondly."

Lindsey slaps her husband's chest. "How do you know they still remember you?"

"Max told me."

"Were you and Max ensorcelled together?"

"Not that I know of."

Larissa is still gaping at Nevan. "You honestly don't hate me?"

He shrugs both shoulders this time. "No, I honestly do not."

"So you might, ah, help me?"

"If my wife agrees." He looks at Lindsey, and she nods. "All right, we will help. What seems to be the problem?"

Larissa backs up to me, her sexy ass molded to my groin. I really don't want to get a hard-on in front of Lindsey and Nevan, so I move sideways until Larissa is molded to my side instead of to my dick.

As quickly as I can, I relate the two incidents with the bounty hunters. Then I glance down at Larissa, raising my brows. "Should I explain the rest? Or would you rather do it?"

"I can handle it." She lifts her chin, which I'm starting to think isn't always a stuck-up gesture. Sometimes I think it's her way to cope with fear. "The Four Winds did something to me. I'm not sure what, exactly, but I have no magics and I seem to be mortal. Janus employed his temporal powers to send me backward in time. I've been living in the mortal world for two years."

"Doing what?" Lindsey asks.

Larissa lowers her gaze to the floor. "Cleaning toilets in a seedy motel."

Nevan stares at her without expression.

Lindsey blinks quickly several times. "Oh. I see."

And Nevan busts out laughing.

CHAPTER TEN

Larissa

I WAIT FOR NEVAN'S LAUGHTER TO SUBSIDE, BUT INSTEAD, HE STARTS laughing harder until his eyes are watering and he's holding his stomach like it hurts from his guffaws tensing the muscles there. What is so hilarious? I'm trapped in the mortal realm, apparently in a human body, and I'm forced to perform loathsome, menial labor to keep from starving. That is not entertaining.

Maybe he was lying when he said he doesn't hate me. Nevan might want to humiliate me as punishment for my sins.

I shut my eyes. My sins are too numerous to count, stretching back for more eons than any being in the Unseen has ever lived through, and I can never atone for what I've done.

Nevan finally stops laughing.

Lindsey elbows him in the side. "That was rude, honey."

Miraculously, the baby doesn't stir. Maybe he's used to his father being an obnoxious twit.

Nevan wipes his eyes. "Can't help it, love. Hathor cleans toilets. When I was in residence at her temple, she wouldn't even peel a grape herself."

"My name is Larissa now," I say.

"Do you have a surname?"

Nevan's question makes me remember Travis's reaction to the surname I'd chosen, and I suddenly don't want to say it out loud.

So of course, Travis blurts it out. "She's calling herself Larissa Robustelli."

And of course, Nevan bursts out laughing again.

What is so funny about the name Robustelli? I don't see the humor in it. Men are such morons.

Lindsey smacks her husband's chest again. "Cut that out. Travis brought Larissa here because she needs help, and that's what we do—help people. Right?"

"We guard the portal to the Unseen," Nevan says. "When did we become private detectives?"

Though she whispers her response, I can hear it anyway. "If you ever want to have sex again, stop harassing Larissa."

Nevan straightens and rolls his shoulders back. "All right. We will assist you. Now, you say sylphs and a harpy came after you. Correct?"

"Yes," I confirm. "The harpy said there's a bounty on me."

Travis conjures his ridiculous plastic bag and the silly folded-up paper—his so-called evidence—and holds them up. "I collected evidence from both scenes."

Nevan leans forward to squint at the items. "Is that a harpy talon?"

"That's right."

"What good will that do us?"

Travis clenches his jaw so tightly a muscle ticks there. "It's evidence. We have no idea why there's a bounty on her head or how these hunters found her. The harpy talon might have some of Larissa's blood on it, so maybe that can tell us something."

Nevan takes the folded-up paper and unwraps it. "Are these flakes of blood hers too?"

"No. Those are from the sylph assholes." Travis makes a face. "No offense."

"Your opinion of sylphs makes no difference to me."

The back door swings open, spilling bright sunlight into the shop, and a figure enters. With the light behind him, the man is in shadow. I can tell it's a man, but that's all.

As the door shuts, I finally see the man's face.

Oh no, no, no. Who summoned him?

Max strides halfway to us, then freezes. His focus lands on me, and he narrows his gaze while compressing his lips. "Who's your new mate, Travis?"

He doesn't recognize me. How can that be? I guess I look a lot different now than I did the last time he saw me. Max speaks with the same British accent as Travis, but he uses the proper British words. Travis insists on talking like a Southerner despite his new accent.

Travis moves in front of me, facing the other incubus, almost as if he's protecting me. "Don't go postal, okay?"

"Postal?" Max says, his forehead crinkling. "Harper hasn't explained that term to me."

"He's telling you not to murder Hathor," Nevan helpfully announces.

Max stares at Travis, his eyes wide. "Did Nevan just say Hathor?"

"That's right," the former sylph says. "Travis thinks she might be human now."

Will Nevan ever shut his mouth?

Ugh. I can't cower behind Travis forever. Sooner or later, I'll have to talk to Max. So I step sideways, revealing myself.

Max doesn't move any part of his body except for his eyes, rolling his gaze toward me. "Yes, I recognize this creature now. Hathor."

"I prefer Larissa."

"Larissa?" he says like he's never heard that name before and it feels strange on his tongue. He takes three large steps toward me, halting an arm's length away. "What game are you playing this time?"

"No game. Something has happened to me, and I…" How can I ask for his help? After all the things I'd done to him. Naturally, Max recognized me even in my new human form. I'd spent more time with Max than with any other thrall I'd ever ensorcelled. "I could use your help, if you feel comfortable with that."

"Comfortable?" He takes another step, cutting the distance between us in half. He's so close I can smell the unique scent of him, the one I'd reveled in when I had him under my thumb. "I ought to wring your ruddy neck."

"Go on. I deserve it."

He fists his hands, almost as if he's imagining wringing my neck, then he relaxes his fingers. "That would be the easy way out for you." He veers his attention to Travis. "Tell me what the bloody hell is going on here."

While Travis explains, I can't help staring at Max. I'd forced him to want me, but all those times we'd been together, I convinced myself he must care for me, or he wouldn't have enjoyed sex with me so much. Yes, I had deluded myself. I'd even thought I loved him. But how can a person love another when magic is involved? Still, Max had made me laugh and given me something I had never experienced before. He had been my friend.

But it was all a lie, one I crafted.

Once Travis is done talking, Max eyes me again. "If you're human, what have you been doing to earn a living? Mortals need to make money."

Why does everyone have to ask that question?

Before Nevan can blurt it out, I tell Max the truth. "Cleaning toilets in the kind of motel where people only go to have sex without being seen."

Max lifts his brows. One corner of his mouth curls up into a slight smirk.

Wait for it… Any second now…

Laughter erupts out of him.

This time, I don't take offense. Max absolutely should laugh at my misfortune. He was damaged by my depravity more than anyone else, and I won't begrudge him his cynicism toward me.

He doesn't laugh for anywhere near as long as Nevan had. Then he sighs and scratches his head. "All right. I will help you."

"What?" I can't help feeling stunned. Max will help. He offered. Voluntarily. "That's… I don't even know how to thank you."

"Try not ensorcelling me ever again. That will do." He leans in, his face so close to mine that I can see the swirling colors in his irises. "But don't expect forgiveness."

I swallow, but my throat has become so tight and dry that I can't speak. I shake my head, hoping he understands the gesture.

Max moves in front of Travis and slaps his arm. "You have excellent taste in women, mate. Who's next? A harpy? Oh no, you've already tried it on with every kind of elemental slag." He tips his head in my direction. "Try something daring and shag a nice girl."

"At least Larissa hasn't tried to kill me."

"Harper only did that once, and it was before she gave up fighting her desire for me." Max cants his head, sharpening his gaze on Travis. "I hope you know what you're doing."

"So do I," Travis says. "But ya know, I ain't the type to leave a woman in distress, even if she is a former evil goddess. Y'all could cut her some slack."

Why is he suddenly speaking Texan again? He seems to revert to that whenever he's anxious, which would mean he hadn't been as at ease back in that alley as he wanted me to believe, when he tried to seduce a mortal girl. That man really needs to stop fighting what the Unseen wants. It will only cause him more anxiety.

I don't care if it does. I swear, I don't.

He sounds completely ridiculous speaking those words in a British accent.

"Do we have a plan?" Max asks, scanning his gaze over all of us. When no one speaks, he grins and claps with a little too much enthusiasm. "Bloody brilliant! We jump into the deep end yet again with no life preservers and cement shoes on our feet."

I really did not miss his sarcasm.

Travis raises his bits of so-called evidence. "I've got these."

"What is that?" Max asks, eying the items askance. "Tell me that's not a harpy's talon."

"It is. And I think that's Larissa's blood on it. We need to get this analyzed."

"Do I look like ruddy elemental CSI?"

"Harper shouldn't let you watch TV." Travis sighs and wags the plastic bag and envelope. "You know people who can analyze stuff. I can't take Larissa into the Unseen because I have no idea if she could survive that."

"If she has a touch of the Unseen in her she can."

"Yeah, thanks for stating the obvious. How do we find out if she's got that?"

Max rolls his eyes. "You ask Janus."

"Oh, perfect," I say. "Ask a god who hates me. He's the one who shoved me back in time so I could enjoy two beautiful years of living in a cesspool."

"Don't be so precious," Max says. "Maybe if you hadn't participated in destroying him, he'd be more likely to help you now."

Travis stomps his foot so hard it shakes the floor. "Enough! If you can't lend a hand, Max, then go home and beg Harper to screw you."

"Calm down, Travis. I will help, even if she is Hathor." Max almost spat my original name. "Janus will help too, I think. He might be up himself, but he's not a half-bad bloke. It's worth a try."

"Where can we find him?" Travis asks.

"If we go to the portal, I'm sure he will turn up eventually."

Travis grasps my hand. "Let's go."

Max vanishes, and Travis spirits us away after him.

Chapter Eleven

Travis

WE LAND ON THE PATH THAT SKIRTS THE WATERFALL AND THE WOODEN railing that surrounds it. The river disgorges its contents over the twenty-foot red sandstone cliff and into the waters of the pool below, where foam bubbles here and there on the surface. Behind the cascade lies a small cave that houses the portal to the Unseen. I've seen it before, and gone through it before, but the waterfall always makes me uneasy. Maybe because I died on the edge of a pool not unlike this one, with my blood slowly dripping away, taking my mortal life with it.

And then I was forged.

"What's wrong?" Larissa asks.

I realize I'm still holding her in my arms and let go, taking a step back. "Nothing. I'm fine."

Max is standing a few yards away alongside the railing.

"What do we do now?" I ask. "Holler for Janus?"

He shrugs. "Never tried to summon him before. The bloke has a tendency to show up whether I want him to or not."

"I'm not just going to stand here hoping he decides to come so he can exchange lame sarcastic comments with you." I take another step away from Larissa, throw my head back, and shout as loud as I can, "Janus!"

My bellow echoes off the trees and the cliff.

"That won't work," Max says. "Janus doesn't care if—"

A figure materializes in front of us.

Janus, the onetime Roman god, stands there dressed in a toga with gold torques around his biceps and a gold belt around his waist. He wears gold-trimmed sandals too.

The god raises one brow at me. "Why have you summoned me so discourteously?"

When I'd first met Janus, his Italian accent had thrown me. I mean, he's not Italian. He's a god who was once worshiped by the Romans, but he doesn't have any ties to modern Italy as far as I know.

Of course, I've developed a damn British accent, so I probably shouldn't look down on how Janus talks.

"We need your help," I say, though I don't walk toward him. The god's eerie gold eyes give me the creeps, and I'm not too manly to admit that. In my head. I would never say it out loud. "Let me explain the situation—"

"Do not trouble me with your petty inconveniences."

"Why not? You like to follow Max around like you're his high-and-mighty puppy. I've got a serious problem that could affect both worlds." No idea if that's true, but it sounds good, and I'm desperate for someone to lend a hand.

Janus veers his attention to Larissa. His lip curls. "Hathor."

"She's mortal now," I say. "We think she is, anyway. That's why we need you, to tell us if she can survive crossing the veil so we can get answers."

"This…creature assisted in my destruction." He waves a hand toward her. "Why should I care what becomes of her?"

"I don't give a shit if you care or not." I stalk up to him. "You will do this, or I'll tell Lindsey you refused to help."

Yeah, I'm playing the guilt card. Lindsey is Janus's descendant, and she once housed his orphaned powers inside her. Janus has become attached to Lindsey and her son, Liam. He won't want her to be upset with him.

I hope.

Janus glares at me, grinding his teeth so loud I can hear it.

I think only a god can do that.

Finally, he sighs and waves an arm in a dismissive gesture. "Go on. She may cross the veil without harm, but I cannot promise that will remain true once she is on the other side."

"Don't you need to sniff her to make sure?"

"Sniff?" He scoffs. "Only elementals need to do that to detect a touch of the Unseen. I simply know."

Since he said that in an imperious voice, I'm beginning to understand why Max calls him, among other things, "bloody annoying but not half-bad otherwise."

"Okay," I say. "Thanks for the assist. I think we can take it from here."

"Good luck," Max says. "I'm going home to shag my wife."

And he disappears. Looks like that's all the help I'll get from him.

Fine. I can handle this myself. My cop senses have kicked in again after a long dormancy, so… No problem.

Janus disappears.

I grab Larissa and whisk us onto the ledge that backs the waterfall. "We'll need to step through the water to get inside the cave."

"You expect me to get wet? That water is probably cold."

My mind shows me an image of Larissa, drenched, with her nipples poking out through her wet shirt. I'd glimpsed her nude backside the other night, but I hadn't seen her in the shower.

"Yes, Your Highness," I say, "you're going to get wet. But don't worry, I'll warm you up afterward."

"No, you will not."

"Shut up, Larry."

I hug her to me and leap through the cascade.

We land inside the cavern where the deafening rumble of the waterfall is muted by magics that I've never bothered to figure out. The floor is even, except for the water-filled pockmarks scattered across it, and the rough-hewn walls have been cut out of the cliff in a way that looks artificial, though I've never asked anyone about that. With the Unseen, it's better not to ask too many questions. I'll get answers I'd rather not hear.

Gentle light fills the cavern, seeming to come from the air itself, though I have no idea if that's how it works. The light doesn't sparkle or shimmer. It simply *is*.

Raising one hand toward the rear wall, I close my fingers tight and then snap them straight.

The portal telescopes open.

In stark contrast to the glow in the rest of the space, the rear wall of the cavern harbors a blackness deeper than the abyss of a black hole in outer space. Within the darkness, fingers of glistening onyx wriggle and writhe as if they want to latch on to anyone or anything that might venture too close. Pinpoints of brightness explode and dissipate within the blackness, over and over, while slithering tongues of iridescent blue, green, and purple lick at the air.

This is the portal to the Unseen. And yeah, it's creepy.

"What is that?" Larissa asks as she stares at the seething darkness.

"It's the portal. How can you not know that?"

Though I'm still holding her to my body, she manages to kick my shin. "I was a goddess, you dumb lug. Why would I ever visit the mortal world? I never left the Unseen, not in all my existence."

"I thought some of the people you ensorcelled were human. How did you kidnap them without leaving the Unseen?"

She kicks me again. "I did not kidnap anyone. They were mortals who had stumbled onto a portal and found themselves lost in the Unseen, or elementals who wanted to find shelter in my temple."

"Ah, of course. That makes it perfectly okay for you to brainwash them."

"Would you shut up and take me…wherever it is you're taking me."

I can't resist shifting my hands down to palm her ass. "I haven't done that yet, Your Highness. But when I do take you, I guarantee I'll be the one in charge while you beg me to make you come."

Wanting to have sex with her doesn't mean I like her. A salamander needs sex, and I might as well get it from the most convenient source. Doesn't hurt that she's beautiful and sexy. But there is the problem of her mouth, the one that spews obnoxious things on a regular basis, not to mention the peevish looks she gives me and the way she calls me a dumb lug and an oaf. So, I would need to strap duct tape over her mouth, cover up her face, and tie her down so she can't kick me anymore. Sometimes I wish I knew how to ensorcell someone. Well, not just anyone. *Her.*

If I expected Larissa to get high and mighty on me again, I was dead wrong.

She pushes up onto her tiptoes and wriggles against me, rubbing her breasts on my chest and her groin into my cock. "Never had anyone dominate me during sex. Might be fun."

"Thought you needed to be in charge. The great goddess commanding her helpless thralls."

"It's not really commanding if they've been magically compelled to do whatever you want." She lowers her head so all I can see is the strip of her scalp exposed by the part in her hair. "Being dominated isn't always a pleasurable experience. Having your control stripped away without your consent... I can't believe I did that to so many innocent people, knowing full well how it would affect them."

"You've been an innocent yourself for the past two years. Maybe you've learned a lesson or two from that experience."

"Innocent?" She lifts her head, those catlike eyes shimmering in the soft light within the cavern. "Maybe I was an innocent, long ago, but I barely remember those days."

The part of me that still feels like a mortal balks at the question I want to ask her. My mother always told me it was an insult to ask a woman her age, but I can't help wondering. And the salamander in me thinks it's perfectly fine to pose the question. "How old are you?"

"Do you think I kept count?"

"I guess that depends on how old you are."

She twists out of my grasp, which only works because I let her do it. "Enough questions. Take—Escort me to wherever it is you're planning to go."

"Oh yes, milady," I say with heavy sarcasm while I bow before her, "it will be my honor to escort you to Ennea's laboratory."

She puckers her lips, then relaxes them as she lifts her brows. "Ennea? She's a fae witch, isn't she?"

"Yes." I wonder how she knows that since I'm positive Ennea has never met Hathor, but then the truth smacks me in the face. "Max told you about Ennea, didn't he?"

"Of course he did. We were very close, and we had long conversations."

"While you had him ensorcelled. Yeah, I'm sure you two were best buddies." I lean in, narrowing my gaze on hers. "That's why Max remembers you so fondly that he curses your name whenever someone mentions you."

She turns her head away. "Maybe our friendship wasn't real, but it meant something to me."

Did she… No, she couldn't have fallen in love with Max. That would mean she had feelings, and everything I've heard about Hathor suggests she cares about no one but herself. Of course, everything I've heard about her came from Max. She had enslaved him with magic, multiple times, so his opinion of her is colored by those experiences. And the woman standing in front of me is no longer a goddess. She's lived among mortals, as a mortal, for two years. Is that long enough for her to mend her ways?

I haven't always acted like an upstanding citizen either. Maybe I never took complete control of another person's mind, body, and soul, but I have done things that I wish I could take back.

Since I can't decide if I want to know more about this woman, I opt for the safer choice. Grasping her wrist, I lead Larissa through the portal.

The journey takes a split second, and though most mortals can't see the black tunnel that ferries us into the Unseen, I can see it. The portal deposits us inside a clearing rimmed by trees that resemble nothing seen in the mortal world, with moss-like leaves drooping from their branches. The sun blazes above us like a glittering diamond and hovers in a sky that shimmers a deep sapphire blue. No matter how many times I visit this world, I never get used to the way it looks.

Behind us, water pours out of a boulder almost as tall as I am to spill into a small pool. That is the portal. From this side of the veil, when the portal is closed, it doesn't seem impressive at all.

Larissa glances around with a slight smile on her lips. She must feel like she's come home, but the happiness disintegrates within seconds. Then she gnaws on her lip as she cringes against me. Having an entire world full of people who want to avenge themselves on you could make a person…tense.

I take us away, but I can't materialize inside Ennea's lab. It's warded, and though the spell that created the wards recognizes every visitor's intentions and grants access if they're deemed safe, I have no idea how the magics will react to Larissa. To be safe, I set us down near the hillside that conceals Ennea's lab. Keeping one arm around Larissa, I thump my fist on the hillside.

"Ennea!" I shout. "It's me, Travis. I have someone with me. Can we come in?"

The hillside shimmers, and part of it vanishes, revealing the cavern inside. Ennea stands there, hands on her hips. "Well, get your butt in here, Travis. You're letting a draft in."

I keep a hand on Larissa's back as we enter the laboratory, and the doorway telescopes shut behind us. Tables and shelves stocked with ingredients for spells and potions fill the space, and the smell of various unidentifiable substances gives the room a strange, but not unpleasant, atmosphere. I've always like Ennea's lab. It suits her. The witch belongs to a tribe of fae who call themselves leprechauns, though they look nothing like the ones in movies. Ennea has bright-green eyes that glow faintly when she's casting a spell. Naturally, she's adorable. All leprechauns are, I think, though I would never tell her brother Tris that.

"Sit if ya like," Ennea says in her unusual accent. It's something like the Bronx and something like Chicago, but not quite either. "Or stand. Makes no nevermind to me."

Larissa glances around the cave that houses Ennea's lab, her eyes wide and her skin a shade paler. Is she afraid of what the witch might do to her? Well, I know she worries about what all those people she enslaved might do if they see her, but as far as I know, she's never done anything to Ennea. They haven't met before.

"This is Larissa," I say, laying an arm across her shoulders without meaning to do it. "She used to be, ah…"

"For Ra's sake," Larissa hisses. Whatever anxiety she'd been feeling a minute ago seems to have lessened. She steps away from me and squares her shoulders. "I used to be Hathor."

Despite her fear, she fessed up. The woman has gumption.

"Oh," Ennea says, her eyes flaring wide briefly. "I heard you were missing in action."

"Yes, I kind of was."

Ennea hops onto a tall stool and wiggles until she's comfortable. "All right. Tell me what you're wanting me to do, then tell me everything I need to know so I can do it."

Chapter Twelve

Larissa

I TELL THE STORY AGAIN, THIS TIME TO A WOMAN I HAVE NEVER MET BE-fore today and who would have every reason to despise me. Maybe I hadn't ensorcelled her, but she must know the stories about me. Since she and Max are friends, he probably told her all about me. So I can't understand why the witch wants to help me. I'm evil, aren't I? Or I was evil. Not sure what I am now, but I spent too many eons doing terrible things that will surely curse me to suffer eternal torment if I should die as a mortal.

As a god, I could never die. That's not always a good thing.

Once I finish my story, Ennea leans forward on her stool to pin me with her gaze. "You kinda glossed over the whole banished-from-the-Unseen part of the equation. I need the deets, hon."

"Deets?" I have no idea what that means. "Are they creatures that assist you with your spells?"

"No," she says with a laugh. "I meant the details. Tell me exactly what went down when the Four Winds did whatever they did to you. You can skip the part about them throwing you in prison. What happened after that?"

"I was teleported into their temple, and Janus was there too. They all gathered around me and started chanting." I hunch my shoulders, spreading my arms with my palms out. "Then, whoosh. I was in the mortal world. Naked. In an alley that wasn't the most pleasant place to wind up when you have no clothing on."

Travis's gaze veers to me. He doesn't blink, just staring at me. "How could they do that to you? Leaving a woman alone and defenseless is bad enough. But naked? You could've been—" He freezes, then speaks carefully. "Did anyone hurt you?"

"No, not successfully."

"What does that mean?"

"One odious man tried to assault me, but I grabbed the lid from a metal garbage can and whacked him over the head with it. Then I stole his clothes." I shake my whole body like I can shake off the memory that way. "They stank, and I think the man was infested with fleas. No one else tried to touch me."

His lips twitch upward at the corners. "Nobody messes with Hathor, eh?"

I feel a strange warmth in my chest when he says that.

Ennea flicks her gaze between me and Travis. "You two are friends or something, huh?"

"Not exactly," I say. "Can you figure out what was done to me? If I'm human or something else?"

"Sure thing. Gimme a minute to whip up a spell."

While she goes about her business, flipping through a large book and humming tunelessly, Travis shepherds me over to a corner of the lab away from where the pretty fae is working.

"Don't worry about Ennea," he says. "She's the best witch around, and she won't hold it against you because you used to be, ah, not the sweetest person in the world."

"I was an evil bitch. Go on, say it. The truth sets you free, right?"

"Not always."

"For me, it's not ever. I don't expect anyone to forgive me, much less accept that I don't want to be that evil hag anymore."

He pulls his head back, blinking swiftly. "You don't want to be a goddess anymore?"

"I don't know. But I absolutely will not ever again abuse other creatures for my own pleasure." I look down at my hands and realize I'm wringing them. "Honestly, I never got any pleasure from the things I did, anyway."

Travis opens his mouth but doesn't get the chance to speak.

"Ready to go," Ennea calls out. "Come over here, Larissa."

I shuffle to the high table in front of her, crossing behind it to stand beside her. "You called me Larissa."

"Kinda figured that was your preference. It's what Travis calls you."

"Yes, I do prefer my new name. The old name feels...wrong."

Ennea stares at me briefly, then pats the stool she'd been sitting on earlier. "Park your butt here, hon."

I hop onto the stool.

Travis has approached the other side of the table. He watches me, not Ennea, while the witch waves her hands in the vicinity of my head and chants softly in the fae tongue.

I have no idea what she's saying, but her lilting voice relaxes me.

After a moment, she lowers her hands. "All done."

"What's the verdict?" Travis asks.

Ennea nudges me with her elbow. "Ain't it cute when he goes all cop and starts spouting the jargon?"

No, "cute" isn't the word I would use. Travis is…something else.

The incubus plants his hands on his hips and frowns at Ennea. "You know what I was asking."

"Chill, hon, I'm getting there." Ennea sets a hand on the table, drumming her fingers. "She is mortal, but not exactly human."

"Is she still a goddess?"

"Not sure."

His frown deepens into a scowl while his eyes become slits. He speaks through clenched teeth. "After all that spellcasting bullshit, that's the best you can do?"

"Sorry, hon, I did my best. If you want more answers, I recommend seeing an oracle."

I leap off the stool, backing away from her. "No, not that. The oracles despise me."

"This one won't," she says. "Trust me. Bob's good people."

Covering my face with one hand, I try so hard not to moan like a pathetic wuss. "But I tried to ensorcell him two thousand years ago."

"He don't hold grudges, hon. Besides, Bob's the only oracle who can handle this kind of screwy magic."

Travis comes around the table to me. He clasps both my hands. "I won't let anybody hurt you."

Ennea's brows shoot up. She looks from Travis to me and back to him. "Can I have a word?"

He follows Ennea into a corner of the room. Their conversation seems intense, given their expressions and gestures. Finally, the witch raises her hands and shrugs.

And Travis stalks up to me. "Time to pay Bob a visit."

He transports us out of Ennea's lab and straight to the edge of a forest much darker and bleaker than the surrounding woods. Even in the middle of the day, the oracle's forest exudes darkness and danger, and night always reigns within its precinct. This is a tactic for discouraging casual passersby from entering the oracle's domain, but it's more than that too. Only those who desperately need to speak to the oracle will forge ahead through the dangers that await them if they proceed into the woods.

Travis wraps his hand around mine. "Ready?"

I nod.

We cross the boundary of the oracle's precinct, into the eerie confines of the black forest. Viscous black liquid oozes out of the gnarled bark of the thick trees, all of which measure wider than Travis is tall. A stench reminiscent of disinfectant, though much more pungent, clogs the air.

"Keep an eye on the sky," I tell him. "The kerkopes haunt these woods. The oracle might not be homicidal, but those creatures are."

"I know that. Why do you keep talking to me like I'm a mortal who's never been to this world before?"

"Because you act like one."

"And you act like a spoiled princess."

I groan out a sigh. "Can we please not argue right now? We need to find the oracle's lair."

"Lindsey told me where it is."

"How? I never saw you talking to her alone."

"Not today." He throws me an annoyed sideways glance. "Before."

"Before what?"

He snorts. "You, for one."

I give up. The man insists on making no sense. I've lived with mortals for two years, but none of the others I've met irritate me as much as he does. Does that mean I secretly like him? According to the idiotic so-called comedies on TV, that's what it must mean.

No, I don't feel that way. I would gladly have sex with him, but that's all.

We reach a stream that looks as toxic as the trees, because it is, but it's too wide for me to jump across the water. Travis picks me up, cradling me to his body, and leaps across the fetid stream to land on the opposite shore. Then he sets me down.

That was rather impressive. I know Max can jump like that, but I had no idea Travis could. Most salamanders I've known aren't that athletic except in bed.

He clamps a hand around my upper arm and urges me to walk alongside him as we move deeper into the forest. Flapping sounds high in the trees suggest kerkopes hide up there, waiting for a chance to dive-bomb us. I've seen such attacks before, but those creatures never dared to touch me. Now, they probably would. I am no longer a god, but merely a woman. Vulnerable. Fragile. Easily ripped apart.

Travis won't let that happen. Will he?

Something swoops low overhead.

He pulls me into his side and peers up into the darkness.

I think he just might step in if something or someone attacks me. He intervened when the sylphs and the harpy came for me.

We survive the forest and reach a small hill.

"This is it," Travis announces. "How can you know the oracle but not know how to get here?"

"I met Bob on a few occasions, but not at his lair. I had minions to come here and make requests for me."

"Requests?" He gives me a dubious look.

"Maybe it was more of a demand. Does it matter right now?"

"Not sure. Guess that depends on how offended he was by your demands."

I wave toward the hill. "How do we get inside?"

"Easy." He approaches the slope, gesturing for me to join him. "Wait for it."

"Wait for what? The dirt to speak to you?"

He compresses his lips and squints at me.

A portion of the hill dissolves, revealing a set of steps that lead to a door recessed into the earth.

Travis stretches out an arm toward the opening. "Ladies first."

I descend the steps, and the door swings open. I head down the corridor inside the hill, which has a barrel ceiling and smooth rock walls. Light that emanates from no visible source casts its wan glow over us, but that hardly bothers me. Elementals love the light-from-nowhere trick. Travis catches up and walks alongside me, which gives me another odd sensation of warmth in my chest. I should not start to rely on him to protect me. If he learns some of the hard truths about me, from the oracle or someone else, he won't want to shelter me anymore. I won't blame him if he feels that way.

But haven't I changed? I'm not the one who can judge that.

"I've never been to the oracle's lair before," Travis says. "But Lindsey told me it used to be disguised as a boulder, then Bob upgraded to a hill so Ken the oracle wouldn't have one up on him."

"Fascinating."

He grabs my arm, forcing me to halt. "Better ditch the all-powerful goddess attitude before we walk into Bob's lair. I don't think ticking off an oracle is a smart choice right now."

"Sorry. I'll bite my tongue."

"I can think of better things to do with your tongue."

The man really shouldn't be making suggestive comments right now, considering that we both might die horribly if the oracle deems us unworthy. Of course, a salamander can't help himself. Travis flirts with every woman he meets, I'm sure, because that is his nature.

But he didn't flirt with Ennea or Lindsey.

We start moving again and reach a large bronze door that swings open for us. Oracles love theatrics. Maybe I used to enjoy that kind of thing too, but I now find I don't appreciate it anymore. How strange.

Travis walks carefully as we cross the threshold into the oracle's inner chamber, like he thinks that will prove to Bob that we're no threat. I could tell him that's a pointless effort, but arguing right now seems like a dangerous idea. I'm sure Bob views this as his sacred space, but I've lived too long in this world to be impressed by such things.

We stop near the large bronze bowl that hunkers in the middle of the chamber, held up by legs fashioned to resemble the feet of a big cat. Amber flames stretch their tongues upward from the bowl, the fire flickering several feet high, and the rough texture of the metal casts shimmering reflections of the light. Bob always has loved drama. I never succumbed to that. No, of course not. My temple had been covered in images of me towering over my subjects while they genuflected before me, but no, that wasn't showmanship. It made my thralls happy to gaze upon my image whenever they liked.

Probably because I had them ensorcelled.

Okay, maybe I did enjoy a bit of drama. Not anymore, though. And I might have experienced a twinge of nausea when I remembered my temple and the beings I had imprisoned there.

The oracle Bobanzhistilanovitz, aka Bob, saunters out of the shadows on the other side of the bronze bowl and halts several feet from its rim. The oracle gazes into the flames. "Took you long enough to get here. I've been expecting you for a long time."

"I would've arrived sooner," I say, "if you didn't use such moronic theatrical tactics to conceal your lair. An acid river? Please."

"I wasn't talking to you, Hathor." He veers his gaze to Travis and thrusts out one arm to point a finger at the incubus. "I meant him."

CHAPTER THIRTEEN

Travis

MAYBE I SHOULDN'T BE SURPRISED BY WHAT BOB JUST SAID, SINCE Lindsey had come here before with Max and the leprechaun Tris, but I am surprised. Stunned, actually. Bob had been waiting for me to show up here? Why? I'm not that important. As part of Team Lindsey, the group of allies who helped her save the world twice, I'd done some minor heroic things. Nothing that makes up for all the mistakes I've made. Definitely nothing that should attract the attention of an oracle.

But he'd pointed at me. Said he'd been waiting for me to come. Why the hell would he do that?

"You must have me confused with someone else," I say. "Maybe Max."

The oracle shakes his head and sighs. "No, Travis, I meant *you*. I've known for ages this time would come, but I had no foresight concerning how long you would take to come here once the precipitating event occurred."

"Look, we're not here to talk about me."

"I know." He taps his forehead, smiling slightly. "Foresight, remember? I've been expecting Hathor too, though the Oversoul didn't see fit to show me when that would happen. You may have come here to chat about her"—He sneers slightly when he glances at Larissa—"but first, we need to discuss you."

"Are you going to be fair to Larissa? She told me you hate her."

"Hate?" Bob puffs up and aims his flame-bright, glittering green eyes at Larissa. "I don't despise you, dear. I am above such emotions."

She makes a derisive sound. "Come off it, Bob. You wouldn't let me into your precious lair because I turned down your advances."

The goddess of sex refused an oracle? I thought she did the deed with anybody and everybody.

Bob folds his arms over his chest. "I didn't proposition you, dear. Losing your powers seems to have addled your mind."

"Enough," I say. "Can we talk about the reason for this visit? Don't give a crap about your petty, eons-old grudges against each other. I would've thought two uber-powerful beings like you guys would show a little more maturity."

Bob lifts one brow at me.

Larissa turns her gaze down to the floor and kicks at it with the toe of her boot.

Score one for the formerly human former sheriff. Cops know how to make people shut the hell up.

But I still can't get over Bob's clothes. He's wearing a navy-blue suit with shiny black loafers, and his gray hair is slicked back. The oracle reminds me of a gangster in an old movie from the forties. I guess I'd expected him to wear flowing robes and have a crown of laurels on his head or…something.

I step closer to the huge honking bronze bowl to aim my cop stare at Bob. "Are you going to help us or not?"

"Help? That's not my thing. I provide insight."

"Great. Give us some of that." I suddenly feel like I'm channeling Lindsey, since she often spoke to vaunted beings from the Unseen as if they were just average Joes. But I have my own way of dealing with these people.

Bob's lips slant upward at one corner. "I had a feeling you'd be a handful. Both of you, actually. It goes without saying that Hathor will cause me grief."

"If it goes without saying, why did you say it?"

He chuckles. "Fair point. Now, shall we move on to the main issue?"

"Yes." About damn time.

"I know you both believe you came here to learn about Hathor, but you're really here to talk about you, Travis."

I snort.

"Don't be rude, salamander. You're lucky you came to me and not Ken. He's prejudiced against your kind." The oracle stretches out a hand, hovering it over the flames in the bowl. "You, Travis Blackwell, are the reason for this visit. Your destiny affects many others—most notably, the maddening creature who now calls herself Larissa Robustelli." He aims a disappointed look at her. "Honestly, that was the best alias you could come up with?"

We agree about one thing at least. I'm starting to like this oracle.

Larissa screws up her mouth and hugs herself.

I move closer to her, draping an arm around her shoulders. "Can we skip the lead-in and get straight to what we need to know?"

"Your destiny began on the day you imprisoned the woman you claimed to love and harassed her for years after. The time has come to atone and forgive."

A chill trickles down my spine. He seems to know things about me I've never told anyone, but I guess that's an oracle's shtick. Still, it leaves me feeling uncomfortable because I have no idea what other secrets he might blurt out.

"Just to be crystal clear," Bob says, "I mean forgiving yourself. You helped save two worlds, twice, but you still struggle with your transition from human to elemental. Here's my advice for you." Bob leans forward, fixing his unblinking gaze on mine. "Cut that out."

I guess I'd expected an oracle to be more…oracle-ish. Calm. Soothing. All-knowing but above the petty issues the rest of us deal with. But no, he's just like every mortal on earth and every elemental I've ever met. I can't think of anything to say to Bob. Cut it out? Like I can wave my hand and get rid of all the baggage I've accumulated over a lifetime.

"He refuses to acclimate," Larissa says. "And the arrogant man is too stubborn to admit he needs help."

"I need help?" I say. "You're the one who has bounty hunters on your tail."

"Every time you speak, you sound ridic—"

"Silence!" Bob bellows, his voice so loud and powerful that Larissa and I both freeze. The oracle's shout echoes off the stone walls, and his eyes have begun to glow brighter. He thrusts a hand into the amber flames, making them surge higher with a whoosh and a crackling sound. "Listen carefully, because I will say this only once."

Larissa presses her body to my side.

I wrap my arm around her more securely. Yeah, the oracle's commanding voice could cow a gnome, and those bastards are huge, angry beasts that can cause earthquakes by stomping their feet. So no, I don't feel unmanly for cowering a little bit.

Bob pulls his hand out of the fire, straightens his suit, and clears his throat. "The path ahead is forked. Choose the wrong direction, and all will be lost. Let your hearts dictate your choice, not your heads. Be honest and forthright with each other, or you will do more than destroy yourselves. You will doom two worlds."

Maybe I'd been hoping Lindsey was the only one who had to figure out how to save the worlds. But no, it looks like I have to steer the ship this time. Fan-frigging-tastic.

"As for what has become of Hathor," Bob says. "She is mortal, but it's unclear whether that is a permanent condition. The bounty hunters can track her now because their masters spent months searching for a way to do just that. It took an enormous amount of dark magics to accomplish the feat, but the leaders of several races in the Unseen cooperated on that task. Now, they compete for the prize. Bringing Hathor in would be the biggest coup any of them has ever achieved. As for the rest of your questions, the Four Winds won't allow me to see."

"Perfect. We came here for answers and got a giant goose egg."

"That's not a bad thing."

"Goose egg means zero. Zilch. Nothing."

Bob groans and grasps his forehead. "I know that, salamander. Haven't you heard of the goose that laid the golden egg?"

"Oh. Sure."

He backs away from the bronze bowl, inching closer and closer to the darkness out of which he had emerged moments ago. "I've told you everything I'm permitted to say. Heed my words, or all is lost. And remember this. As a dear friend once told me, humanity is more than a condition of slowly approaching death."

Bob disappears into the shadows.

What the fuck? Slowly approaching death? I thought oracles were supposed to give sage advice, not issue vague threats. Or maybe I'm misinterpreting his less-than-clear statement.

Larissa slips her hand into mine. "Let's go. He won't come back to give us the answers we want."

"Yeah, I know. It's up to us to figure out what in tarnation he meant."

"That's what oracles do. You'll get used to it."

We exit the oracle's lair hand in hand, making our way down the corridor and out the door. It vanishes behind us, replaced by the hillside, as if the entrance had never existed. The little hill hunkers there like it contains nothing more unusual than dirt and grass. We hurry through the dark and disturbing forest, with its stench of decay and ammonia, neither of us wanting to spend any more time than necessary in this place. I realize Bob uses this unsettling landscape as a way of deterring casual interlopers. But did he have to make it quite so disturbing?

Wings flaps overhead. Kerkopes, I imagine. Lindsey had described the creatures to me once, and they sound like beings I'd rather avoid. A chill raises every hair on my body. My brother, Calder, had become one of the kerkopes when he was forged, while he lay dying alongside a pool of water in Texas. Now I've become an incubus. Was I always destined, or maybe doomed, to undergo the forging and become inhuman? Is it my punishment for the things I've done in the past?

Larissa and I leave the dark woods and step out into the waning light of the evening sun. Soon, it will dip below the horizon. Night is not a quiet time in the Unseen. All the worst creatures emerge at sunset to hunt for prey.

"We should find someplace to hide you," I tell Larissa as we halt in a clearing. "Max's lair is warded, so I think we should go there."

"Max won't want me in his home."

"If I ask him, he'll do it."

"You two are close, huh?" She eyes me while smirking just a touch. "Have you and Max ever had sex?"

"I get naked with women all the time."

"That's not what I mean." She sidles up to me, rubbing her body against my side, and speaks in a sultry voice. "Have you and Max ever had sex with each other?"

"What? No, of course not."

She glances upward and makes an exasperated noise. "You and Max are two of a kind. He didn't want to get it on with another male unless I ensorcelled him to do it."

"And you wonder why he hates you."

Biting her lip, she averts her gaze. "Yeah, I know. I was horrible to everyone."

I remember earlier, when she vowed she would never again abuse another being for her own pleasure. Then she'd said, "Honestly, I never got any pleasure from the things I did, anyway." Realization shimmers through me as I consider that statement again. I'd dismissed it as nothing at the time. Now, I start to wonder.

"Did you enjoy getting it on with your thralls?" I ask.

She wraps her arms around herself. "Rather not talk about it."

"Bob said we need to be honest and forthright with each other."

"Oh, I could throttle that oracle." She rubs her arms and aims her gaze at the ground. "No, I did not enjoy it. I don't think I have ever experienced true pleasure of any kind—sex, drugs, even spells don't make me feel anything. Happiness and sexual fulfillment are alien to me."

For a moment, I can't speak or move. Though I stare at her, she still refuses to look at me and keeps rubbing her arms as if she's cold. I conjure a soft blanket and drape it over her shoulders.

Her head pops up. She blinks rapidly, her gaze glued to mine. "What are you doing?"

"You look cold, so I got you a blanket."

"But why? You can't stand me."

I scratch my cheek and grimace. "Well, maybe that's not strictly true."

"Honest and forthright, remember?"

Yeah, I'd like to throttle Bob too. "Okay, I don't hate you. I've gotten used to you, and maybe I kind of think you're an all-right person. When you aren't acting like a pretentious goddess."

"Gee, thanks. I don't hate you either. You aren't half-bad when you stop calling me Larry and Your Highness."

"Did we just admit we like each other?"

"Let's not go overboard. We tolerate each other, and I suppose that's a good start."

I gaze up at the bright colors of sunset, their shades much more intense than anything I'd seen in the mortal world. "When I kissed you, did you feel anything?"

"Well...maybe something. A teeny bit."

Can't stop myself. I smirk at her. "Only a teeny bit? You had your legs wrapped around me, and you were rubbing yourself all over my cock, and you were making noises I can only describe as—"

"Okay, fine. I felt a big something." She looks straight into my eyes. "I think I might have gotten…aroused. Highly aroused. But that's never happened to me before, so I can't be sure."

"I have the solution." I grasp her hips and tug her closer. "Let's try that again. If you start to feel tingly and hot, and you get wet down here"—I push my hand between her thighs—"then you'll know for sure I get you turned on."

Her breaths quicken. "Please, do that. I'm dying to know what a real orgasm feels like."

From the other side of the clearing, someone starts clapping.

She jerks away from me, staring wide-eyed at the area from which the clapping originates.

I hold up a hand to shield my eyes from the glare of sunset, but I can't see whoever's over there, hidden in the shadows of the trees. "Show yourself."

A figure ambles out, halting halfway across the clearing. Larissa and I stand at the periphery. The man has deeply tanned skin that's dusted with shimmering flecks of gold. His black hair hangs in wild waves around his face and reaches his broad shoulders. He has the physique of a typical elemental, but somehow, I sense this being is not like me. He exudes a kind of power no elemental could achieve.

He stops clapping, though he seems enormously pleased with himself.

"Oh no," Larissa says, almost whining. "Go away. Haven't you harassed me enough? I bet you sent those bounty hunters after me."

"Hunters?" the man says with a dismissive wave of his hand. "I don't need to bother with those vile creatures. I knew all I needed to do was wait, and eventually, you would find your way back to the only world that counts."

The being speaks with a British accent, like me and Max, but that's the only similarity. This guy moves like he's used to everyone being wowed by his presence. He kind of reminds me of a male model strutting his stuff on the runway. I only know what those guys do because I once dated a girl who loved all that fashion garbage. I couldn't care less if I'm in vogue, or whatever they say.

"Who the hell are you?" I demand.

He tosses his head, flicking his hair.

I thought only stuck-up women did that.

"Why should I speak to a salamander?" he says with disdain in his voice. "Hathor, darling, it's time to come home."

"Home?" she says, scuffling closer to me. "You imprisoned me for nearly two thousand years."

"Are you planning to hold a grudge forever? Come on, we both know I give you the best sex you've ever had."

"No, you don't. I never felt anything for you, much less experienced an orgasm."

He stares at her for a second or two, then busts out laughing. "I am the best lay in the multiverse. Of course you came for me."

"I faked it, you arrogant asshole."

I smack my fist into the other palm, creating a loud enough noise they both look at me. "Who are you? Tell me now, or I'll crush your skull."

The bastard laughs again. "Crush me? You have an inflated view of your strength, puny salamander. I am Kamadeva, the Hindu god of pleasure."

"Comma-day-vah? What a stupid name. Is your brother called Parenthesissy?"

"Hathor can explain to you how my name is spelled. Assuming you are literate." He shakes his head. "Never can tell with your kind. Salamanders are the lowest creatures in the Unseen."

"Guess you love gnomes, then. And what about those slimy kerkopes? You're enamored of them too, I guess."

Kamadeva stalks up to me, stopping inches away. Since he's as tall as I am, he can glare into my eyes without lifting his head. "Go find a nymph to rut on like the filthy animal you are. Hathor and I are gods, so far above your kind that you can't see my big toe. She belongs to me."

"You arrogant, condescending—"

"Shut up!" Larissa screams. "I belong to no one."

Kamadeva backs up several paces, his eyes whirling with shades of blood red and metallic silver. Ice-blue flames flicker in his irises. "Do not anger me. Hathor knows what my rage looks and feels like, but you are unfamiliar and ignorant. I give you one last chance to leave us, incubus, before I destroy you."

"Like to see you try, Comma. A jerk named after punctuation doesn't scare me."

"My name is Kamadeva. K-A-M-A-D-E-V-A. What's yours? Mr. Wanker?"

I roll my shoulders back and glare at him. "Travis Blackwell."

"Never met an incubus who has a surname. Travis isn't a very…seductive name. Can't picture any female orgasming while screaming 'Travis.' Do you get any action at all?"

"Fuck off, Limp Dick."

"Kamadeva. Do you have hearing problems?"

Larissa screams, louder than before and without any words. She just screams and screams while the racket echoes off the trees and vibrates my eardrums. Even the Hindu god winces. When she finally stops, her cheeks are pink—from exertion, I think—and she's breathing hard.

"I'm standing right here," she hisses. "Would either of you care to address the woman you're arguing over?"

"No point," Kamadeva says with a shrug. "You belong to me."

He takes one step toward Larissa.

And I whisk us away.

CHAPTER FOURTEEN

Larissa

TRAVIS TAKES US TO A MOUNTAINSIDE THAT HAS A SMALL CLEARING AT its base. The mountain is so large I can't see the edges of it or guess its circumference. I don't know why Travis has brought us here, but he must have a good reason. As much as I complain about him, I realize he's intelligent and strong, in more than his body. He stood up to an oracle and a god. And he did that for me.

"Where are we?" I ask.

"You'll see." He thumps his fist on the mountainside. "Open the door. It's an emergency."

A small opening the size of a ship's porthole opens in the mountainside at the height of Travis's head. Max's face appears in the opening. "Why should I let *her* inside my home?"

He throws a sideways glance at me.

"Because I'm asking," Travis says. "And you trust me."

"And because I say so," a redheaded woman says as she hops up to look through the small opening. "It's my house too, Max."

"Harper, that creature is—"

"Powerless and in trouble. Are we still the good guys, or have you gone over to the dark side?"

"That female thing—"

"Is a woman called Larissa who used to be Hathor. Get over it, Max. And open the door."

Max grumbles, then the door telescopes open. He grudgingly waves for us to enter.

The woman beside him ushers us through an entryway into what seems like a combination living room and bedroom. She wears leather pants, just like Max does, but with a pink T-shirt while he goes shirtless. Since I know he prefers to go naked, he must've put on pants because he's uncomfortable with me on the premises. I notice another doorway but can't tell what lies beyond it. The perfect amount of warm light fills the room, with no visible source. Two chairs flank a small table, and a crimson chaise sits against the wall, while a large bed covered with a fur blanket is tucked against the opposite wall.

I'm in Max's lair. He never took me to his place back when we knew each other, in the biblical sense. Why would he? I rarely left my temple, and he only left it on those rare occasions when he escaped my clutches. I had clutches? That makes me sound like a villain, but I guess I had been one. Of course, even Max doesn't know the whole truth about our time together.

Harper sits on the edge of the chaise while Max hovers near the entry-way, a few feet from his wife.

I'd met Harper when my bounty hunters captured her and Max. I'd only wanted him. But even then, they came as a package deal. She's beautiful, strong, and now powerful thanks to whatever the obsidian fae did to her. She died and eventually came back as something more than human. Max had grieved for her so intensely that I couldn't help wondering if I had ever cared for anyone with that kind of passion, or if I'd ever cared at all. Were my feelings for Max an illusion? Did I convince myself he meant something to me so I could excuse my own behavior that way? I couldn't ensorcell someone I honestly loved. Could I?

My gaze flicks to Travis, who's just sitting down on one of the chairs.

I looked at him for no reason at all. It has nothing to do with what I'd been thinking about.

Travis leans over the table, looking at me when he pats the arm of the chair adjacent to his.

And I shuffle over there to sit down. The chair has nice padding. It's a bit large for me, but then, it was designed to fit a sylph. Nevan had lived here before he met Lindsey, and they shared it after they became a couple. Even when Nevan became king of the sylphs, he lived here with her instead of in the palace. Now, they're both mere mortals and live in a house or something. Everything I know about these people comes from what Max told me, and he hadn't always been super-specific. I do know Max moved in here after Nevan married Lindsey.

My gaze travels to Harper, who is smiling at me. "Nice to see you again, Hath—Larissa."

"Nice?" Max says, his lip curling.

Harper elbows him in the side. "Behave, Max."

Travis sits forward, resting his elbows on his knees. "We need a place to crash—a safe place—and this lair is warded."

"You want to cohabitate with me and Harper?" Max says, gaping at Travis.

"Only until we figure out what's going on and how to stop it."

"How long will that take? I don't want that creature in my home any longer than absolutely necessary."

"I know." Travis studies the floor for a moment. "Can the wards keep out a god?"

Max leaps to his feet. "You've angered a god? What the bloody hell is wrong with you?"

"This was a bad idea," I say. "We should go."

"No," Max groans. "I might despise you, but I can't stand by while bounty hunters and apparently gods try to capture you."

Harper clasps her husband's hand, giving him a grateful smile.

Why should she be grateful? I'm causing them both a great deal of trouble. They might get injured or even killed.

I jump up. "No, this is wrong. I won't risk anyone else's life in the vain hope of saving mine. Maybe I should just surrender to Kamadeva and end this."

Travis rises and grasps my arm, pulling me toward him. "You are not surrendering to that jackass."

Max shoves a hand through his hair and growls. "You can't go out there. Stay here while we try to come up with a plan."

"Can the wards keep out a god?" Travis asks again.

"I have no bloody idea." Max frowns. "But I think we're about to learn the answer to that question."

Though I want to tell Max to open the door and let me out so no one else will get hurt because of me, I know these people will not let me do that. They are heroes. Saving lives, saving worlds, is what they do. I'm just a former goddess who may or may not stay human forever, or at least until my mortal body gives out.

Harper stands, scrunching her face as if she's thinking hard. "Maybe Max and I should pay Ennea a visit and see if there's a way to beef up the wards."

"Shouldn't we stay here to protect these two?" Max asks.

"Are you sure the wards will hold if Kamadeva batters them?"

Max sighs, shutting his eyes briefly. "All right. Let's go see Ennea."

Harper and Max vanish. The wards are designed for them, clearly, so they don't need a doorway to come and go.

"Uh, what happens if we need to leave this place?" I ask. "Never had to think about wards before. Not sure how they work. I mean, I had them around my temple precinct, but nobody explained how they functioned. It didn't matter to me."

"We can't leave until Max and Harper come back."

"Isn't that dangerous?"

Max reappears. "Harper reminded me that you lot might need an escape hatch, as she calls it. This will let you come and go as you wish."

He tosses a small silver disk to Travis.

"What is this?" Travis asks, turning the disk between his fingers.

"Something I procured for Tris, a sort of key. Harper insists we invite the annoying leprechaun over for dinner at least twice a month, and he whines like a baby if he has to wait thirty seconds to be admitted into the lair or allowed to leave. I conjured it from his lair, but if he asks, you have no idea what happened to his key."

Max disappears again.

Travis stuffs the disk into his pants pocket. "Well, at least we have a get-away plan."

"What do we do now?"

"Beats me." He glances at my breasts, and his lips curve up in a sensual smile. "But I can think of one thing we could do to pass the time. I did promise I could make you come."

"We can't—Not here. What if Max and Harper come back?"

"They'll get an eyeful." He tugs me into his muscular body, the elemental heat of him penetrating my clothes and my skin to sink deep inside me. "I heard you hosted orgies in your temple. How can you be shy about getting it on with me?"

"I don't know. Everything feels different since I was dumped into the mortal world."

He slides his hands down to my bottom, cupping my ass cheeks. "Let's see how much I can make you feel."

I gasp when he slips a finger between my buttocks.

Travis keeps that finger wedged between my ass cheeks while he cradles the back of my head with his other hand. His lips descend on mine, hot and demanding, and he thrusts his tongue between my parted lips to tease the roof of my mouth. I moan and wilt against him. Kissing has never felt like this before. I open wider for him, moaning again when he glides his tongue around mine and shifts his hand away from my buttocks to shove it inside the waistband of my jeans and inside my panties, his rough palm exciting the bare skin on my bottom.

I clench his shirt and nip at his tongue.

He groans so deeply that I feel it in my sex.

Yes, please, more, make me feel. I can't speak the words, but I think them so hard that I wonder if he can hear it. With that hand inside my jeans, he hoists me up and rushes backward, dropping onto the bed on his back with me sprawled over him. I don't need to open my eyes to know what happened. I feel the silky fur of the blanket on my arms. He flips us over, his body pinning me to the bed, and rips open the button and the zipper on my jeans, then he plunges his hand inside to cup me between my thighs, where wetness coats my flesh. I've noticed that kind of thick liquid on other females, but I've never experienced it myself. I tingle there too, and every inch of my skin feels sensitized as if the slightest touch will make me scream with ecstasy.

Travis shimmies down my body until his face hovers above my groin. "Gonna devour you, Larissa. Eat up every last bit of your cream while you writhe and scratch me and beg for me to make you come."

He pushes his fingers inside my open waistband, seeming like he's about to pull my jeans down.

An explosion detonates right over our heads. The entire mountain trembles, and bits of dirt and rock splatter down around us.

Travis shields me with his body, though I can hear the fragments pelting him.

"What was that?" I ask, breathless from more than his touch.

"Not sure." He rises onto his hands and knees, glancing up at the ceiling. "Maybe it was just an earthquake. Do they have those in the Unseen?"

"I've only ever felt an earthquake when an angry elemental caused it. Gnomes, for one."

Another detonation rocks the mountain, sending more debris splattering down on us.

Travis covers my body with his. "Need to get out of here."

I feel him rooting around between our bodies until he finds his pocket and extracts something. The silver disk, I assume. Then he teleports us to the doorway, still holding me to his body. The wards prevent him from whisking us directly away. We need to open the door first.

Yet another bomb-like blast detonates overhead, and the ceiling caves in, carving out a cylindrical tunnel straight up through the mountain. Earth and rocks slump onto the floor as Travis and I struggle to stay upright through the concussive waves of the quake.

A being thumps down onto the debris pile. He shakes his head, shedding the dirt that had concealed his red hair. He shakes his entire body too, cleansing his reddish-brown skin. Wearing only a white kilt with an ornate belt, he rolls his shoulders back and smiles with feral satisfaction.

"Who the hell is that?" Travis asks, sounding bewildered.

I swallow hard, but my throat remains tight. My heart races, and I can't seem to pull in a whole breath.

Setesh hops off the debris pile and saunters over to us. He fixates his attention on me and only me. "Hathor, my *neferet*, I found you at last."

Then he teleports me into his arms and kisses me.

Chapter Fifteen

Travis

THE BEING WHO CRASHED STRAIGHT THROUGH A MOUNTAIN AND THE wards finally releases Larissa. She seems to be in shock, and I assume that's why she didn't fight off the red-skinned freak. Does he think he's King Tut? Dressing like a pharaoh. What an asshat. I can feel the wards are still in place, but the skirt-wearing lair crasher got in anyway.

Larissa staggers backward, right into me.

I grasp her shoulders. "You okay?"

"Uh-huh." She keeps staring at the sunburned cretin. "Why won't you leave me alone? First it was Kamadeva. Now you, Setesh. For Ra's sake, I'm not even a goddess anymore. After thousands of years away from all of you, suddenly I'm a prize for you to fight over."

So the ass in the skirt is called Setesh. Even his name annoys me.

I clutch the silver disk in my hand, the one Max gave me, and try to activate it so we can escape from this lair. But nothing happens. I feel a faint zing of magic, then it fizzles out. The guy in the skirt must've somehow dampened the disk's power or drained it. Why, then, are the wards still in place?

"Your current state of helplessness," the freak says, "made it possible for us to track you down once you entered the Unseen. The elemental tribes thought to employ bounty hunters, but that only proves what hapless fools they are. A god such as me needs no such assistance. Now that you are something closer to human, we could smell you as soon as your feet touched down in the realm. Mortals are pathetically easy to find."

He speaks with an odd accent. Maybe it's Egyptian, since he wears a kilt like the ones I've seen in tomb paintings from ancient Egypt. I'm not a history buff, but Lindsey had once convinced me to go with her to a museum exhibit in Dallas. That feels like centuries ago. It was literally in another lifetime, for me.

Larissa pushes closer against me. "Eros is coming for me too?"

Her voice is hushed and infused with a fear I haven't heard before. She handled Kamadeva like a pro, but Setesh has clearly set her on edge—and the mention of Eros has frightened her. Who are these bastards? They must've done something to her, long ago, something so terrible it can make a former goddess cringe.

"Did this Eros jerk-wad send the harpy and the sylphs?" I ask.

Setesh deigns to look at me, but he lifts his chin to glare down at me over his birdlike nose. "Of course not. I told you, true gods do not require the assistance of filthy elementals. Eros believes himself to be so clever and so powerful that he does not need to hire lowly creatures like harpies and sylphs to aid him. He created his own army of beasts that will do his bidding without question and without payment." Setesh tips his head down to peer at Larissa. "I enjoyed a great laugh when you commandeered one of his minions and ensorcelled the beast so he might serve you."

"What kind of beasts are these hunters?" I ask.

"The sort that will sink their fangs into your throat and drain the blood from your body."

"Vampires?" Oh, that's right. I remember Max talking about the vampire Gundisalvus, who had served Hathor. He's dead now, along with every other being that had been trapped inside Hathor's temple when the obsidian fae reduced it to rubble and dust. The magics employed by the obsidian fae had destroyed them all, which is the only way elementals can die. A temple crashing down on them wouldn't do it. But dark magics can.

"Bloody hell, what have you done to our home?"

The salamander who spoke those words has just materialized with his wife hugged to his side. Harper glances at Setesh, and her brows crinkle. When Max catches sight of the wannabe pharaoh, he flattens his lips into a slash.

"Another tosser who wants to get his hands on dear old Hattie?" Max says. "Go back to your godly apartment in the sky or wherever you live. This is *my* home."

I glance at Max. "Should you be harassing the man who busted a hole in a mountain and breached your wards without breaking them?"

"Why haven't you fled yet? I gave you a door key."

"The thing doesn't work," I hiss, hoping Setesh can't hear me.

"Dark magics," Max grumbles. "I hate that rubbish."

Setesh smiles with smug certainty. "You are all trapped now. I reconfigured the wards. Any elemental may enter this place, but none may leave without my permission."

That's just perfect. We're trapped in this lair with a skirt-wearing psycho.

Larissa looks at Max, and he stares at her, seeming confused. All I can see of her face is her cheek and her eyes. It looks like she's rolling them upward, then to the side, then upward again. Is this a secret code between the two of them? Max doesn't seem to understand, so I guess not.

Suddenly, he freezes, cants his head, and blinks once slowly.

Max jerks his head up and focuses on the god. "So Teshy, tell me what your grand and brilliant plan for us is. I like to know what sort of eternal torment I'm in for so I can cancel my golf plans."

"Golf?" Setesh says, squinting at Max. "You speak nonsense, incubus. But I will happily tell you my plans." He stretches out an arm to point at Max. "First, I shall dismember your body. Then, I shall dismember your woman's body. After that, I will dismember his body."

Setesh swings his finger in my direction.

"You're seriously into dismemberment," I say. "Can't come up with anything more original?"

"It's his thing," Larissa mutters. "His exploits inspired the ancient Egyptian myth about the god Setesh killing his brother Osiris and dismembering the body, then scattering the pieces far and wide. Isis collected all the pieces and reassembled Osiris so she could have sex with his corpse and bear their child, Horus."

"That's disgusting."

Setesh chuckles. "Isis always was twisted. Necrophilia does not appeal to me. But I fucked Isis once a few millennia ago, and she was surprisingly good in bed."

"As fascinating as your life story is," I say, "can we get on with your evil plan? I'm getting bored."

"You are anxious to be dismembered alive, eh? I shall happily oblige you."

"Before you start chopping, I'd like to know what you plan on doing with Hathor."

It feels strange to use that name. She is not the goddess anymore. She's a woman with frailties and feelings and wounds hidden deep under her skin.

Setesh sighs. "Obviously, I will ensorcell Hathor and make her my thrall. She will spend the rest of her life, assuming she remains human, catering to my needs. And she will enjoy it. In fact, she will beg me to let her swallow my glorious member countless times per day. She will also beg me to defile her in every sadistic manner I can think of."

Like hell he will.

Glorious member? He seriously said that.

The jerk-wad in a skirt told us the wards will let anyone in. I wonder if that goes for objects too. If I can conjure something useful… He can still smite me with his little finger, I'm sure, but at least I'll go down fighting. What should I conjure? An endued weapon would be great, but I don't know where to find one of those.

Oh yes I do. Can't believe I didn't think of it before.

I picture Lindsey and Nevan's home, their bedroom, and the closet in which they keep her endued Bond Arms derringer inside a lockbox. The weapon has interchangeable barrels that fit either .357 rounds or shotgun shells, but I think only the .357 rounds are endued. Though I have never attempted anything like this before, bringing an object to me through wards, I focus all my energy and power on a single task. *Bring me Lindsey's gun.*

A twinge of…something passes through me. But the gun does not appear.

Focusing even harder, so invested in the task that a cold sweat breaks out on my brow, I command the weapon to come to me and hold one hand down at my side with the fingers curled as if I'm holding a gun. The derringer is a small gun, so I should be able to hide it in my palm. I keep my gaze trained on Setesh, since I don't trust that bastard any further than I could throw him—which would be about three inches, I'm guessing.

An object fills my open hand. Cool metal. A short barrel with a cylinder, and a trigger guard brushing against my thumb. Damn, I did it. I've conjured Lindsey's endued derringer. Though I'm pretty sure I can't destroy a god with it, maybe I can at least injure him enough that he loses his hold on whatever magics he summoned to trap us here.

His belt buckle, emblazoned with an image of a bird, shimmers briefly.

Could that buckle be the anchor for the spell he used to trap us? I'm no expert on magic of any kind, much less the dark variety, but it seems improbable that his belt shimmering had nothing to do with the fact I just conjured an object from inside the wards. If I could ask Max…

I don't need to, do I? I've got a former goddess pressed against my body. But I kind of doubt Setesh will let me have a chat with her.

"May I kiss Hathor once before you dismember me?" I ask Setesh. "To say goodbye. Salamanders are very sentimental."

Peripherally, I notice Max lifting his brows. Yes, all right, I made up the thing about salamanders being sentimental. Maybe some are, I don't know. But I'm betting Setesh knows almost nothing about our kind, since he's an almighty god. Besides, I'm sure he will love watching me say goodbye to Larissa and surrender to him.

"One kiss," the god says. "A brief one."

Larissa turns toward me, laying her hands on my chest. I sense a question in her eyes, but I've got one of my own. I wrap my arms around her waist and lift her feet off the floor, bringing our faces into alignment. She gazes into my eyes, her brows furrowed. Her hair ought to hide what I'm doing well enough that Setesh won't catch on.

I press my lips to hers, lightly, so I can still whisper to her. "Does his belt buckle control the wards?"

"Maybe. I have seen him use it to enhance his spells."

"So, if I can disable him and steal the buckle, maybe I can unlock the wards."

"It's possible."

Although I should pull away from her, I do the exact opposite. Can't stop myself. I crush my mouth to hers and slide my tongue between her lips to taste her one more time, just in case my plan blows up in our faces.

"Go to Max," I whisper to her, then I take a step back. "I'm ready. Butcher me first."

Larissa doesn't hesitate. She hurries over to Max and Harper. He lays an arm over her shoulders in a protective gesture I wouldn't have expected from him, not with the former goddess who had repeatedly enslaved him.

I'm grasping the derringer behind my back, hoping it looks like I'm casually holding one arm behind my body. But not for long. I swing the weapon up, aim it at the god's torso, and fire five rounds into his chest.

Blood spurts out of him, then trickles down his flesh in miniature rivers. He gasps and flails his arms while his knees give out.

I might not have much time, so I rush at him and tear the buckle off his belt. The buckle's magic tingles in my palm. I drop it on the floor and fire the last round from the revolver straight into the metal. It shatters like glass, spraying bits on Setesh, who has just crumpled to his knees.

The silver disk in my pocket pulses. The magic is alive and ready.

Maybe I shouldn't bother, but I can't help myself. I lean over the gasping, gurgling god and snarl, "Don't mess with a cop, you arrogant bastard."

Then I rush to Max and the girls, activate the silver disk, and whisk us all away.

CHAPTER SIXTEEN

Larissa

THE FOUR OF US EMERGE AT THE EDGE OF THE POOL THAT MARKS THE POR-
tal, right next to the boulder. Its waters spill down into the pool, swirling
and bubbling. I'm sure Travis plans to take me back into the mortal world
in the hopes it will be harder for Setesh and Kamadeva to find me there.
Max and Harper have lost their home because of me, and I'm not sure I
deserve to be protected. But I'd experienced a kind of epiphany back there
in that lair. I realized I don't want to die.

Max and Harper step away from me and Travis, who has his arm
around me.

"Not sure how I feel about this," Max says. "You and Hathor getting so
chummy. But even a former evil cow doesn't deserve what Setesh or Kamadeva might do to her. Never met those blokes before, but I've heard the
rumors about them."

"They are even worse than the rumors let on," I say.

He nods. "Good luck, you two. I'm taking Harper to Lindsey and
Nevan's house. It's outside the boundaries, which means elementals can't
get there. As for gods, I don't have a ruddy clue. But it seems like the safest
place." Max eyes me, then looks at Travis. "You and Hath—Larissa could
come with us."

"No," Travis says. "We need to stay away from all of you. It's too dangerous, especially since bounty hunters can track her here."

"Oh, I forgot to give you Ennea's gift." Max holds out his hand,
palm up, and a necklace appears there. "She made this for Larissa. It
should make it more difficult for the hunters to track her, though
Ennea couldn't promise it will work all the time. This was a rush job,
after all."

"We appreciate it." Travis accepts the necklace, closing his fist around it. "Now, you guys go. Be safe. And tell Lindsey I'm sorry for stealing her gun, but I'll get it back to her soon."

Max nods, then raises one hand to curl his fingers and snap them straight, activating the portal. He and Harper walk through it hand in hand.

The portal remains open.

Before we cross the veil, Travis lowers the necklace over my head, letting it rest on my upper chest. The metal feels cool, and the Eye of Horus pendant attached to it gives me a strange feeling of déjà vu. I had experienced the entirety of the ancient Egyptian empire, from its founding to its disintegration, and my beloved friend Horus had witnessed it with me. Seeing the pendant, I can't help thinking of him. I have no idea where my friend went after the empire fell, but I know he'd gotten sick and tired of consorting with other gods whose depravity made him long for a simpler life. I had been depraved too, but somehow, Horus always saw the good in me.

Did the other gods destroy him? As I had helped them do to Janus?

My throat constricts. I haven't thought about Horus in such a long time.

"Hey," Travis says, brushing the backs of his fingers over my cheek. "What's wrong?"

"I'll tell you later. Can we please get out of the Unseen right now?"

"Absolutely."

He clasps my hand, leading me through the portal.

We step out into the cave behind the waterfall, and Travis scoops me up in his arms to carry me through the cascade and leap across the pool below and the wooden railing to whump down on the dirt path.

"Impressive," I say. "You're getting more comfortable with your incubus powers every day, aren't you?"

"More so lately." He sets me down, then wraps his arms around me. "I know a place where you've never been before, so I bet it'll take a good while before any hunters can track you there even if the necklace doesn't work."

"Where are we going?"

"You'll see."

He spirits us away, touching down again in the middle of a desert with strange-looking cactuses that resemble trees. Mountains hem in the valley, but they lie far distant from where we stand. The sun burns down on us from within a clear blue sky, but I see hints of smog along the horizon. Yes, I've become familiar with smog since I've lived in Phoenix. It's one of my least favorite things about this world.

"Where are we?" I ask.

"The Mojave Desert. Those are Joshua trees," he says, pointing at the trees I'd noticed a moment ago. "They're a type of cactus. Anyway, there are no natural water features in this area, so no elementals can come here—unless they have dark magics on their side."

"Not terribly comforting."

"I know. But it's the best I can do. Maybe hiding out in the desert will at least even the scales, but maybe it'll tip them a little bit in our favor."

"Thank you, Travis. I don't know what I'd do without you."

"You'll never need to find out." He peers over my shoulder, then smiles faintly and nods. "I see a place where we can crash tonight."

I know he can breach the boundaries because Lindsey gave a few of her elemental friends that ability before she gave up being the Janusite. The god Janus wanted his powers back, and Lindsey was, apparently, more than happy to relinquish them. Back before Max met Harper, he had come to me to satiate his sexual hunger because he'd let himself starve for too long. Naturally, I ensorcelled him. My skin itches when I remember that. But while Max was with me, he'd shared the story of the Janusite and how she gave up immense power to be with the man she loves and start a family with him. Lindsey and Nevan truly do have an epic love story, one worthy of becoming a legend.

Max and Harper have that kind of love too. Eternal. Powerful. Unbreakable.

I will never find that. My past sins will curse me to die alone.

But for now, I have an incubus protecting me, and I can pretend he might care for me in some small way. The fantasy keeps me going despite the bounty hunters, Kamadeva, and Setesh.

Travis teleports inside the little house he'd pointed out a moment ago. It looked small from a distance, but from the inside, it feels cozy. Dilapidated, but cozy. I suppose he couldn't find a vacant luxury hotel out here in the middle of nothing. Whoever had abandoned this place left behind a recliner, a love seat, a kitchen table with two chairs, and a full-size bed tucked into the corner. The house consists of one room. The tiny kitchen still has a stove, but there's no fridge. The bathroom seems to be a portable toilet shoved into the corner beside the stove.

Oh, lovely. But at least we're relatively safe here.

"Stand by the door," Travis tells me.

"Why?"

"Because."

Despite the fact that was not an answer, I move over to the door. He wants to be in charge, so fine, I'll let him. For now.

He walks into the center of the room and stops. Then he stuffs the little revolver he'd conjured earlier into his waistband. And he just stands there. Not doing anything. For a long, long, long moment.

"What are you doing?" I ask. "Listening for mice?"

"Shut your trap. I'm trying to concentrate."

I lean back against the door and watch him do absolutely nothing.

A bed appears in the center of the room. It's the one from Max's lair, the salamander-size bed with lots of cushioning and a lush fur blanket. Next, a picnic basket appears. Though its lid is shut, I can smell the food inside it. Fried chicken, I think. God, that smells good. My tummy starts to rumble because

I haven't eaten in so long that I can't remember when I'd last consumed anything resembling food.

Travis faces me, his lips stretched into a smug smile. "How d'ya like it?"

"Like what? The bed you stole from Max and the food you stole from…where exactly?"

"Not sure. You need to eat, so I got you some food. 'Thank you' might be a good thing to say right now."

I wander over to the bed, eying it with suspicion. "What are you planning to use this for?"

"Showing you what sexual pleasure feels like."

Though a delicious little shiver tingles down my spine, I feel compelled to point out the obvious. "Should we be doing that when bounty hunters and gods are after me?"

"Yes." He grabs the picnic basket and sets it on the bed. "Sit down, Larissa. Let's eat, and when you're ready, we can make love. The necklace ought to at least slow down the hunters."

"Please. You don't even like me, which means all you want is to screw me and devour my sexual energy."

His lips pucker briefly, then he sits down on the bed, his head bowed while he examines the contents of the picnic basket. "Fried chicken, potato salad, and apple pie. Hey, there's a thermos in here too."

I give up and drop my butt onto the bed next to him.

Travis opens the thermos, peers into it, and sniffs the contents. "Lemonade. Pink lemonade, I think."

"Are there paper plates and napkins?"

"Yeah." He glances at me, a slight smile on his lips. "Ready to satisfy your hunger?"

"What about yours?"

"Later."

We enjoy our picnic on the bed without talking. I can't talk since I'm too busy wolfing down the food. Travis doesn't need to eat, but he samples the offerings—to keep me company, I think. When my tummy has had enough, I take one more swig of lemonade and sigh. Food hasn't been a source of pleasure for me over the past two years, since I couldn't afford to buy good stuff. I lived on bread that tasted like its main ingredient was sawdust and luncheon meat that tasted like it had been soaked in urine, not to mention frozen dinners that I think might've been mummified thousands of years ago. The occasional hamburger from a fast-food restaurant didn't taste much better.

But the food Travis brought me… Oh my word, it tastes like heaven.

The time has come to explain things to Travis. Since he insists on protecting me, he ought to know the truth.

"I need to tell you a few things," I say, staring down at the fur blanket because I can't look at him while I speak. "Once you understand what I used to be, I won't complain if you want to leave."

"Not leaving. Don't care what you tell me."

"We'll see." I turn away from him with my legs dangling off the bed and gaze out the dirty window at the desert outside, where the sun is setting. "I wasn't born like mortals are. No one forged me either. The primordial gods were the first beings to come into existence in the multiverse, but they grew bored with only each other for company. They decided to create more gods. Eros created me from nothing, using the magics inherent in the multiverse to bring me into being. I had no mother or father, no childhood spent learning how to become a mature being. I had no idea how many gods existed because all I knew was Eros."

The bed shimmies a little as Travis edges closer. I can't see him, but I know he's inches away from me now.

"I knew nothing about magic," I say. "Eros never taught me. Instead, he used his vast powers to ensorcell me so that I would adore and worship him, let him do anything he wanted to me, and I would love doing it. For more than three thousand years, I was his slave. He had no other consorts, no minions to do his bidding, only me. And heaven help me, I loved every moment I was with him. I know I was ensorcelled, but still, all I can remember of that time is how good it felt to be treasured by Eros. Even today, I know what he did was horrible, yet I can't remember ever hating him for it, not until eons later. I hate myself for not being strong enough to break free of his control."

"He brainwashed you. That's not your fault."

"Maybe not, but that isn't the end of the story." I wrap my arms around myself, feeling suddenly cold, though I don't think it's because of the air temperature. "I knew only Eros for thousands of years, longer than even I could count. Then another god found out that Eros had a sex slave, and he grew jealous. Setesh rescued me from Eros, but then ensorcelled me in the same way and for the same purpose. I adored and worshiped him too. For two thousand years. At that point, I still didn't realize I was being manipulated. I thought I genuinely loved Eros, then Setesh."

"Larissa…"

"Sex with Setesh was like being devoured by a beast that is never full. Day and night, I worshiped him and reveled in our intimacy, believing we shared a deep and meaningful love." I drop my head into my hands, my shoulders quivering because I'm about to cry. But no, I will not do that. I need to hold it together long enough to make Travis understand. I raise my head and swipe away the tears. "Even when I found out Setesh was seducing many other women, I still adored him. But then Kamadeva took me from Setesh during a protracted battle that left many innocent people dead. Mortal people. This was during the Stone Age, as mortals call it. At least Kamadeva didn't ensorcell me. Instead, he imprisoned me in his temple deep in the jungle in the mortal world, locked me in a chamber there, and came to me only when he wanted to taunt me and make me feel like a useless lump of nothingness. He tried to have sex with me, but I only found out much later that he prefers men."

"As long as they're ensorcelled, I'm sure."

"Probably. Anyway, he thought I was too weak and stupid ever to escape from him. I was his trophy he would trot out to show the other gods and elementals how he had bested both Eros and Setesh."

Travis lays a hand on my shoulder. "You must've gotten away from him eventually."

I flinch and scoot sideways to get away from him, though I don't fear his touch. The memories have scoured away the shell I've hidden behind for so long. "One day, I got lucky. Kamadeva was called away to a duel—with Setesh, of course. He wanted me back. Everyone in the temple was outside, in the courtyard, to watch their idiotic battle. Weeks earlier, when Kamadeva had taken me out to show off his prize, I stole a small dagger from one of his minions. The man didn't even notice when I took it. I hid the blade under a loose block in my cell's floor, and during the duel, I used the knife to pry the lock on the door open and flee the temple. The duel raged for nearly four days, based on gossip I heard much later. By the time Kamadeva noticed I was gone, he couldn't find me."

"You've got brains and skills," Travis says, almost sounding proud of me. "And courage too. How long has it been since you got away from Kamadeva?"

"Ten thousand years."

Silence echoes between us. Though I don't look at him, I can guess what his expression looks like. Shock. Maybe disgust too.

He has no idea how old I am, but it's time I tell him. "I was created more than seventy thousand years ago."

CHAPTER SEVENTEEN

Travis

"S EVENTY THOUSAND YEARS?" I SAY, TRYING MY DAMNEDEST TO WRAP my head around the idea. She has been alive longer than any human civilization has ever survived. Longer than all of them combined. Christ, she's more than ancient. She is…a primordial god. Maybe she didn't call herself that, but it must be true. Eros made her. He was a primordial, so she must be too.

Not that it matters. She is prehistoric, period.

And I still want to have sex with her. I've gone crazy. But I won't seduce her now, I can't. Not after the horrific story she just told me. I want to hold her, to comfort her, but that seems like the wrong move too.

"What happened after that?" I ask. "How did you keep those gods from capturing you again?"

"I dived headfirst into dark magics. It seemed like the only thing powerful enough to protect me. I spent millennia perfecting my skills as a spellcaster and sorceress." She won't look at me, but she inches a little closer. "By the time Kamadeva found me again, I was too powerful for his old tricks to work. I used my magics to give him a beating that sent him scurrying home with his tail between his legs. Later, Setesh tried to ensnare me again, but I walloped him too. And by the time Eros came, I had amassed so much power, fueled by the devotion of the ancient Egyptian civilization, that even the great god himself was no match for me."

"That's why they waited until now to come for you again. When you're powerless and vulnerable because you've become a mortal."

"Yes, I'm a weakling now. Helpless to defend myself."

"That's not what I meant. You have no supernatural powers, but you are not helpless."

"Because I have you to protect me." She finally glances at me sideways. "I appreciate what you're trying to do, but I can't stand feeling like my own destiny is beyond my control."

I can understand that, after what she's been through. But she doesn't seem to realize one important fact about this world. "Not having unbreakable magics doesn't make you weak. Lindsey might've been invested with Janus's powers, but she was still mortal and easily killable. That didn't stop her from fighting. Even without Nevan, she could outwit her enemies and wound them enough to slow them down for a long time."

"Yes, but she did have powers. I don't."

"That's bullshit." I slide over to sit beside her and hold her hand. "Power doesn't come only from magic. It's something you have inside you. Your mind, your heart, your determination. Surviving for two years in the mortal realm took a hell of a lot of guts. You were dropped into this world with nothing, not even clothes, but you survived and kept going. Never forget that."

"But I—"

"If you're about to explain to me why you're a wuss, don't bother. I've seen your inner strength. Now it's time you recognized it too."

Her shoulders sag. "You don't understand. How can you? Your life has been normal, and you've never become a monster out of fear and rage. I did. For thousands of years, I terrorized the Unseen."

"Sounds to me like those three god wankers are way worse than you ever were."

Her mouth kinks up on one side, forming a sly little smile. "You just used the word wanker. That's a British thing. Max loves to use that word."

"No, I—Well, I heard him say it earlier. It got stuck in my brain."

"Or maybe you're finally starting to acclimate to your new life and accept that you've changed."

"Don't hold your breath."

Her half-smile broadens, though it doesn't quite become a grin. "You're embarrassed, aren't you? Someone caught you talking British, and you—"

"I am not embarrassed. It's weird, that's all."

"Mm-hm." She studies me while tapping one finger on her thigh. Then she straightens, her eyes alight with interest. Not the sexual kind, unfortunately. "I just remembered something Bob said about you. He mentioned you imprisoned the woman you claimed to love and harassed her for years. What is he talking about?"

Why does she have to remember that? Damn that Bob.

But I guess it's time I told her and got it off my chest. The oracle claimed I need to atone and forgive. I already apologized for what I'd done and died to save the worlds. What else can I do? Explain it to Larissa, that's what.

I slump forward, my elbows on my knees, and stare down at the scratched and uneven floor. "I met Lindsey Porter back in Texas, when I was a police officer in a small town. She had just moved there. We both went to the same restaurant for lunch, and we ended up sharing a table because the place was so busy that there weren't any others available. That's how we became friends. I fell in love with her, but she saw me as only a friend. Still, I guess I thought eventually she'd feel for me the way I felt for her."

"But she didn't. Max told me—"

"Would you stop talking about Max? I'm telling you *my* story."

"Sorry. Please go on."

The more time I spend with Larissa, the angrier I feel every time she mentions Max, but we can deal with her romantic obsession later. I need to finish my story first, before I chicken out. "So, I had a thing for Lindsey. I was too much of a coward to tell her, though. I guess we would've gone on like that forever—but then my brother came home from the big city."

"That would be Calder. The one who was forged and joined the ranks of the kerkopes."

"Right. Calder was younger than me, but he'd always been good at sweet-talking. He never had trouble getting a date. When he met Lindsey, I completely disappeared from the picture. Not that I'd done a damn thing to try to win her over." I drop my head and sigh. "But I knew I had no chance at all once Calder asked her out. They fell in love, got engaged, and then…"

"He died."

"I thought he died, anyway. It was years before I found out what had really happened to him. All I knew was that he told me he was spending the night with Lindsey, then he disappeared." I suddenly feel like insects are crawling all over my skin, nipping and clawing at me, but I resist the urge to scratch myself bloody from head to toe. "As far as I knew, Lindsey was the last person to see Calder alive. So I…arrested her. Locked her up in a cell. Interrogated her. I wish I could say I was at least doing that because I was desperate to find my brother. But if I'm completely honest, I did it because I was jealous. I believed Lindsey was having sex with Calder."

"You believed? That implies it wasn't true."

"I didn't find out until years later, after Lindsey became the Janusite, that she had never slept with Calder. She was a virgin until she met Nevan."

Larissa leans into my shoulder, and I can't help wondering why she seems to want to comfort me. We haven't gotten along so well most of the time.

But I need to act like a man, even if I'm not technically a man anymore. I sit up, take a cleansing breath, and tell her the rest. "My boss fired me for holding Lindsey without evidence of a crime, much less murder. Lindsey never knew I'd lost my job, still doesn't know. She left town suddenly, and I had no idea where she went. I had just enough savings to keep me going while I conducted my own investigation to hunt her down. It took six months, but I finally found her in Michigan, at the rock shop. I, ah…moved there. Got myself elected sheriff. Honestly, it wasn't that hard to get the job since no one else wanted it."

"Max said—" Larissa winces. "Sorry, I'll try not to say the M-word any-more. But I, um, heard you weren't very nice to Lindsey at that point."

"It's all right, you can say Max told you. He's right. Lindsey must've told him how I hounded her for three years. At the time, I would've denied it, but I real-ize now I did that to her because I still thought I loved her. I know that sounds bloody stupid, but I somehow believed I had a chance with her now that she was alone and vulnerable. Christ, that makes me sound like a bastard."

"Because you were one. No offense." She smiles with her lips sealed and bumps her shoulder into me. "You did it again. You spoke British."

"No, I didn't."

"You said 'bloody,' and you weren't talking about a murder scene."

I can't even start to think about that right now. If the Unseen wants me to change, apparently I will. Not sure how I feel about it, but having no choice is what I deserve.

"You said you 'still thought' you loved Lindsey," Larissa says. "That sounds like you're not in love with her anymore."

"Don't know that I ever was, really. I was obsessed with her. When she met Nevan, not only did the old jealousy rear up again, but I had to deal with the revelation that the supernatural exists—and that Lindsey was having sex with a jungle fairy."

Larissa laughs softly. "Jungle fairy? I've never heard of those."

"That's what I called Nevan, just to annoy him. I called him Kevin too, but he didn't appreciate that either. He responded by hurling me into a tree. Guess I deserved that."

"Yeah, you did."

Groaning, I shut my eyes. "Naturally, I tried to arrest Lindsey again, twice. Well, the first time I was taking her in for questioning but didn't lock her up. The second time, when a dismembered body turned up in the boot of her car, I tried to arrest her—but Nevan teleported her away."

Larissa is smiling in that cheerfully self-satisfied way she'd done a mo-ment ago.

"What did I say now?" I ask.

"Boot. You were talking about the trunk of Lindsey's car, I'm sure. But you called it the boot."

I groan again, then I set aside my annoyance with the Unseen and finish my story. "I called in my deputies, and we scoured the woods for Lindsey and Nevan, but they were gone. Then, as I was heading back toward the rock shop, I passed by the falls and saw the two of them jump through the water. It wasn't easy, but I managed to climb onto the ledge and jump through the waterfall into a cavern I didn't know was there. I had to find Lindsey, that was all I thought about. She and Nevan were gone, though."

"Through the portal."

"Yes. Then I...waited for them to come back. And I sort of...expressed my feelings for her, in a ruddy awful way, but I could tell she was already falling for Nevan. I was too late again. Eventually, I gave up and admitted to myself I'd never really loved her. But I could tell she loved Nevan, much more than she'd ever loved Calder. I think my brother's forging damaged him deep inside, so that the monster he became was more than a new physical form. It scoured out any goodness he might've had inside him and replaced it with every awful thing a person can feel. My obsession with Lindsey paled next to what Calder did to her after his forging. He tormented her mercilessly, killed a man as part of his plot, and physically tortured her in the hopes he could convince her to become like him."

Larissa turns toward me, her gaze intent on mine. "You still haven't forgiven yourself, for anything."

"I should've protected Lindsey when Calder was trying to drive her insane. I should've—I don't know. Somehow known and stopped him. But he had become something I refused to believe in, until I had no choice anymore."

"You did save Lindsey. You died doing that."

"No. I cocked it up and got caught by the evil bitch who had been Nevan's wife thousands of years ago. She slit my throat. There was no heroic moment. I got caught, I died, Max forged me. The end."

"Your story is not over. Neither is mine. I think that's part of what Bob was trying to tell us. We need to stop fighting it and see where this leads."

"Where what leads?"

"I don't know. Oracles are so annoyingly cryptic. Maybe he meant this path we're on together, trying to stop something terrible from happening." Her gaze goes distant as if she's remembering or thinking, maybe both. "Kamadeva and Setesh want me. They will go to any lengths in the moronic battle they're determined to fight. I wouldn't put it past them to destroy the mortal world in their zeal to win. Bob said we would doom two worlds if we can't make peace with each other, and I think he meant that we will be too distracted to stop doomsday."

"Because we're arguing instead of searching for a solution."

"Exactly." She bites her lip, avoiding my gaze. "Mind if I ask you a question?"

"Go on."

"Why have you been hiding out in the mortal world? Do you even have a lair in the Unseen?"

"No, I don't. Is there some elemental law that says I must have an underground hideout? I like the outdoors, not holes carved out of mountains. Luxury hotel suites are even better, though."

"Okay, but why hide out—"

"Because I needed to get away from my old life. Find a new path. Figure out how the hell to live for the rest of eternity as an incubus."

"How's that going?"

I shrug. "Not sure."

"May I ask one more question?"

"Since when do you request permission?"

Her lips twitch like she might smile, but she doesn't. "Are you attracted to me?"

"I'm an incubus. Being attracted to women is a primal instinct. I can't help it."

"But do you...um..."

Since I'm an idiot, I didn't realize until this very second that she's asking if I want to have sex with her. The former goddess is anxious about it, worried I'll say no, so she can't quite get the words out. She told me earlier that sex with her thralls never gave her pleasure and that she didn't think she had ever experienced a genuine moment of happiness or sexual fulfillment. But she also told me she loved shagging Eros and Setesh, so I need to ask her a question.

"If you loved sex with those god wankers, why did you say you've never experienced a real orgasm?"

"Because it wasn't real with them. I was brainwashed, like you said, and they both used magic to make me climax for them. Since I escaped from them, I haven't had an orgasm. I'm incapable of enjoying sex anymore. Even kissing eventually stopped feeling good."

But when we kiss, she feels it. I can tell. A salamander can sense things that no human male could. I know she gets aroused when she's near me, and I know she was ready for me to fuck her back in that alley, after the sylph attack. When I pull in a deep breath through my nostrils, I stifle a groan as the aroma of her desire inundates my senses. She wants me. Maybe I want her too, for more than the simple reason I gave her a moment ago. Right now, I won't analyze my need—or anything—because I would love to be the first being, human or elemental, to give her real, intense pleasure without any gimmicks.

I slide a hand over her leg, my fingers teasing her inner thigh. "Larissa, I want to give you something you've been denied for too long. Let me be the one who shows you pleasure, starting with the sexual sort, since I know you want me. I can smell it. Your desire is intoxicating, and you have the most sensual body I've ever seen. Kissing you excited me more than my incubus instincts would account for, and I need to explore every inch of you to find out exactly how good we can make each other feel."

She's breathing harder, her lips parted, and her eyes have darkened.

I push my hand further between her thighs, then I brush my lips over hers. "I want to make love to you, Larissa. Right now. Do you want me?"

"Yes. I want you, please, now."

That's all I need to hear.

Chapter Eighteen

Larissa

GENUINE PLEASURE IS AN ALIEN CONCEPT TO ME, WHICH I'D TOLD TRA-vis earlier today. But he wants to make love to me. Though I don't know what exactly that means, I need him to touch me, to tease me, to coax pleasure from my body until I can't breathe anymore. I need him to make me feel. I have no idea what sexual pleasure feels like when I'm not influenced by dark magics. Yes, I understand the biology of sex. But experiencing it myself, with the only being who has ever made me feel anything genuine… This might be a huge mistake. I don't care anymore, though. I need this. I need him.

Travis picks me up and lays me down on the bed, on my back, spread across its length. My clothes vanish. So do his. I lie naked atop the fur blanket with its silky texture teasing my skin. I've laid on fur blankets before, not to mention sheets made from fabric woven by a fae tribe that creates the threads by harvesting silk from a type of worm found only in the Unseen. Nothing in the mortal world could ever be as silky as that fabric, but I never experienced satisfaction when I rolled around in sheets made from it. Nothing I ever conjured or procured had made me feel as good as this blanket does.

"Is this an enchanted blanket?" I ask.

Travis kneels at the foot of the bed, about to climb onto it, but stops when I ask him that. "Enchanted? Not as far as I know. It's just a fur blanket."

"Oh. But it feels…divine."

"Why do you sound surprised?"

"Because I've never experienced anything like this. I'm actually enjoying the sensation." I wriggle to make the fur slide across my skin, and shiver with delight. So this is what pleasure feels like. If a blanket can do this to me, then…

Travis crawls up the bed on his hands and knees until he crouches over me, his face hovering above mine. "If you like fur, just wait till I'm inside you."

"Do I have fur inside my body?"

He chuckles. "No, baby, you don't. I meant I'll make you feel better than that blanket did."

"I see. Honestly, I have no idea what the inside of my body looks like, but you must think I'm an idiot for asking that question."

"No. I think you've been deprived of all the good things in life." He bends his arms just enough to make his flesh graze mine and his erection rub across my belly, moistening my skin. "You deserve to feel good."

He nuzzles my neck, just under my ear, and purrs almost like a cat, the vibrations exciting my skin. Every hair on my body shivers and stiffens. My nipples are hard, and I can feel how wet I am between my thighs. He drags his lips down my throat, then places soft kisses on my skin as he moves down my body, until his head is between my breasts. I clench the fur blanket, my breaths coming harder and faster, and my pulse revs up too. He turns his head to the side, rubbing his hair on my skin, making me choke back a moan.

This is what sex should feel like. It's amazing so far, but I know he hasn't gotten to the best part yet.

He cups my breast, kneading tenderly, and circles his hot, wet tongue around my nipple without touching it. My fingers grip the blanket so hard my knuckles ache, but I don't care. A tingle sweeps over me from head to toe while he teases the underside of my breast with his thumb, awakening nerves I never knew I had. By the stars, this feels so incredible. His skin is hotter than any human male's would be, heated up by his incubus powers, though I doubt he knows that's why his skin scorches. It never burns me, though. The magics that endow him with all his elemental and incubus instincts prevent that hot body from singeing me.

"Oh, yes," I breathe as he finally pulls my nipple into his mouth and suckles it. My back arches, and my sex throbs.

He releases my stiff peak and blows a gentle stream of air across it, making me shiver. Then he slides down my body, licking and kissing and nibbling on my skin, plunging his tongue into my belly button, all while he keeps his hands on my sides and inches ever lower. When he reaches my mound, he dives his face into the hairs there and sucks in a deep breath through his nostrils. Groaning deeply, he lifts his face to gaze at me with eyes hooded by desire. Shades of copper, silver, and crimson swirl in his irises, the shades more intense than I've ever seen before with any incubus. Does that mean he wants me more? I haven't forced him to want me with magics, so whatever he feels right now is genuine.

The salamander driving me crazy with pleasure surges forward to shower kisses over my belly, then he lays his body on top of mine and shimmies lower until his face is positioned between my thighs, just below my mound. He hauls in another deep breath, his lips curling up slightly as he…relishes the aroma. Of me. My body. The secretions I can't control. He groans and pushes my thighs apart with the gentle pressure of his palms and gazes up at me over my hips.

"Fuck, Larissa," he growls. "I love the scent of your desire, but I need to feast on you now."

Before I can respond, he shoves his head between my thighs, between the slick folds there, and starts to lave my flesh with his tongue, rasping it up and down, side to side, latching on to my nub only to release it and thrust his tongue into my opening.

My back arches so wildly that only my head rests on the bed. I clutch his head while he keeps tormenting my flesh, grunting and growling like he can't get enough of doing this to me. A strangely thrilling kind of tension builds inside me, stealing my breath, forcing my back to flatten into the bedding.

Travis lifts his head, his lips glistening, and licks his mouth clean. "Mm, you taste so damn good."

"Please. I think I was about to—"

"Yes, you were. But I'm not ready for you to come yet. I want that to happen while I'm inside you."

Oh my word, I want that too.

He shifts off my body to lie tucked up against me on his side.

"You can't stop," I say, probably sounding pathetically desperate.

"Don't worry. I'll make sure you feel all the pleasure I can give you." He settles a hand over my collarbone, then skates it down my body oh-so-slowly, his skin touching mine with a delicacy that only heightens my arousal. I gasp for breath, my chest heaving, and clamp my teeth down on my lip. His palm skims lower and lower, grazing the hairs on my mound. He moves that hand onto my inner thigh and drags it down to my knee. "I'm going to show you right now."

"Show me what?"

He crawls over me to kneel between my legs, then grasps my ankles to encourage me to bend them. I can't look away from his eyes, the way they swirl like a shimmering, fiery maelstrom, their colors blending and separating in a mesmerizing whirlpool. He leans over my body, his hands planted on either side of my shoulders, his gaze bound to mine.

And he thrusts inside me.

I cry out, throwing my head back.

"Lock your legs around me," he says.

Helpless to resist anything he wants, I wrap my legs around him and hold on, my heart beating so hard and fast that I feel a bit lightheaded.

Travis moves inside me, in and out, taking his time with every thrust, his focus always on my face, my eyes, even while he pulls his hips back and pushes deeper into my body. His cock feels so good, hard and hot and pulsing in a way no mortal man's ever could, every sensation propelling my need to greater heights while I clutch his arms and abandon myself to this incredible feeling.

I know an incubus can make a woman come even harder when he unleashes his seed inside her body, but I've never experienced that. Despite having sex with salamanders many times, including with Max, I had to pretend I enjoyed it. What sort of sex goddess would I be if I felt nothing? So I faked it. For more millennia than I could count. But now, here, with this man I couldn't stand when I first saw him, my body is coming alive in ways I never could've imagined.

"Travis, please, I need to—"

"I know exactly what you need. Don't worry, I won't push you too far."

"But I can't—It's so—" I whimper, unable to silence the pathetic sound.

"Hush, it's all right." He lifts one hand to caress my cheek. "I won't leave you hanging."

And then he does something I never would have expected.

He drops onto his elbows and kisses me. It's not a hot, tongue-thrusting kiss either. He makes love to my mouth while he makes love to my body, his cock gliding in and out in time with the leisurely strokes of his tongue. I throw my arms around him. He sneaks a hand between our bodies, easing it between my folds, and massages my clit.

My entire body jerks and goes rigid. I scream into his mouth while white-hot pleasure explodes inside me, firing electrical shocks down my nerves and straight into my sex. My body pulsates around him, and he growls as his release jets out of him, the heat and power of it making me come harder, scream louder, but his mouth still muffles my cries. His climax goes on and on, and my body reacts, shooting lightning-hot pleasure down every nerve.

By the time we both stop coming, all I can do is lie here, limp and dazed. Holy shit. Is that what incubus sex is supposed to feel like? I had no idea anything could be so…mind-blowing.

Travis rolls off my body, lying on his side again, his body tucked snugly against mine. He kisses me sweetly. "How did you like your first real orgasm?"

"By the stars, I never—It was so much more—" I give up trying to find the right words and just say, "Wow."

"You deserve to feel that way every single day."

I suddenly realize the sun has set, and the light of a full moon bathes us in its glow even through the dingy glass of the windows. "I think I understand what Bob was trying to tell me when he said being human means more than slowly approaching death."

"Glad you understand, because I don't."

"It means that even if I become immortal again, I can still be human, in my heart. Everything I've learned and experienced over the past two years, that won't vanish if the Four Winds turn me back into the goddess Hathor." I lay a palm on his cheek. "I'll still be Larissa Robustelli, the woman with a stupid alias. I'll still be the woman you wanted to make love to."

"Of course you will. You're not who you were before. Even if you start calling yourself Hathor again, you will never be the evil bitch who enslaved people."

"I hope you're right. Going back to the way I was… No, I don't want that." I rub my thumb across his bottom lip. "You've taught me what being human really means."

He smirks. "It was a cracking shag that did that, eh?"

Grinning, I tap a finger on his chin. "You spoke British."

"Maybe I've learned a thing or two from you. Like how to be an elemental." He flops onto his back, hands linked under his head. "So let the Unseen do what it wants to me. I won't stop being me because I talk differently. Even being a salamander can't fundamentally change who I am."

"Exactly. The Unseen wants to guide you to becoming your true self."

"Are you saying the other world has a brain?"

"No. The Oversoul initiates the change."

He eyes me with a strange expression. "What is this Oversoul?"

"That which underpins the universe and maintains balance without interfering in everyday life."

"Not sure I understand."

"We can talk about that more later." I roll on top of him. "More sex now, please."

He turns serious as he threads his fingers through my hair. "Did you love Max?"

"No. I suppose I was obsessed with him, though I wanted it to be more." I fold my hands on his chest and rest my chin on them. "Any fondness I thought I saw in him was strictly the effects of the ensorcellment. With you, I feel like it's real."

"It is. You haven't enslaved me with magic. I'm here with you because I want to be." His mouth slides into a wicked smirk. "Now, about that more sex idea…"

A gale abruptly roars to life outside, battering the walls.

Is that a sudden windstorm? I might believe it, if not for the unease crackling through me. That's when I realize the necklace is gone. Travis must've accidentally removed it when he magically stripped my clothes off my body.

I open my mouth to tell him that, but the realization comes too late.

The house explodes.

Chapter Nineteen

Travis

THE ROOF TEARS OFF THE HOUSE AND FLIES INTO THE SKY WHILE THE walls peel away too, careening end over end across the desert until I can't see them anymore. The roof has vanished into the heavens. We lie naked on the bed I'd conjured, both of us too stunned to move or speak. The wind that seemed to precipitate the explosion, or whatever it was, has diminished to a whisper. The second I regain my wits, I conjure our clothes and stand up, with Larissa crushed to me, while I send the bed away.

Then I try to whisk us away.

And slam into a barrier.

I fall backward onto the floor with Larissa on top of me. Her gaze darts here, there, and everywhere while she struggles to breathe but only manages to make gasping sounds. I fly to my feet, holding her to me, and squint into the moonlit night. Nothing. I see nothing.

She closes her hand around the necklace Ennea enchanted for her. "You sent this away with my clothes."

"I what? Bloody hell, I fucked up again."

"Not your fault."

A high-pitched sound—like a plane hurtling down, about to crash into the ground—grows louder and louder above our heads. I drag Larissa into the kitchen, huddling by the stove as if that will protect us. Is it Kamadeva again? Or that kilted twat Setesh?

"Can gods cross the boundaries?" I ask.

"No idea. I never left the Unseen when I was a god, so I never tried to violate the boundaries."

If Setesh could penetrate the wards in Max and Harper's lair... I should've guessed a god could pierce the boundaries in the mortal world too.

The high-pitched noise is so loud I want to cover my ears, but I won't let go of Larissa to do that.

A figure crashes down, shattering the floorboards. The male creature has fallen into the crawlspace under the house, though his body above the waist is visible. His blond hair shimmers in the moonlight as he scratches his chin. "Didn't realize there would be an empty space beneath the floor. My grand entrance hasn't gone the way I planned, but I can adjust."

He springs out of the hole and dusts off his gold toga-like garment, though it hangs off one shoulder. Gold chains encircle his waist, and more gold secures his clothing in the form of clips while a gold torque encircles one of his biceps. He wears gold sandals too. And he speaks with an odd accent, but I've never been good at identifying things like that. His accent isn't like Janus's, but he is wearing a toga, so maybe he's Greek.

"Who the bloody hell are you?" I demand.

"I'm certain Hathor remembers me." He smiles at Larissa, but it's not a friendly expression. It's more like a lion opening his jaws before he devours his prey. "Don't you, my pet? After everything we meant to each other—"

"You are insane," she hisses. "What we meant to each other? Please. You ensorcelled me for thousands of years, Eros. I hate you."

"Do you?" He shrugs. "That hardly matters. Once I ensorcell you again, you will adore me."

I move in front of Larissa. "Like hell she will. You are not taking her."

Eros tips his head left and right, studying me with unnerving curiosity. "You will not be able to stop me, salamander. I am a god. You are…a pitiful creature."

Why does it surprise me that gods are full of themselves? I should've guessed they would be. Having more power than anyone else in the multiverse must go to their heads.

He waves his hand in a vague gesture. "I have surrounded this place with impenetrable wards. Surrender Hathor to me, and I might spare your life."

"Sod off."

I'm beginning to like the British words.

And I'm starting to wonder if Eros used the same trick as Setesh. Do his wards keep us in, but let us conjure things? The disk Max gave me won't get us through Eros's wards, though. I can't just stand here listening to him prattle on about how powerful and awesome he is, which means I need to risk getting us both killed in the hopes that the wards are tied to him and might fall, or at least weaken enough for us to escape, if he's injured.

Worth a shot. I can't ask Larissa how she feels about my plan, but I suspect she'll be on board. Anything to stop Eros from enslaving her again.

I summon Lindsey's derringer and more ammo, conjuring rounds into the empty chambers while sending more into my pocket. Since I keep the weapon behind my back, Eros can't see it. I think. "Why don't you try ensorcelling yourself? You can wank off mumbling about how much you adore you."

He sighs, the sound full of melodrama. "I grow tired of this conversation."

The bastard raises a hand, holding it palm up toward Larissa. "Come, my pet. Don't be tiresome and force me to bring you over here."

I pull the gun out and fire five rounds of jacketed hollow-point ammo straight into the god's chest.

He stumbles backward while blood pours out of his chest to coat his torso. His legs give out, and he smacks down on his knees, breathing hard, teeth gritted and lips peeled back into an angry sneer. "You cannot destroy me, tiny salamander. I am not *a* god. I am *the* god."

Oh no, he's not full of himself at all.

I try to teleport us away, but the wards prevent it. They don't knock me back like last time, though. They sort of...stretch. The wards have weakened. Eros doesn't wear a belt buckle, like Setesh, but I wonder if one of the metal clips holding up his dress—sorry, his toga—might be what's keeping the barrier in place. Or maybe it's the gold torque on his arm. I'll try both.

Raising a hand, I summon my fire and hurl a blast of it at His Majesty.

The flames engulf him from head to toe, and *the* god howls and swats at the fire.

I shift into salamander form and race to Eros, then skitter up his body amid the flames, which don't bother me at all, and bite down on every metal clip I encounter, though I don't taste any magics in them. When I reach his torque, I clamp my teeth down on the gold band. Power zings through me, sharp and ice cold. So, the almighty Eros hasn't created an impenetrable barrier after all. It depends on the torque strapped around his biceps.

A second before I shift back into humanoid form, I sink my "tiny salamander" teeth into the tosser's flesh, just to hear him howl even louder.

Then I'm me again, conjuring the derringer and firing the last round in the cylinder straight at the torque on Eros's arm. The metal shatters, but not because of the gunshot. The hollow-point ammo smacks into the torque, but it's the sudden release of magics that makes the gold band explode.

And the wards crash down.

We're gone before Eros can snarl a curse at the "tiny salamander."

I take us to the first place I think of—Phoenix. Maybe that wasn't the brightest idea, but I had a split second to decide where to go. No, it wasn't my idea. It came from outside of me, which means...

"Did you wish to come here?" I ask.

We've ended up in the parking lot of a rundown, two-story motel of the kind that offers rooms by the hour and accepts cash with no credit card as collateral and no questions asked. It's dark here, and the neon sign that identifies this place as the Midtown Oasis Motel flickers intermittently. A smattering of vehicles occupies the parking lot.

"You think I brought us here?" Larissa says, sounding annoyed instead of grateful that I got her away from *the* god. "Why would I do that? The bounty hunters know I've been living in Phoenix. Might as well have detonated a nuclear bomb over our heads to let them know I'm back."

"I had literally no time to decide where to go, but I sensed the idea originated outside of me. Is there any reason why you would want to come here? I have no idea why we're standing in front of a sleazy motel. I've never seen this place before."

"Okay, I'm sorry." She glances around, her features crimping. "This is where I work. Must've accidentally wished to come here because my subconscious wanted that. Don't ask me why."

"So you don't swim in the sewers for a living after all."

"No, I clean the rooms here. Which isn't much different from the sewers, actually."

"Well, at least you're away from Eros and those other two twats."

She smiles, her cheeks dimpling. "You've really embraced your new self, haven't you? All it took was a 'cracking shag' to loosen you up."

"Don't flatter yourself, Larry. You aren't *that* good. I am, but you're not."

"Typical. All you salamanders are so full of yourselves." She freezes, her smile disintegrating. "Don't you think it was a little too easy? The way you outwitted Setesh and Eros? I mean, one god falling for that trick is somewhat believable. But two? And Eros is one of the oldest, most cunning gods in the multiverse. Not even Zeus could defeat him."

"Maybe I'm just smarter than the gods of the Unseen."

She gives me a look that implies I am a foolish nincompoop.

"All right, yes, I agree," I tell her. "That did seem a bit too easy. I don't like to look gift horses in the mouth, though. Getting too close gives them a chance to bite my nose off. Are you sure you don't know why we materialized here?"

"Hello, subconscious desire. That means I have no—" Larissa scans the row of numbered doors that comprise the motel's first floor. Her attention stalls on one room, and her eyes widen. "Dani."

She sprints toward the room in question.

I run after her while glamouring into a more suitable appearance. As we approach the room, I suddenly realize the shadow beside the door hides a small child—a little girl. She has her knees drawn up and her arms wrapped around them.

Larissa drops to her knees on the sidewalk and lays a hand on the girl's arm. "Dani, what are you doing out here by yourself, at night? Where's your mom?"

The girl shrugs. "One of her friends came. They went inside for a while, but after he left, Mom didn't come get me. I knocked on the door, but she didn't answer. Her friend was dirty."

"Dirty?"

The girl nods.

I glance at the concrete in front of the door, and everything inside me freezes. A few small, red stains color the sidewalk, but it's the blood on the door handle that activates my cop instincts.

Larissa and I glance at each other at the same instant. Her face has gone pale, as if she recognizes something awful has happened here. I don't need to say a word to her. She puts on a brave face for Dani, then scoops the girl up into her arms. "Let's go to the lobby and get some snacks. You must be starving."

"What about Mommy?"

"My friend Travis will find her."

Larissa heads toward the far end of the building, where the lobby must be.

As soon as they disappear inside that building, I teleport into the room. It takes me a moment to understand what I'm seeing. Blood. All over the bed. A knife. Covered in blood. A woman. Her eyes wide and vacant. I stumble over to the bed and press a finger to her throat, but I don't feel a pulse. I check her wrist too, but still nothing.

She is dead.

And the bastard who murdered her escaped.

The little girl… We can't leave her here. Social services will take her, and God knows what will happen to the kid then. I have sodding supernatural powers, don't I? Coming up with a plan to save a child shouldn't be that difficult. But Larissa and I have gods on our tails, nipping at our heels, waiting for the first chance to pounce.

I can think of only one thing to do. I conjure the cell phone I rarely use and dial a number I swore I'd never call again. I've asked too much of her already.

"Hello?" Lindsey answers drowsily.

"It's Travis. I need a huge favor. It's urgent, and it involves a child."

"Tell me what you need." She sounds wide awake now.

Once I've explained the situation to Lindsey, she insists I bring Dani to her. She thinks, and I agree, that the bounty hunters and gods are unlikely to be able to track Dani. She isn't a former goddess. She's only a child, a scared little girl who needs our help.

I zip out of the motel room and sprint down the sidewalk toward the lobby, bursting through the door.

The young man behind the desk looks surprised, though Dani is too busy tearing open a packet of chocolate-covered peanuts to notice. When Larissa sees me, I know she knows.

"Come on," I say. "We need to go."

She grabs Dani's hand and whispers something to the girl, then they both follow me outside. I lead them into a shadowed area near the parking lot. I don't need to say a thing.

Larissa lifts the girl into her arms and says, "Close your eyes. We're going to take a quick trip to a place where you'll be safe."

How did she know that's what I plan to do? I'll have to wait until later to think about that.

Dani squeezes her eyes shut.

I throw my arms around them.

We reappear inside Lindsey and Nevan's house in Michigan. It's outside the boundaries, which will keep bounty hunters away, though there is a slight risk one of those arsehole gods could find this place. But I have to assume they're too caught up in their quest to control Larissa to figure out I've stashed an orphan at my friends' house.

Lindsey and Nevan understand the risks. I would've taken Dani to Max and Harper, but I have no idea where they are. Setesh destroyed their home, after all. Nevan doesn't get annoyed with me. I think he and Lindsey realize this is a potentially world-ending problem Larissa and I need to deal with, and neither of them can say no to sheltering a little girl. Larissa insists on giving her enchanted necklace to Dani, just to make sure none of the baddies can find the girl and use her as leverage.

She's leaving herself vulnerable. To protect a child.

I'd been so wrong about her when we first met.

This time, I ask Larissa where she thinks we should go before I whisk us away. She suggests something...odd.

A heartbeat later, we're standing among the ruins of a temple—where, I don't know—with a large building to one side and the remnants of other structures scattered behind it. The large building must be an ancient temple. It towers above us, making me feel like the tiny salamander Eros had called me. A full moon bathes the complex in milky light that's bright enough to reveal everything around us.

"What are we doing here?" I ask.

Larissa turns in a circle, surveying our surroundings. "This was one of the last temples ever built to honor me."

"Are we here so you can reminisce?"

"No." She faces me, standing up straight. "For thousands of years, the ancient Egyptians worshiped me as their beloved goddess. The energy of their devotion echoes through this place."

"So we're here to make you feel better about yourself."

The moonlight lets me see it when she frowns at me, but I don't need any help to hear the huffy noise she makes. "Must you always be so rude? No, we're not here for that. I told you, this place echoes with the power of my subjects' devotion. When mortals worship gods of the Unseen, that adoration gives birth to magics. That means power. Understand?"

"You think you can get your powers back by standing here?"

She makes a growly huffing noise this time. "You are so dense sometimes. I'm hoping the faint magics that linger here will make it harder for Eros, Kamadeva, and Setesh to find me. Plus, this temple is outside any boundaries, which means the bounty hunters shouldn't be able to track me either."

"Okay, this does sound like a reasonable plan. For now."

"Thank you."

I follow while she wanders among the ruins, occasionally touching a broken stone block or pausing to gaze up at the gigantic temple with a soft, wistful smile on her lips. Questions keep popping into my mind, so I decide to interrogate her. A little.

"How do you know Dani, the girl at the motel?" I ask.

"Because I work there. Her mother is—was a prostitute. She would lock Dani out of their room while she dealt with her clients." Larissa stops walking and bows her head. "Now she's an orphan. Alone and scared, at the mercy of a world that doesn't care about anything."

"She's not alone. She's with Lindsey and Nevan." I come up behind her and slip my arms around her waist. "We'll find a good home for her, once this is over."

"How?"

"Magics, of course. You are so dense sometimes."

She doesn't laugh, but I swear I see her lips curve up the tiniest bit.

I lower my head, resting my cheek against hers. "Why do you care about a little girl? If you're a cold-hearted evil bitch, you wouldn't do that."

"Even I couldn't leave a child to suffer alone."

"But Dani knows you and trusts you. That means you've been watching out for her for a while." I pull her tighter against me. "You've changed."

"Doesn't matter if I have. The fact that I exist could wreak havoc on this world." She wriggles a little, like she's uncomfortable, but I don't think it has anything to do with me holding her. "I kind of like the people here. I don't want them to suffer because of me. Bob said capturing me would be the greatest coup ever, which means I am endangering this world by being here."

"Those god wankers found you in the Unseen. You won't be any safer there, and I doubt it matters which world you're in if they track you down."

"You have no reason to be here with me. Go, find someplace safe."

"I will not leave you."

"But—"

"Never."

Awareness stiffens every hair on my body. Something is out there, cloaked in the shadows to hide from the false daylight of the full moon. I prick up my ears, so to speak, and listen for the slightest noises. Shuffling. Breathing. Faint growling. When I sniff the air, I smell...

Blood.

What on earth?

Sunlight blinds me, and I throw a hand up to shield my eyes from the brilliance—but the sun isn't there in the sky. The light comes from...everywhere. It illuminates a circular area that surrounds the temple complex. And inside that cone of light, I see vampires.

Today just keeps getting better.

A figure drops out of the sky to touch down twenty feet away. Eros grins.

Bloody hell.

Chapter Twenty

Larissa

OH NO, NO, NO, NO. WON'T THIS JERK EVER GET THE PICTURE? I HATE him. I will kill myself before I ever let him ensorcell me again, and I've been around too long to be as gullible as I was when he created me. I know how to evade his magics, especially here in a temple dedicated to me. Maybe I feel a little queasy when I think about humans worshiping me, but right now, I need the protection of the residual magics left behind by their devotion. The temple might've let Eros and his minions in, but I doubt they can get out again.

Especially if I can do what I think I might be able to do. This is my temple, after all.

A horde of vampires has gathered behind Eros. Slavering, hissing, odious creatures who will do anything if the reward is great enough. They care only about drinking blood.

"Take your dogs and leave," I shout at Eros. "I will never be yours again."

He laughs. "Of course you will. And this time, you will accept my gift."

"Are you insane? I didn't want vampires the first time you offered them to me with cute little red bows on their heads." Okay, he didn't actually put bows on their heads. But he acted like he'd given me the greatest gift the multiverse had ever seen. Hideous, blood-sucking beasts? Oh please.

"They are magnificent creatures."

"In what world? Pasty-faced monsters with fangs? I didn't want your zombies then, and I don't want them now."

Eros scowls. "They were magnificent when I created them—until that little toad Setesh perverted my creation. He was jealous of the glorious gift I'd manufactured for you."

"Whatever. I still don't want vampires."

"But you welcomed one into your temple."

"No, I used him for my own ends. He was the best tracker, after all."

"I sent Gundisalvus to you as an offering, proof of my devotion to you."

Devotion? What a load of bullshit. Eros always had been great at slinging the crap. But if he wanted to impress me, he might've, oh, informed me he'd sent the pasty-faced, red-eyed vamp to me. I thought Gundisalvus came to me on his own.

"I understand why you dislike my vampires," Eros tells me. "But I have at long last found a way to restore my gift to its original form. You have no idea how many eons it took me to harvest enough magics from the bodies of sorcerers and witches so that I might undo what Setesh did to my beloved children."

He waves an arm in a sweeping gesture, indicating his horde of slavering monsters. "Watch, and you will at last witness the vast scope of my power."

"The power you ripped out of the brains of elementals. Gee, I'm so impressed."

Eros turns sideways to us and his vampires. He raises both arms, tips his head back, and bellows in ancient Greek, his voice booming off the ruins around us.

The sun-like light he had created suddenly erupts in a blinding flash.

I shut my eyes and turn my head away. Travis keeps his arms around me, even after the blinding light dwindles into a sun-like glow again.

"What the bloody hell?" Travis says, his jaw slack.

At first, I'm not sure what has stunned him. My annoyingly human eyes need a moment to recover from that blinding flash. But as my vision returns to normal, I feel my jaw drop too.

Where the horde of slavering vampires had stood, I see an army of gorgeous, muscular men. When the nearest one smiles with a hunger that makes me want to cringe, his long, sharp canines glisten. He runs his tongue over those teeth in an almost sensual way.

Hot vampires? I thought those only existed in movies and romance novels.

"Now you see," Eros declares. "My gift is splendid."

Someone claps slowly, the sound reverberating around us.

Kamadeva saunters toward us from the opposite direction from where Eros stands with his army of hot vampires. "Aren't you the clever one? But you can't be stupid enough to believe I'll let you get the upper hand."

He snaps his fingers.

The vampires burst into flames one by one, screaming and rolling on the ground in a vain attempt to douse the fire on their skin. Some of them rush into the darkness inside the temple, but I can't see if they save themselves that way. The ones left outside swiftly crumple into blackened heaps on the ground.

Kamadeva laughs and points a finger at Eros. "The look on your face is priceless, mate."

He laughs even harder, bent over because his guffaws are so powerful.

"What have you done?" Eros demands.

Kamadeva grins. "I made them allergic to sunlight, even the fake version you created."

"You will pay for this, you insipid runt."

Eros rushes at Kamadeva just as Setesh whumps down between them.

"I prefer darkness," Setesh says. "It is my element, you know."

He flicks his wrist, and the sun-like glow vanishes, plunging us into night again. The abrupt shift is disconcerting—for everyone except Setesh. The moon still glows high above us, but my eyes can't adjust fast enough for me to see what's going on. I hear scuffling and grunting, the explosive gasp as someone gets belted with a powerful fist, and various other noises that indicate a struggle.

Are all three gods battling each other with fisticuffs? I've never seen such a thing. And I can't see it now, not yet. Gods don't...punch each other. They wield spells and curses, maybe use lightning bolts or endued weapons. Not fists.

Travis whispers in my ear, "I think you were right. The residual energy from how much your devotees worshiped you is dampening their powers. Why else would they get into a fistfight?"

"What should we do? They might cause a disaster just by punching each other."

"Let's get inside the temple. The leftover magics might be stronger in there."

"Then what?"

"We'll wing it."

His answer doesn't make me feel any better about the situation, but I don't have any ideas either. Guess we'll "wing it" together.

We hurry up the steps and into the temple.

Shapes writhe in the deeper darkness within the structure. The moon's glow had provided light outside, but in here, I can't see anything. My eyes need time to adjust, but Travis isn't content to wait for that. He conjures a lantern flashlight and switches it on, revealing the scene.

Vampires, everywhere vampires.

I count two dozen, though I'd only seen a handful run for the temple. But then, I'd been distracted by the three evil jerks fighting over who gets to ensorcell me. The vampires seem confused, many of them squinting at the light from the lantern and shielding their eyes, others writhing on the floor as if what's happened to them causes intense pain, and still more stumble around like they can't regain their equilibrium. Oddly, I can understand their confusion. They were abruptly changed, with no explanation and no time to adjust—just like what the Four Winds did to me.

Yes, I empathize with vampires. It's very strange. The once loathsome creatures are now attractive and muscular. Will they still be rotten beasts who tear people's throats out for the fun of it? Or has Eros's spell changed them at a deeper level that might make them behave differently? Time will tell, I suppose. What Kamadeva did to them doesn't help.

Travis sweeps the lantern over the vampires more slowly. "I almost feel sorry for these guys. Is that crazy?"

"No, I don't think so. They've been fundamentally altered without their consent. Whatever they were before, they're suffering now."

"Should we…help them somehow?"

"I'm more worried about the three asses outside."

Travis clenches his jaw, squeezing words out between his teeth. "Them. How do we defeat gods?"

"We can't destroy them. It took the combined powers of all the primordial gods to get rid of Janus, but that didn't destroy his essence or his powers."

"He was in limbo, I know." Travis studies the vampires for a moment, his gaze narrowed. "Think these guys might hate our god buddies enough to help us knock them down a peg or two?"

"Not sure we can do that."

Setting the lantern on the floor, he faces me and clasps my hands. "You're one tough chick, Larry. Way back when, you stopped those three from ever ensorcelling you again, which means you have the knowledge to help me knock them back on their arses for a good long while."

"It sounds strange the way you mix British words with down-home ones."

"Nice attempt at evasion, but it won't work." He leans in close, his swirling gaze locked on mine. "I believe in you, Larissa."

A warm shiver rushes through me. Has anyone ever believed in me? I'm positive the answer is no. I never had friends or even lovers, only innocent beings I bespelled so they would adore me. Now, I have someone who wants me and believes in me of his own free will. Travis has given me more than my first orgasm. He gave me his trust.

I can't let him down.

"Let me think," I say. "The level of magics I was used to employing might be out of your reach. That's not an insult. It's a simple fact."

"I get it. You were a goddess, but I'm a lowly salamander." He pulls me into his body. "Though if you ask me, you're even more of a goddess now."

He palms my ass.

Every incubus has a one-track mind. It's in their DNA.

If they have DNA. I never thought about that before.

"Sex later," I say. "Let me think now."

"I can think while I'm shagging."

His increasing use of Britishisms is a touch disconcerting, but I like it. "Afraid I can't think while you're inside me."

The salamander sighs. "All right. I'll go over there and check on our new mates. Find out if they might cooperate with us."

He conjures the little endued gun and hands it to me. "I put more rounds in the cylinder. But I'd rather you shout for me instead of firing, if you have the option."

"I'll be careful. Maybe I should go with you."

"Don't want you getting too close to the vamps until I figure out what sort of state they're in. Stay by the lantern."

"Okay."

He saunters off toward the vampires.

And I lean against a stone column while I consider our options. The endued revolver did slow down Eros and Setesh, but I doubt that will be enough. We need more firepower. Well, Travis is a salamander—a fire elemental—though I don't know if he has mastered that element yet. Max had told me stories about how Travis struggled to adjust to his new life, including his tendency to set things on fire accidentally. He seems quite adept now, at least in terms of teleporting and conjuring. Maybe he's mastered fire too. Other salamanders I've known, including Max, can run at lightning speed while fully aflame. They have powerful pheromones too, but I'm not sure how that might help us now.

Still, I'm starting to get ideas. Travis might hate them, but he hasn't come up with anything yet.

Any plan involves the high probability that we will die in a gruesome and horrifically painful way, or become ensorcelled, or both. The thought of ensorcellment terrifies me almost more than the possibility of torture.

Suck it up, Larry. Time to pull on your big girl pants.

Outside, I hear crashes, booms, and hoarse bellowing. The gods are still at it. Well, at least that distracts them from what Travis and I plan to do.

I glance over to where Travis is kneeling beside a vampire who's curled up in a fetal position on the floor. He doesn't want me going over there, but I can't just stand here waiting for him. I don't want to wait. Besides, I have an endued weapon, which means I can dust these vamps if they mess with me. Most of them don't look capable of sitting up, much less lunging for me.

With the gun in my hand, I walk toward Travis.

To get to him, I need to wend my way through the vampires. Some of them glance at me, but most are in too much agony to do anything except moan. I bump into one vamp who's standing in the middle of the group, breathing hard but more alert than the others. He scratches his scalp, mussing his dark hair, and his stunningly pale blue eyes dart back and forth.

I start to move past him, but he shoots out a hand to grasp my upper arm.

"Please," he says, his voice low and raspy. "No sun."

"You can stay in here where it's dark." I offer him a small smile. "You'll get used to the change. I know what it's like to be altered suddenly. It's hard, but you can adjust."

"Hathor," he says slowly, like he can barely pronounce the syllables.

The vampire speaks with a slight German accent, but I bet that will change. The creature is different, so the accent will follow. The Unseen will make sure of that.

"No slave," he says.

"You can be whatever you want. Don't let anyone force you to bend to their will." I'm not sure why I'm comforting this creature, but I feel an odd kinship with these vampires.

I start to move away, but he grabs my hand. His cold fingers close around mine. "Protect you. Die for you."

Since I have no clue how to respond to that, I give him another small smile and hurry toward Travis. Maybe I shouldn't have rushed away when a vampire offered to die for me, but his statement made me uneasy. A newly altered vamp might not have full control of his powers, his senses, or his hunger for blood.

Travis is examining a different vampire now, one who lies sprawled on his back, eyes half-closed.

"How's it going?" I ask as I reach Travis.

"I'm no expert on vampire physiology, but I think they'll survive. Not sure any of them can teleport, though, not yet. I might need to give them a ride."

"But are any of them battle-ready?"

"Some might be, but—" He grimaces. "I think they need to feed first."

The booms and shouts outside have grown louder, seeming closer to the temple than before.

"You and I can't feed them," I say. "They'll drain us dry, whether they mean to or not."

"I know." He gazes down at the vampire, studying the creature with his brows knit together. Then his lips slide into a sly smile, and he looks at me. "Oh, I've got a great idea."

"Which is?"

"Ever tried to conjure a gnome?"

Chapter Twenty-One

Travis

LARISSA GAPES AT ME LIKE I'VE SUGGESTED WE SHOULD INVITE A BUS-load of schoolchildren to stop by and let the vamps feed on them. Gnomes are horrible creatures. As far as I can tell, they will work for anyone if the price is right. They helped the harpy Aello when she wanted to kill Lindsey and destroy both worlds, and the beasts nearly decimated the sylph army in the process. A gnome dragged Nevan over a boundary, destroying him, and one almost killed Lindsey too. The huge, hulking bastards also smell awful and don't seem to know the meaning of the word hygiene.

Yes, I hate gnomes.

So no, I won't feel bad about letting vampires feast on them. But I will instruct the bloodsuckers to leave the gnomes alive. If they don't obey my orders, well…I've got bigger problems.

"You can't be serious," Larissa says. "Conjure a gnome? Summoning a firearm is one thing, but conjuring a living being… I've only seen it done a handful of times. Your targeting has to be precise down to the molecule or the being you summon might show up dead or horribly disfigured."

"They're sodding gnomes. I don't care if they're more deformed and awful when they arrive, as long as they've still got blood pumping through their veins."

She tips her head to the side. "You had a bad experience with gnomes, didn't you?"

"Yes. If you'd watched one of those monsters destroy your friend, you wouldn't worry about damaging them either."

"Oh, you're talking about when Nevan was destroyed. Max told me all about the big battle with a harpy and an army of gnomes."

"Max has a big mouth."

"He had no choice. I ensorcelled him."

Since we've moved past her past, sort of, I decide not to get testy because she's prattling on about her beloved Max again. I'm not jealous. It's annoying, that's all—and unfair. Max rarely said anything about Hathor, except how evil she was, so I don't have regurgitated stories to throw in her face the way she does with her Max tales.

All right, maybe I'm slightly jealous.

But I've got one up on Max. I gave Larissa her first taste of sexual pleasure.

"I'm going to conjure a gnome," I tell her, "and see how it goes."

"Better hurry. The battle outside is coming closer."

"Right. Time to do this." I glance around at the vampires lying on the floor, standing up, and slumping against stone pillars. "I should get a little further away from these guys first."

When I start walking, Larissa follows me. I stop and turn partway toward her, holding up a hand. "No. You stay here. I won't have a gnome squashing you under his foot."

"Good point. I'll hang out with our new friends."

"Maybe you should hide in a corner." I gesture toward a vacant area behind a wide pillar. "Over there."

She flattens her lips and squints at me.

"You're not a goddess anymore," I point out. "You're a lot more squashable than I am."

With a huff and a brief scowl, she whirls around and marches into the corner I'd suggested. She's probably cursing at me under her breath and wishing she had powers so she could toss me into a wall or something.

I jog over to an empty area that's a good ways from the vampires and Larissa.

Then I do it. With arms down, held slightly away from my body, I spread my palms and focus all my energy on bringing a gnome to me. Pain bites into my brain, but I concentrate harder, gritting my teeth and squeezing my eyes shut while sweat rolls down my temples. Magics from outside of me gather on my skin and sink beneath it, amping up my innate powers. The temple is helping me, I think. *Brilliant.*

An explosive thud shakes the entire building.

When I open my eyes, all I see is dust. It plumes up from the floor, disguising whatever had rocked the building. The cloud of debris gradually settles, revealing what the dust had concealed.

A gnome crouches there, knees bent, ax raised. His gnarled, massive body resembles a deformed tree.

I've done it. I conjured a gnome.

Rather than pumping my fists in the air to celebrate my achievement, I shout to the gnome, "Hey! Over here, mate. I'm the one who brought you to this place."

The gnome straightens to his full height, towering over me, and turns this way. His lips peel back from his brown, ragged teeth. "Why have you summoned me, minuscule salamander?"

I'm shorter and less tree-like than he is, but I'm hardly minuscule. And I'm getting bloody sick of other elementals and those god arseholes calling me puny and tiny and pathetic.

They're about to see how wrong they are.

"Do you like the gods Eros, Kamadeva, and Setesh?" I ask the gnome.

"I would crush them with my little toe if I could." He snarls, and spittle dribbles from his lips. "Tell me why you have summoned me, or I will crush you with my pinky finger."

He wiggles his pinky at me.

It's large, but not big enough to terrify me. Not even the stench rolling off his finger intimidates me.

"Yes, you're very terrifying," I say. "I'm cringing on the inside. Sorry, but I don't have time to chat with you. Now, would you like to hear my offer? Or should I holler to the gods outside that a gnome is trying to steal their prize?"

"What prize?"

"Those creatures." I point to the vampires, who now look nothing like they did earlier. I'm banking on the gnome's stupidity and hatred of gods. "Those blokes are Eros's favorite toys. How do you feel about that particular god?"

"Want to crush his skull with my mouth, but gods are indestructible."

"Well, I've brought you a veritable feast of elementals who are crushable."

All the racket outside has grown even louder. The gods will breach the temple soon, if they can stop beating on each other long enough to realize that.

The gnome glances at the vampires. "What are they? Never saw ones like them before."

"Eros made them. He dearly loves his new pets." I lean in to speak in a pseudo-whisper. "Wouldn't you love to tear apart the god's little darlings?"

"Yes," he growls, drawing the word out. "Then I will crush you with my pinky."

"Sounds like a plan." I wave toward the vampires. "Go on. Have your fun."

The gnome jogs toward the creatures he assumes are helpless and hapless. His footfalls shake the temple, but at least there's no debris cloud this time. He skids to a halt at the edge of the gathering of vampires and licks his lips.

"Wake up, bloodsuckers!" I shout. "I've brought you dinner."

For a moment, no one moves—not the gnome, not the vampires, and certainly not me. I can see Larissa hiding behind that pillar, but she doesn't move either. Then all hell breaks loose.

Vampires swarm the gnome, who flails his arms and stamps his feet while the bloodsuckers latch onto various parts of his body. Some climb up his trousers to feast on his torso, while a few manage to reach his neck and sink their fangs into arteries.

I zip over to Larissa.

She rushes into my arms. "Now what?"

"I summon a few more gnomes, if I can. Can't believe it worked the first time."

"Well, I tried to help you. Think it worked."

"You don't have powers. How did you help?"

She hunches her shoulders and focuses on my chest. "The residual magics here belong to me, or the me I used to be. I hoped that if I prayed for those magics to help you, they would."

"When exactly did you pray?"

"Right about the time you squeezed your eyes shut."

And then I'd felt a surge of energy. She helped me. Without powers. I guess this temple belongs to her whether she's a god or a mortal. It makes a kind of sense. The people who worshiped at this temple worshiped her, not the place, and their adoration empowered the temple.

Now it's empowered me, thanks to her.

I kiss her forehead. "Thank you. I couldn't have done it without you, Larissa."

She smiles shyly and still won't look at me.

"Mind giving me a boost to bring in more gnomes?" I ask.

"Whatever I can do."

"I wonder if it would be easier to do this if we kiss while I conjure those buggers."

She lifts her head, smiling with nothing at all like shyness this time. "Might be fun to find out."

With both hands under her arse, I lift her off the floor so I can seal my mouth over hers. She locks her arms around my neck, then clamps her thighs around me too. While our tongues collide and our teeth clash, I hold my hands out and spread my palms to summon the magics.

The thunderous sound of gnomes hitting the floor feet-first reverberates through the temple. One, two, three, four. That seems like enough, so I stop conjuring and wrap my arms around Larissa to kiss her so deeply, for so long, that the entire multiverse seems to disappear. When I finally force myself to stop, I see vampires gorging on gnomes. Those bloodsuckers look much livelier than they had a little while ago. Instead of limping or lying slack on the floor, they leap around with swift, graceful movements as they evade the crush-ready feet of the gnomes.

I set Larissa down and shove two fingers into my mouth to whistle. The ear-splitting sound pierces the melee and causes all the gnomes and vampires to disentangle from each other and look at me.

"Now that the vamps have full tummies," I say, "who wants to go out there and wallop a few gods who think they own the multiverse?"

They stare at me for so long that I start to worry they're about to attack me instead. But then the gnomes glance at each other and gnash their teeth, and the vamps bare their fangs.

One bloodsucker hollers, "Kill Eros!"

"Kill Setesh too!" another screams.

"Rip Kamadeva's head off!" yet another suggests.

The gnomes raise their axes and shout in unison, "Crush the gods!"

Well, that'll work.

Every creature in the temple, except for me and Larissa, barrels out the main entrance.

I lead Larissa out onto the portico, where the massive columns hide us. On the steps that lead into the temple, the three gods are being assaulted by gnomes and vampires intent on ripping them apart. I doubt they can do that, but maybe they can at least wound the bastards enough that they won't be so worked up about Larissa anymore. If we're lucky, the gods will limp back to their lairs or temples or whatever and convalesce for a few centuries.

Kamadeva has just been walloped by a gnome's club. He staggers backward, then clenches his fists and glowers at the gnome. His eyes begin to burn a fiery red. And then, his body begins to swell and rise until he stands twice as tall as the biggest gnome. The god spreads his arms and smacks his fist into the palm of the other hand. He roars, the sound so fearsome it shakes the temple and the ground.

Setesh flings a ball of seething fire at Kamadeva. It engulfs him and seems to absorb the magics that made him enormous. His body shrinks back to normal, and he wastes only one second before he conjures a sword and drives it straight into Setesh's heart.

Assuming the gods' hearts are in the same place as mine.

"We need more firepower," I tell Larissa. "The gods are getting even angrier, and I'm not sure the gnomes and vampires can handle them."

A sword appears in my hand—long, red, double-edged, and throbbing with magics. An endued sword? There's a note tied onto the hilt, so I tear it free and unfold the paper to read the familiar handwriting: "A gift from Max and Nevan, with an assist from Ennea and Bob. Kick those gods' asses. Lindsey."

God bless her. And Nevan, Max, Bob, and Ennea. I'll give them all big wet kisses when this is over, if I survive it.

Another sword appears in Larissa's hand. She jumps, then opens the note attached to her blade. "It says this is a gift from Nevan, Max, Ennea, and Bob. Lindsey signed the note."

"Yeah, I got the same thing. They're endued weapons."

"More than endued." She raises her sword, her lips curving into an almost lustful smile. "It's super endued."

"Never heard of that."

"Only a handful of elementals can craft a spell like this. It must've required help from an oracle too, which explains why Bob is mentioned in the note. Can't believe they did this so fast." She waves her weapon in sweeping gestures as if she's testing its weight. "I've never used a sword before."

"It's easy. Slash and run, and try not to get in the way of your opponent's weapon." I brandish my blade. "I'm no expert either."

The sound of a gnome falling detonates in the air and makes the earth tremble.

I glance toward the melee. Eros has slain a gnome, but the vampires are swarming him now.

Time to enter the fray.

Larissa raises her sword at the same I raise mine—and we rush headlong into battle.

Chapter Twenty-Two

Larissa

How can it be this hard to defeat three men when we have a horde of vampires and gnomes on our side? Our sole hope is to force Eros, Kamadeva, and Setesh to use so much magic and energy that they deplete themselves. The gnomes love beating on the gods, and the vampires simply want to drink blood. They're swarming Eros, their creator.

The noises of the battle become so thunderous that I can't hear anything else.

I have a sword, but I don't know what to do with it. I mean, I know I should skewer something or someone. But who? Eros has his hands full with the vampires, which leaves Setesh and Kamadeva to fight each other and the gnomes. Travis has joined the gnomes, but he's not having much luck pushing through them to reach the gods.

The stench of blood and sweat and foul magics fills the air.

I stand on the steps of the temple and watch the battle raging several tiers down. I need to do something, but only one idea springs to mind. I race down the steps, skirting around vampires as I wend my way toward Eros. Maybe I shouldn't do this, but my mind replays every moment of my millennia-long enslavement to Eros, and a vengeful impulse grips me so hard that I can't breathe for a few seconds. Then I dodge the vampires and make a beeline for my target.

Eros has just dispatched four vampires in such quick succession that I had trouble following the movements. The headless bodies lie sprawled on the steps with the accompanying heads rolling down toward the ground. The god is streaked with blood from head to toe, and he bares his teeth like a rabid animal.

I barrel through the vampires.

Eros notices me and grins, but it's an evil expression, not a cheerful one. He believes he almost has me. I keep my sword down so he might not notice it and call on every iota of magic left inside this precinct. How I can do that, I don't know. But I sense the residual energy draining away as it floods into me. I've waited an eternity for the chance to cause Eros as much pain as he caused me, but now that I'm rushing toward oblivion, I suffer a powerful, if brief, impulse to stop and think before I attack a god.

I stand ten feet from him, my sword raised, my chest heaving.

Will vengeance help me heal? Does it matter? Eros must be stopped. That's all I know for certain.

Screw godliness. This being is not worthy of anyone's devotion.

Eros's gaze locks on to mine at the instant I lunge for him.

"How sweet," he says, sidestepping my strike. "The creature I gave life to now wants to take mine. But I cannot die, you silly girl. I have more power than all the other gods combined."

"Bullshit. You're nothing but a bully." I gasp as a revelation slams through me, and I know I must ask, "Why didn't you come after me once I'd escaped from Kamadeva?"

I hadn't been powerful yet at that point. He could've abducted me from the other god's clutches quite easily.

"Why bother?" Eros says. "I had minions and didn't need your affection any longer."

"So why bother trying to kidnap me now?"

"Because I created you. Hathor belongs to me."

He says my original name like Hathor is someone else, like he's not talking to me right now. And that's when I'm positive, beyond any doubts. I'd suspected it before, during the eons when I was free of these bastards, and I'd sort of let Travis believe I knew it for a fact. But Eros's response confirms it and justifies my belief.

"I'm more powerful than the three of you," I say. "Hathor possessed more magics than either you, Kamadeva, or Setesh. That's why no one came after me until I was stripped of my powers. You were afraid of me. Still are, I'm sure. That's why you three play these idiotic macho games to see who can grab me first, and why you don't just grab me and go."

"You know not of what you speak, child. Come with—"

"No." I brandish my sword, aiming it at his chest. "Time to prove I'm right."

I rush at Eros, screaming like an enraged harpy, and ram the blade straight through his heart.

Eros freezes, his eyes wide and his mouth open.

Then he tumbles down the steps backward, landing on the ground below on his back with the sword protruding from his chest. He splutters and gasps, but can't get up.

"My children," he croaks as blood dribbles from his lips, "take me away to my temple."

His "children," the vampires, bound down the steps to encircle Eros. They hiss and gnash their fangs while saliva drips from their honed tips.

A knife-sharp blade of brilliant light shoots down from the sky, piercing the moonlit night straight to the earth mere feet from where Eros lies wounded and surrounded by his formerly devoted "children." Silence descends with such suddenness that it feels as if we've all been plunged into the deepest abyss in the deepest ocean on earth. The air feels thicker too, though not from humidity. The viscosity stems from the magics employed to interrupt the battle.

Four beings float downward within the beam of light, their long robes barely fluttering. They touch down within the beam and rake their gazes over every being that still haunts this place.

The Four Winds have arrived.

Miriella, Javren, Lartellon, and Zerith remain silent for longer than I can gauge.

"There will be no more bloodshed," Miriella announces. "You have invaded the mortal realm for wicked, selfish reasons, and you have abused your powers in an attempt to acquire one who does not wish to be appropriated. Cease your pointless battle. We declare it null and void."

Setesh leaps into the air, landing inches from the beam of light. "I am the rightful owner of the creature now calling herself Larissa."

"No being owns another," Miriella says. "We have allowed the self-appointed gods to run wild, immune to the power of the Great Bargain. No more."

Kamadeva joins Setesh at the periphery of the beam that holds the Four Winds. "The Bargain itself grants us immunity. Nothing can change that—unless you want to convene a realm-wide meeting in the Unseen to vote on altering the Great Bargain."

Miriella points a finger at Kamadeva. Her expression and her voice turn austere and unforgiving. "We crafted the Bargain. We are the essence of the Unseen, and our power supersedes that of all other beings in that world. The mortal realm is your playground no longer. Cease your actions willingly, or we shall impose our will on you."

Two gods laugh. The third still lies in a puddle of his own blood, gurgling and thrashing his head.

Setesh roars and rockets his body into the air, flying on a trajectory aimed straight at me.

Just as he whumps down an arm's length away, Travis rips through the crowd at lightning speed, his entire body aflame and the endued sword on fire too. Before Setesh can lunge for me, the salamander grasps the sword's hilt with both hands, plunging it into the god's chest. The blade protrudes from Setesh's back, while the hilt is flush with his torso. The god wheezes and struggles to get hold of the hilt to pull it out, but he starts to teeter, and his fingers fall away from the sword. He hits the ground on his side, eyes wild.

Kamadeva bolts toward me, but Travis tackles him while still aflame from head to toe. He slugs the god in his gut three times, until Kamadeva slumps onto the ground.

I wonder for a moment why none of the gods tried to teleport to me, but I know the answer. The magics of this temple complex prevented it, just as I'd suspected earlier. I can still feel the leftover power inside me, though it's far weaker than earlier.

The Four Winds cast their gazes on each fallen god in turn—and they sigh in unison.

"As you wish," Miriella says as she surveys Eros, Kamadeva, and Setesh. "You have brought this upon your own heads. Judgment shall be given in our temple."

The Four Winds raise their arms in unison, and a humming sound originates from their vicinity.

All three gods vanish. But the swords that had felled them remain, lying on the dirt in twin puddles of blood.

Miriella looks at me. "You have done well, Hathor, as did the salamander. We will decide your fate soon, but first, you have more to experience and endure."

All four beings disappear, and the beam of light snuffs out.

More to endure? When I heard those words, my first instinct had been to assume Miriella meant I need to suffer. But "endure" doesn't mean that. It means to keep going in the same manner as before. The Four Winds have delayed their judgment of me until I've endured my current condition for a bit longer, and until I've experienced something else. What, I don't know. Time and fate will tell.

Although the gods and the Four Winds have left, the vampires and gnomes are still here.

Travis jogs up to me. "Are you all right?"

"Fine, yes. How are you?"

"Brilliant." He grins. "We both stabbed a god."

"Can't tell you how good it felt to skewer Eros."

He moves beside me, sliding an arm around my waist, and gazes out at the creatures who now stand idle and seemingly baffled. "What should we do about them?"

"Can you send the gnomes back where they came from?"

"I can try to un-conjure them." He slings his other arm around me, tugging my body into his. "With a little help from Larissa the Badass Ex-Goddess."

"Should we do this the way we did it last time?"

"Yes."

I throw my arms around his neck, and he grasps my bottom to hoist me higher. Our mouths collide, the kiss hungry and wild. I feel the energy crackling around us, inside us, enlivening our kiss and penetrating our bodies, the power hot and liquid like the essence of desire.

Travis pulls his head back, severing our lip-lock. "The gnomes are gone."

"Good." I open my eyes, glancing over my shoulder. "What about the vampires?"

"Not sure what to do with them. I could try to send them home, but I don't know where that is or if I can conjure them to anywhere. There were only a handful of gnomes, but even after the big battle, there are a lot of vamps."

A dozen or more, I'd say. But I don't say that, because Travis can see it for himself.

"Let's call a friend," Travis says. Then he conjures a cell phone and dials a number, his gaze going distant as he waits for the other party to pick up. "Max, I need a favor. How can we ship a bunch of vampires back to where they belong?" Travis nods, listening to whatever Max is telling him. "Right. Thanks, mate."

Travis ends the call, and his phone vanishes.

"Well?" I say.

He smiles with his lips sealed. "Wait for it."

Max appears—at the other end of the concourse. He glances around and makes a peeved face. "Why did I materialize here? I was aiming straight for you."

Travis spreads his arms, indicating our surroundings. "This is Hathor's temple. The residual magics of her worshipers' devotion protect it and her."

Max runs toward us, flaming all the way. "We're at Dendera in Egypt, aren't we?"

"Yes," Travis says. "And you might need a little help with leaving this place. I managed to zip myself from one end of the temple to the other, but everyone else seems to have trouble with it."

"Only you can teleport inside the temple precinct?" Max eyes his friend up and down with a suspicious look on his face. "I wonder why that would be."

And he sounds suspicious too.

I swear Travis blushes the tiniest bit.

"You shagged her, didn't you?" Max says.

"He did, yes," I reply. "Not that it's any of your business."

"Considering how often you ensorcelled me so you could make me shag you for weeks at a time, I think it is my business."

Travis growls. "Can we deal with the issue at hand? Before those vampires decide to invade Cairo."

Max moves alongside Travis, standing sideways to him, and throws his friend a sideways glance. "Just so there are no misunderstandings, I'm doing this because it's necessary, not because I want to do it. So don't either of you read anything into it."

"You said you were happy to help," Travis says.

"That's not what I'm talking about." Max aims a sharp look at me. "Don't say a bloody word. Understand?"

I nod. What is his problem? Still me, I assume.

Max clasps Travis's hand and raises his arm, lifting Travis's too. Then Max raises his other arm to the side, and Travis does the same. Flames erupt on their skin, though smaller than the conflagration that bursts out whenever they run at top speed.

The vampires jerk and gasp.

"Bloody hell," Max moans. "We need more contact. Which does not mean I want to shag him."

He glared at me when he said that.

I roll my eyes. "But you enjoyed it when I brought you males to—"

"No, you magically coerced me to do it. Don't get any ideas about me and Travis getting a leg over so you can watch."

"I'm not interested in that anymore." No, the only one I want to have sex with anymore is Travis.

Max throws his arms around Travis, hugging him tight.

Travis scrunches up his face, but then hugs Max the same way. Flames erupt again, becoming a wall of fire that surrounds them both.

One vampire breaks out of the crowd and barrels toward me.

I glance at the nearest sword, about to run for it.

The vampire latches his arms around my torso, pinning me to him—and he whisks us away.

CHAPTER TWENTY-THREE

Travis

I SEE THE FUCKING VAMPIRE GRAB LARISSA AND DISAPPEAR WITH HER, but I can't do anything about it. Max and I are in the middle of sending the vamps away, and I can feel that we need to finish the task because breaking away from it might rip us apart and the bloodsuckers with us. I don't give a toss about the vamps, but I won't risk my friend's life.

Besides, Larissa and the vamp disappeared so fast that I couldn't have reached her in time even if I'd tried.

The bloodsuckers vanish.

Our flames are doused, and Max hustles backward away from me. He swivels his head left and right. "Where's your evil girlfriend?"

"Larissa is not evil. And a vampire took her, I saw it happen." I march over to my sword, and with a puff of fire, cleanse it of the god's blood, conjuring the clean blade into my hand. "I need to find her. Where the hell would a confused vampire take her? Why does he want her at all?"

Max rolls his eyes. "To feed on, obviously."

My fist tightens around the sword's handle, making my knuckles ache. "How do I find the bastard?"

"No idea. Tracking isn't my forte." Max eyes me warily. "Are you in love with Hathor?"

I stab the sword's tip into the earth. "No, I'm in love with Larissa."

Did I just say that out loud? Why did I say it? Because it's true, I realize with a start. I do love her. It's completely insane, since I've known her for a day or two at most—hard to keep track when we've been fleeing from gods and consulting with an oracle—but I feel like I've known her for much longer. I'd never met Hathor, but I love Larissa.

Max is gaping at me. "You—what? She is evil, Travis."

130

"No, she's not. The goddess you knew no longer exists. Larissa has lived as a mortal, in the mortal world, for two years. She's changed."

"She's ensorcelled you, hasn't she?"

I stalk up to him, hands fisted, jaw clenched. "She is not evil. She is a good person who's been through more hell than even you have. The things those gods did to her… Christ, Max, I don't blame her for going insane for several thousand years."

Max's brows cinch tight over his nose. "What the gods did? She *is* a god."

"Not anymore." I let my head drop into my raised palm and groan. "Eros created her, then he ensorcelled her so she would be forced to enjoy it every time he used her body to get his end away. Then Setesh captured her and did the same bloody thing. At least Kamadeva didn't enslave her with magics, but he did imprison her in a cell, alone, only visiting her when he felt like slapping her around a bit or showing her off like a trophy."

Maybe I shouldn't have told Max all of that, but he needs to understand, so he'll realize we are not fighting for the goddess Hathor, but for the mortal Larissa—an innocent woman.

He stares at me, his face blank. "Are you sure she didn't lie about what the gods did?"

"I'm sure. Don't ask for proof because I can't give it. I feel she's honest and good and deserving of our help."

"You were never this passionate about rescuing Lindsey. Thought you were in love with her."

"No. It was obsession, not love." I grasp his shoulders and give him a little shake. "What I feel for Larissa is real. Will you help me, Max?"

"All right." He eyes the scorched bodies that litter the steps of the temple. "Are you sure those were vampires? I've never seen any who didn't look like they got crapped out of the arse-end of a gnome."

"Eros changed them. It's a long story."

"You can tell me later, then." He grabs Larissa's sword, cleansing it with a wave of his hand. The weapon looks tiny in his hand, since it was designed for a woman who's much smaller than Max. "You mentioned before that the bounty hunters found a way to track Larissa in the mortal world."

"Their masters did, yes. Took a lot of magic to do it."

Max curves his mouth into a sly smile. "Let's go find a bounty hunter. Ennea said you gave her a harpy talon, so we'll pay her a visit first."

He zips away, and I follow.

We wind up at the waterfall behind the rock shop. After a quick trip through the falls and the portal, we emerge on the Unseen side, wasting no time as we teleport directly into Ennea's laboratory.

"Uh-oh," she says, raising her head while still bent over a bubbling cauldron. "Larissa's not with you. That can't be good."

"A vampire took her," I say. "We need to find a bounty hunter. Could you somehow use that harpy talon to, ah…"

"Hunt the hunter? Not sure that's what you need, hon. A way to track her is more like it, but you don't need a bounty hunter for that."

"Can you help me track her?"

"Lemme see what I can whip up for ya."

While Ennea rummages around for whatever ingredients she needs to cast a spell, I drop onto the chair in the corner and slump my entire body.

Max conjures a chair and sits beside me. "The good guys always win, that's what Lindsey says."

"Then I'm screwed."

"Bollocks. You're still part of Team Lindsey."

I shut my eyes and groan. "You weren't there when I was obsessed with Lindsey and harassed her for years. I'm not a good guy, Max. I've made too many mistakes."

"Let me see if I understand this." Max's chair creaks as if he's shifted his weight. "You can forgive Hathor for the thousands of years she spent abusing other beings for her own pleasure, but you can't forgive yourself for harassing Lindsey. That makes perfect sense."

Bob had told me I need to forgive myself, but I still can't manage to do that. He also said my destiny affects others. Have I lost Larissa because I can't get over what I did to Lindsey? Is it my fault?

Max does have a point. I've absolved Larissa of everything she did when she was the goddess Hathor. So maybe it is time I forgive myself. I've made up for what I did to Lindsey, and she granted me her forgiveness, though I hadn't been willing to accept that gift. Not until now.

I fought alongside my friends to save two worlds, twice. I died for the cause. Just because I'd been captured by an evil sorceress doesn't negate the fact that I'd been willing to die to save the people I care about—not only Lindsey, but our friends too, and even the ex-king of the sylphs himself. Yes, I would risk my life for him, though I don't think I'll ever tell Nevan that.

Maybe I'm not a bastard after all.

No, not maybe. I am not that man anymore, literally. I've become a salamander and done more good since that change than I ever did as a mortal cop.

"I forgive us both," I tell Max, looking him straight in the eye. "Larissa deserves to get a clean slate as much as I do."

My friend studies me for a moment, his lips puckering slightly. "I trust your judgment. If you swear Hathor—Larissa has changed, then I believe it."

"I appreciate that, Max."

He relaxes into his chair with a sigh. "But I'm still not shagging you."

Ennea throws her arms up and grins. "Who's the best witch in the Unseen?"

"You are," Max and I say at the same time. And we mean it.

She walks over to us and hands me the harpy talon. "This is now enchanted. It will lead you to your girl, but I can't promise the journey will be smooth."

"How do I use it?" I ask.

"Just hold the talon in your hand, real tight, with your fingers wrapped around it. You'll be whisked away, but like I said, it might be a bumpy ride with a few hiccups along the way." She pats my arm. "You can handle it, hon. Follow wherever fate leads you."

"Fate? I thought it was a tracking spell."

"Don't talk back. I'm doing this for you for free, so show a little unspoken gratitude."

I push up out of the chair. "You're a good friend."

"Much better." She hops up on her toes to kiss my cheek. "Trust the spell, hon. Would I steer you wrong?"

"Never."

Max clears his throat. "Should I, ah, go with you?"

"No, I think I need to do this on my own. But you're a real mate for asking."

He nods, then vanishes.

I transport myself outside, into the woods that surround the mountain in which Ennea's lab resides. I have no idea if using the tracking spell while inside her lab would cause a problem, but getting myself to somewhere else first seemed like the best plan. I conjure my new endued sword, gripping it in one hand while I wrap my fist around the harpy talon.

The world spins around me as the air in front of me seems to melt and twist, like a bizarre version of a whirlpool, but this one hovers a foot off the ground.

I'm sucked into the vortex.

The forces that dragged me into the maelstrom tear at my body, but I grip the talon and my sword even tighter, refusing to give up my only weapon. No, it's not my only weapon. I have fire and elemental strength too. But I can't think about that or anything while I'm hauled downward and my body feels like it's aflame on the inside.

The whirlpool spits me out in the forest. In the mortal world. I don't remember going through the portal, but I must've done. How else could I wind up in the woods behind the rock shop in Michigan? The vampire wouldn't have brought Larissa here. The bloody stupid spell failed.

Both my sword and the harpy talon are gone.

Janus materializes in front of me. "There you are, salamander. I was beginning to think you would not heed the advice of the fae witch."

"What do you mean you were beginning to think that? I only just saw Ennea."

"But I knew of your visit with her long before it occurred."

"How—" I groan, my shoulders sagging. "You're the ruddy god of time."

"Not precisely accurate, but close enough." He tilts his head to the side, raising his brows. "You have begun the transition in earnest, haven't you? Giving up your old way of speaking and accepting the new."

"If you mean do I talk British now, the answer is…sort of. I think it'll take time for me to switch over a hundred percent. Unless I cock it up somehow."

"You will not." He crosses his arms over his chest. "I am not only the 'god of time,' but also the guardian of transitions. Therefore, I can state with utter certainty that you will successfully adopt your new manner of speaking and at last complete the transition from mortal to elemental. My vast powers assure me of this."

Max wasn't exaggerating when he told me Janus loves to proclaim he has "vast powers" and say that in an arrogant voice. Max was also right about Janus being a bloody annoying freak, though not a half-bad bloke. It's the god's eyes that make him freakish. They shimmer like genuine, molten gold.

"No offense, mate," I say to the god. "But I was trying to find a woman, not you."

"The spell sent you to where you should be at this moment." He approaches me, laying a hand on my shoulder. "You have quite a journey ahead of you, but each stop along your route will play a part in ensuring you have all that you need to save the woman you love."

"How do you know I love her?"

The god taps his temple. "Vast powers, my salamander friend."

He didn't sound like an arrogant twat when he said that. He seemed almost…friendly.

"What about my sword and the harpy talon?" I ask.

"Not my concern." Janus moves to stand in front of me, squares his shoulders, and raises both hands. "Now, allow me to send you on your way."

With a flick of his wrist, he does just that.

I'm sucked backward into the same vortex that had hauled me to the waterfall, but this time I tumble end over end as the savage currents rip at my flesh. It feels that way, at least. When the vortex spits me out, I tumble sideways down a hill but don't have any wounds on my body. That's how the supernatural works. Sometimes it bites and you bleed, but sometimes the wounds are illusory.

Maybe I don't bleed, but I do have grass and twigs stuck in my hair and pasted to my body. Hopping to my feet, I brush myself off and survey the area. Though there are trees behind me on the hill I rolled down, ahead of me I see a squat brown building. I've seen that structure before. I know it well, because I'd spent more years inside that building than I care to count. It's the police station where I'd been working when I met Lindsey and my life changed in ways I still don't fully understand. Everything that happened in my life led me to become what I am now, but the events that transpired after Lindsey entered my life would become the most painful of all.

Because of me. Because of what I'd done to Lindsey.

Why has Janus sent me here? He and Ennea both essentially told me to roll with it, whatever "it" might be. So I amble down the hill, glamouring into my old self as I round the corner of the building. I trip on a rock and throw out a hand to halt my fall, but my palm goes right through the wall. I stumble sideways, stagger a few steps, and stop.

I'm inside the building. Inside a jail cell.

What just happened? I can walk through walls now? Maybe Janus killed me with that vortex, and I'm a ghost. No, he wouldn't do that. The god might be annoying, but he's no murderer.

A door opens, and two people walk down the hallway that houses the four cells.

It's me. And Lindsey.

She's handcuffed. I watch the old me, the human me, open the cell door and shove Lindsey inside. He removes the cuffs and shuts the door. The lock clicks into place.

"We'll talk about this later," Old Me says. His Texas accent sounds odd to me now. "When you're ready to tell me the truth."

"I told you everything," Lindsey says, grasping the bars. "Why are you doing this, Travis? You know me. We're friends. You can't honestly believe I'd kill your brother. I loved Calder."

Not long ago, Lindsey told me she never did love my brother. She thought she had, but later, she realized whatever she and Calder had together wasn't real love. Nevan gave her that and showed her what it means to really care for someone and have a connection so deep that logic can't explain it.

I seem to be in the past, thanks to Janus, the god who loves to be cryptic and not explain things before he sends someone on a magical mystery tour of a previous life. I'd been a different person back then. Watching the old me gives me a strange feeling of déjà vu, but also makes me feel like I don't belong here anymore. I'm not the man who arrested Lindsey. I am an incubus.

And I suddenly realize why most elementals choose a new name after their forging. Maybe I should do that, but I'm not quite there yet.

"Tell me the truth," the other me snarls. "You say my brother is dead, but I can't find a body. What did you do with him?"

"Nothing."

In the blink of an eye, the scene changes. I'm no longer in the police station. I've wound up inside a Ford Expedition, the one I'd driven when I was sheriff of Mandan County. Lindsey huddles in the backseat, handcuffed.

Old Me glowers at her over the back of his seat. "I don't get it. Why'd you hook up with a sleaze like Nivea?"

"His name is Nevan. And it's none of your business who I hook up with."

"Guess you're right. And I reckon I should worry more about what you'll do to him than what he'll do to you."

"You have no clue what really happened with Calder."

"Enlighten me."

She glares right back at him.

He drapes one wrist over the steering wheel, his fingers coiled into his palm. "No body, no crime. If you won't talk, I can't help."

"I didn't ask for your help."

This incident happened last year, or maybe it was the year before. So much has happened since then that it's hard to keep track. Lindsey had found a dead body in the woods behind the rock shop, but it vanished. So of course, I hauled her in for questioning and harangued her for hours before I let her go. I'd already had one encounter with Nevan, the bronze-skinned sylph who would sweep Lindsey off her feet. Naturally, I hated him at first sight and did everything I could to make both their lives hell—all because I was jealous. Lindsey had rejected me, but she trusted Nevan from the moment they met.

Watching this moment unfold, I feel no resentment or guilt. This part of my life ended, and I have a new one to live.

I'm jerked away from this event and hurled into another.

No, I can't relive this. Why on earth would Janus or the Unseen or whatever force is controlling this stroll down memory lane want me to witness this? I can't watch. I won't.

But I must do it. I vowed I would see this through to the end.

And here it is. My end.

I'm in the woods in the Unseen. Before me, I see Ceara—the being who had once been Nevan's mortal wife three thousand years ago, but who was resurrected by an insane sorcerer. And that sorcerer had been my brother, in part, melded with two other beings—Notus, the former sylph king who had died ages ago, and Skeiron, Notus's successor who died when Lindsey tricked him into marching across a boundary in the mortal world. Calder had died twice, once as a mortal and again when Nevan snapped his neck, ending the version of my brother who had been twisted into a monkey-beast by the forging.

The moment in which I find myself now happened months later. Ceara wanted to destroy Lindsey by convincing her she was the ultimate cause of the murders committed by the sorcerer. I had stayed behind when Lindsey and our other allies went off on missions of their own. But I'd gotten captured by Ceara. When Lindsey found us, I was on my knees and a mess, thanks to my attempts to fight off the evil sorceress. Blood oozed down my scalp. I remember not being able to move with her magics confining me. We're positioned at the edge of a pool formed by a small waterfall.

"What do you want, Ceara?" Lindsey asks.

Ceara smiles with feral hunger. "Your powers, of course."

"Can't give them to you even if I wanted to. No idea how to do it."

"You will discover a way, given the proper motivation." Ceara conjures a knife into her hand, turning it this way and that so its wide and long blade glints in the light of the rising sun. "Do it, or I will end this mortal's life."

She holds the blade to my throat.

His throat. It's the other me who will suffer unspeakable agony, but I know, though I can't explain how, that I will feel it all again when the moment that fundamentally altered me comes to pass.

The old me makes a disgusted face. "Don't do it, Lindsey."

"Do you bother to think," Ceara says, caressing Old Me's throat with the blade while watching Lindsey, "how many have died in your name? Three young women, whose only crime was their resemblance to you. The man you were to wed, who became a monster because he longed to be with you forever. Two kings. And how many sylph soldiers, in the battle to dethrone Skeiron?" Ceara's voice takes on a vicious edge, as does her smile. "Nevan almost lost his eternal soul because of you."

"Nice try," Lindsey says, "but I'm canceling my reservation at the guilt trip hotel."

Lindsey had shed the past and moved on. But I hadn't been able to do that, not in the time when this moment happened.

I lose track of what's going on in front of me because I can't help wondering if I'd always been destined to meet my mortal end here, in this place and this time, so I could be reborn as something else, someone else. I'd fought the change, clinging to who I had once been. But I can't do that anymore. I won't do it. My future lies not with who I used to be, but with the one person in the multiverse who understands my inner conflict.

Larissa. I belong with her.

But I'm meant to relive my mortal death. I said I'd go along with whatever this journey showed me, which means I have no choice. I must witness the demise of the old me and the birth of a new being.

Lindsey fires her endued derringer at Ceara, but even a .357 round can't pierce the wards around the evil bitch and Old Me.

Ceara's smile twists into a nasty grin. She yanks Old Me's head back and slashes her knife across his throat. Blood streams from the wound as she lets go of him, and his body crumples with his head slumping over the pool's edge, his hair touching the water. Blood starts the process, activating a portal to the Unseen, but only another elemental can trigger the forging.

What happened after that, I've never known, not for sure. Lindsey, Nevan, and Max told me, but I've always suspected they left things out to spare me the full horror of it.

I won't be spared today.

A feeling of being disconnected from reality takes hold of me, and I watch as Lindsey kills Ceara, then falls to her knees beside Old Me. Droplets of my blood drip into the water and spread out on the surface, carried away by the current.

"We have to save him," Lindsey says to Nevan, who crouches beside her. "Must be a vortex around here somewhere, we have to find Tris—"

"No, love, it's too late." Nevan pulls her close, burying her face against his neck. "There are no healing vortexes on this side of the falls."

In the Unseen, he means. I died in the world that would transform me.

Max hovers nearby, and Tris and Ennea appear seconds later. The group begins to discuss how to heal me, but it's not possible. I'm too far gone, too…dead. Lindsey won't accept that I'm gone for good, though. She's still the Janusite in this time, and her bond with her familiar, Max, drives him to do something he swore he would never do again.

"I'm sorry, my love," Nevan tells Lindsey. "I would do anything to spare you pain but there is nothing I can do. Nothing anyone can do."

Max clears his throat. "Not entirely true."

Lindsey jerks her head up. "What? There's a way?"

"There is *one* way."

Nevan's jaw tightens, a muscle ticking there. "No."

Lindsey glances from Nevan to Max and back again. "You have to tell me."

"Travis wouldn't want it," Nevan says gently. "He saw what became of his brother."

He was right, of course. If anyone had asked me, I would've said no—if I'd been asked ahead of time. But honestly, if I'd been given the choice when Ceara took me prisoner, I would have gladly sacrificed my life to save my friends, and I would've volunteered for the forging so I could continue the fight with them.

Their conversation has continued while I was lost in my thoughts.

"Calder was weak," Lindsey says, her face stained with tears. "Travis is strong. He can come through it okay."

"You can't know what will happen," Nevan tells her. "The risk is too great. I will not do it."

Max approaches them, crouching alongside his mistress. "I will do it."

Nevan squints at Max, forcing words out between his gritted teeth. "Don't encourage her. She is grieving and has no conception of what she asks."

"I know what's involved," Max says, his voice calm but his face pinched. "And I understand the consequences. If Lindsey wants this, I will do it."

Sobs burst out of Lindsey, and she lashes her arms around herself.

They discuss the situation for a few more minutes, with Max insisting the forging must happen now or I'll be too dead to come back from it.

Lindsey rises. "Travis would never have gotten involved in any of this insanity if he hadn't followed me. He was always trying to protect me. His death is my fault, and I have to live with that."

But no, it wasn't her fault. Though she knows that now, I couldn't accept that I hadn't fucked up and gotten myself killed simply because I was a fool who didn't deserve to live. Events beyond our control had done this. An evil sorcerer and his insane girlfriend had done this.

The event has rolled onward to the point where they've all agreed I shouldn't be forged. I never heard this conversation at the time, since I'd been bleeding out and on the verge of a death that no one could come back from.

Max rises too, glancing at Nevan. "You should take her away from here."

Lindsey balks, of course, but Max promises to take my remains back to the mortal world. She and Nevan vanish, headed through the veil to the falls behind the rock shop.

But Max doesn't take my body home. He stands beside me and begins to chant in another language, one so old that few elementals know it. This is the forging ritual.

And the agony is about to begin.

Chapter Twenty-Four

Larissa

I ROUSE AFTER A LENGTH OF TIME I CAN'T GAUGE. THE VAMPIRE DOESN'T seem to be adept at teleporting, and the rough ride through the void had knocked me out. It's dark outside, but a big lamp illuminates the interior of this structure. I'm strapped to an armchair, secured with duct tape, inside a house that looks like it's lived in by someone. Not the vampire who brought me here. They don't buy houses in the mortal world. Do they? I never had conversations with his kind because the goddess Hathor wouldn't deign to lower herself to the level of such hideous, slavering creatures. Sure, I'd employed the vampire Gundisalvus as a bounty hunter. But I didn't invite him to tea.

Now the vampires are attractive, sexy males who smell unusually good. Do they now have supernatural pheromones like the salamanders? I have no idea what Eros did to them, so the new and improved vampires remain a mystery to me.

Where is Travis? Is he dead or alive?

He must have survived whatever happened after the vampire abducted me. I refuse to believe he's gone. Max helped him send the vampires back to the Unseen, and now Travis is searching for me. I'm sure someone will help, possibly more than one someone, including Max. He might not trust me or like me, but I think he has finally realized I'm not the worst being in the multiverse anymore.

Maybe I never was the worst. Bad, yes. But not the evilest being in existence.

Eros deserves that title.

I survey the room in which I've been detained. It has a large sofa, three more armchairs, a coffee table plus various end tables, and cheerful decorations. I see family photos lined up on the upright piano, pictures of smiling children and their smiling parents. People live here. What if they come home while the vampire is in residence in this house? What might he do to them?

Nothing will happen, because I will not allow that beast—however sexy and pitiful he is—to harm anyone, especially not children.

Okay, I have no powers. How am I going to do anything?

You've got a brain, don't you? Time to start using it.

I scrutinize my bindings, and the way the duct tape adheres to the soft fabric of the chair. It's not smooth leather, but soft, slightly fuzzy material. How well does tape adhere to something like that? One way to find out. Since the vampire strapped the tape over the arm and partway down each side but didn't continue it under the chair, I wonder if I can manage to dislodge the sticky stuff.

Moving my hand from side to side, I don't feel much give in the tape. Damn.

But my head is free. Tape is strapped across my bosom and seems to be wrapped around the entire chair twice. My tits are squishable. Maybe I can use that somehow...

I suck in a huge breath, which makes my breasts push outward against the tape. A soft ripping sound comes from behind the chair. Did the vamp not run the tape all the way around the chair after all? The overlapping layers of tape might extend only partway around the backside. Hmm...

Sucking in another, bigger breath, I hear that ripping sound again. So I exhale and throw my weight forward. More ripping. Louder this time. Emboldened by my slight success, I repeat the process over and over and over until the tape around my torso loosens on one side. I thrash until the tape comes free on my right side, but my hands and ankles are still bound.

Didn't need my squishable tits after all.

If I can lean over far enough, maybe I can liberate my hands.

The task takes what feels like an hour, though it probably wasn't that long, and I'm sweating profusely by the time I free my right hand. But I did it. Now, I quickly remove the rest of the tape and stagger away from the chair, breathing hard. Lucky for me, the vampire sucks at restraining someone with tape. I suppose that's not surprising. He'd lived in the Unseen and probably saw the mortal world once or twice, if at all. It seems unlikely that Eros would have let his vamps run free, and that jerk admitted he sent Gundisalvus to me as a gift, though I hadn't realized it at the time, which means Gundisalvus had not escaped. Eros let him go, and I scooped him up.

Then I had fed so much dark magic into him that he became even more of a monster. Does that darkness still taint me? Will I ever cleanse myself of it?

Right now, I have bigger problems. The vampire will come back—before dawn. I need to get out of here and find out where "here" is.

Maybe I can climb out a window, but the house must have at least one door that leads outside. I trot through the only doorway I see, which leads into the dining room, then I continue through another doorway. I wind up in the kitchen. Which has a door. One that clearly leads outside. Hallelujah. I unlock the door and swing it open.

The vampire stares back at me.

Shit. I try to kick him in the balls, but he catches my ankle and pushes forward with his entire body, walking me backward into the house so fast that I flail my arms for balance. He backs me up to a storage cabinet, forcing me to bend my knee until I'm pinned with only one leg on the floor.

He studies me with curiosity, tilting his head this way and that in jerky movements as he slides his hand up from my ankle, over my knee, and along the side of my thigh until it meets my hip. "You are Hathor."

I recognize his face and his voice, not to mention his slight German accent. This is the same vampire who spoke to me back in the temple. Just as he had then, he speaks with exquisite care as if he's having trouble pronouncing the syllables. When we'd first met, he said several things that seemed odd.

No slave, this vamp had said in the temple. *Protect you. Die for you.*

Is that what he's trying to do now? Protect me? If so, he's got some weird ideas about how to protect a woman. I might enjoy a little bondage in the bedroom—with Travis. But I don't like being duct-taped to a chair in someone else's house and being held hostage by a vampire who seems not to have all his marbles. I realize whatever Eros had done to him over the millennia, coupled with his sudden change and new aversion to sunlight, might've warped his mind. But an unstable vamp sounds like a dangerous proposition. I need to tread carefully.

"I used to be Hathor," I tell him. "Now I'm called Larissa. What's your name?"

"Cyneric."

He has no trouble pronouncing his own name. I guess he only has trouble with every other word in the English language, though I don't think his name is English. It sounds ancient Germanic. I've lived long enough to remember when ancient Germanic was simply a language with no name. Cyneric might have lived back then. He could be one of the original vampires created by Eros. The bastard had tried to win me back at one point, and he honestly believed giving me the gift of bloodsucking monsters would make me run back to him. By then, I'd been too powerful for him to ensorcell me again.

I'd never seen the attractive vamps. Setesh had cast a spell to deform them just as Eros unveiled the creatures to me. And of course, a massive battle ensued. Jeez, men are such dicks. I wiped the floor with them, so to speak, and they gave up on trying to recapture me.

"Cyneric," I say, "why have you brought me here? Are you trying to protect me?"

"Yes. Protect you." He moves his hand around to my ass. "Show my love for you."

Oh hell no. If he intends to rape me, I'll grab a kitchen knife and cut his heart out. Well, his dick first, then his heart. But I'm not sure that's what he means. English probably isn't his first language, and he's not in top mental form at the moment.

"Show me how?" I ask.

He falls to his knees, head bowed.

Okay, so he wants to worship me, I guess. But I don't want that, not anymore.

"Please get up," I say. "You're not my slave. I'd like to be your friend, but right now, you need to let me go."

He surges to his full height, bracketing my body with his hands. "You must stay here. Safe."

"I appreciate that you're trying to help, but I need to find my friend Travis. He might be in danger."

"No one else matters. I am all you need."

"You can come with me. We can find Travis together."

Cyneric bends his arms, pressing his entire body into mine—including his swelling erection. "I grow hungry."

No way, fang boy. I will not be fed upon by a vampire, a newly changed one who seems to think "protecting" and worshiping me involves sex and a blood transfusion.

He's so tall that I can't see over his shoulder, but I can see under his arm. On the kitchen island sits a set of large kitchen knives housed inside a wooden holder. If I can reach one of those...

"If you're going to bite me," I say, "at least give me some juice or water first. I'm dehydrated after all that fighting and running. Please, I know you don't want to hurt me. But if you bite me now, I might die."

No idea if that's true. I'm no doctor, and I'm still not completely up to speed with how a human body works.

He seizes my wrist and drags me toward the fridge.

We pass by the island on our way there.

Cyneric is focused on getting to the fridge, so I manage to snag a knife and hold it behind my back where he probably won't see it. Though he intends to feed off me, I can't help feeling bad for him. Whatever Eros and Setesh did has altered the vampires with devastating results. They seem incapable of dealing with anything right now and have reverted to caveman-style behavior. Want, have, keep. That sort of thing. I don't want to hurt Cyneric, but I can't let him feed on me when he's in this state. He might kill me without meaning to do it.

Travis must be looking for me. He might not find me in time, though.

We've reached the fridge.

Cyneric yanks the door open. "Take what you need."

God, I feel horrible about this. But I have no choice. I swing the knife out from behind my back and stab it straight into his heart.

He gasps and staggers backward into the refrigerator door, grasping at it but losing his balance. He slumps down to the floor. Eyes wide, he stares up at me while struggling to breathe.

"I'm sorry," I tell him.

Then I bolt out of the house into who-knows-where. Into the night, that's all I know. Somehow, someway, I will find Travis.

Chapter Twenty-Five

Travis

As I watch the other me undergo the forging, I feel every-thing that he feels. White orbs dance around his body and then swarm him, their energy biting into his flesh and searing it until the heat of every wound melds into a single, unbearable agony that engulfs him. His flesh is rent from his body, burned so hot and so fast that it vanishes into the air like smoke—white, glittering smoke. He screams, and it's more agonized than any living thing should sound. I hear it in my head, experience the pain inside me, and fall to my knees while gasping for breath, my ears ringing.

Yet still, I hear his screams. They echo in my mind.

I don't need to relive it now because I remember every second of what happened once the forging began. My bones shattered. My brain liquefied. Yet I remained conscious as the supernatural energies violently transformed me into something else, something not human. Every particle in my body was torn asunder, and even my soul seemed to disintegrate and reform as the change kicked into high gear and I was reshaped, remade, resurrected as a new being. In the last moment before the change consumed me, I prayed for death.

But my prayer wasn't answered. I awoke as a different man. No, not a man, not anymore.

A salamander. An incubus that feeds on sexual energy.

Only my memories survived. As for my soul... I don't know if I still have one.

As the scene plays out before me, the forging subsides, and a nude, copper-skinned male is revealed. Smoke curls up from his skin.

I remember that moment, when I'd realized everything inside me had been transformed. I raised my head with an effort that stabbed new agony through my skull, and I looked at Lindsey.

She and Nevan had stood on the other side of the pool created by the waterfall. The anguish on her face haunts me to this day. I know she didn't want to lose me, and she changed her mind about the forging in the end, but Max's powerful connection to her had made him do the unthinkable. I don't blame either of them. They did it because they were out of their minds with grief, especially after all the things we'd fought through together. We might've called ourselves Team Lindsey before, but only at that moment, when I died and was reborn as something else, did we truly become a team. More than that, we became a family.

In front of me, Max places a hand on the other Travis's shoulder and transports them both away.

Lindsey and Nevan vanish too.

Pain still racks my body, echoes of the torment I'd endured to become what I am now. As much as I did not want to relive that moment, I know I'd needed to go through it again. I've struggled with the transition from human to elemental because I refused to accept I'm not Travis Blackwell anymore. I am an incubus. The five months I've spent hiding out in the mortal world gave me time to adjust and accept the truth. I've gotten better with my powers too, more adept in some ways than Max is. But until tonight, when Janus threw me into the past so I could remember what I've been through, had I finally accepted everything. My guilt was burned away by the echo of the forging that seared through me.

I'm free.

But I'm still calling myself Travis. Max kept his original name, so I don't see why I need to change mine. Staying Travis is my way of memorializing who I was, and that's something I never want to forget.

I rise and stretch, rubbing muscles made sore by the way my body had wrenched with agony thanks to the visceral replay of my forging. Glancing around, I wonder why I haven't been pulled back into the present. I'm still here at the waterfall in the Unseen, and I can still see the bloodstains on the ground, as well as footprints left behind by my friends.

Shedding my old life doesn't mean I have to give up my family. Lindsey, Nevan, Max, and the others will always be in my life. I don't need to hide from them anymore.

"Janus!" I shout. "I'm done here. Bring me home, all right?"

Nothing happens. Has that arse forgotten he sent me here?

"Wake up, Janus! I've seen what you wanted me to see. Take me back to the present."

The world shifts, and I'm sucked through that nasty vortex again, then spit out into…a palace. Or maybe it's a temple. Can't tell for sure. A skylight lets sunshine spill down into the large space, providing natural illumination. Ancient Egyptian motifs decorate every wall, most of them depicting a woman with a crown made of cow horns. Ahead of me, a gold chair decorated with more Egyptian images sits atop a stepped dais. I'm standing just inside the closed doors to this room, but I have no idea why Janus would send me here.

I scan my gaze over the imagery throughout this room one more time. A chill ripples through me. Oh yes, I do know why I'm here.

This is the temple of the goddess Hathor.

A noise I can barely hear spurs me to approach the dais and mount the steps to the throne. The closer I get, the better I can hear the sound. Someone is crying. When I reach the throne, I can see the bare legs and sandaled feet of a woman who's slumped on the floor behind the ornate gold chair. I sidestep the throne, and the woman comes into view.

Larissa.

She was Hathor in this time, though I don't know how far in the past Janus has sent me. She wears almost nothing, just a white bra with gold straps and what looks like a beetle-shaped amulet pinned to the fabric between her breasts. A long strap hangs down from her leather belt, but other than that, she is naked. A gold crown-like headdress lies on the floor beside her along with earrings and a necklace.

Tears stream down her cheeks, and her eyes are red. She sniffles, swiping at her eyes.

I have never seen anyone look as miserable as this woman does. Why would Hathor, the goddess who became too powerful for Eros to ensorcell again, sit here crying? Alone? She has minions who will worship her. She could cheer herself up with an orgy. Max told me she used to love those. But Larissa confessed that she never experienced any real pleasure until I made love to her.

"Oversoul, I beg you," she says. "I cannot do this anymore. Max is gone again. He thinks he escaped, but I let him go, though he will never know that. I always let him go."

She released him voluntarily? I can't figure out why she would do that and not make sure he knew about her beneficent act. Had she honestly loved him? Larissa told me she never had, not really, but the demeanor and words of the woman before me contradict that. She set Max free.

"Destroy me," she says with a sob so intense that it wrenches her entire body. "I do not want to live anymore. I've done too many terrible things. I know there won't be redemption for me in the afterlife, but I'd rather suffer all the torments that a damned soul like mine deserves instead of living as I am."

Larissa is not damned. I know she committed terrible acts, but I now understand why. She told me what Eros, Kamadeva, and Setesh had done to her. After thousands of years of ensorcellment, her mind had been broken. The abused became the abuser. I'd seen that vicious cycle more than once when I'd been a human police officer. Children who were abused often continued that cycle as adults, but they could fight their way back from it. I'd seen it happen. Though the road to redemption is never smooth, Larissa has been on that highway for two years—maybe longer, since I'm watching the old her, the goddess Hathor, begging the Oversoul to destroy her.

She can change. She *has* changed.

And so have I.

The scene shifts around me. Now, I'm in a corridor that's decorated with Egyptian motifs, standing before a set of closed doors.

Both doors swing open, and Hathor exits. Then the doors shut behind her.

She sags against them, eyes shut, biting her bottom lip that's trembling. Tears trickle down her cheeks. "Oversoul, I beg you. End my existence. I don't want to defile Harper, or anyone. Why did I send bounty hunters to find Max and bring him to me? It was selfish. I did it because I missed him, and because I want him to care for me. But Max despises me, and he should."

This is the moment when everything changed for her. I can feel it. She's about to reach a decision that will alter more lives than her own.

She opens her eyes, and I swear she's looking at me. Then she shakes her head and pushes away from the doors. "I should free my thralls. I know I should. They deserve to be liberated, but if I do that, I can't know what will happen to them, or to me. Other gods are just waiting for me to show weakness, and to them, mercy is a failing. The second I release my people, the gods will swoop in to claim them. Max and Harper might be taken too. I can't allow that."

Hathor is on the cusp, about to change everything. I tense, waiting for it to happen.

She walks away.

But I know she'd been about to do it. Maybe she needed stronger motivation, and I know that's about to come crashing down on her, literally.

I'm thrown into another moment. Hathor stands outside, on the edge of the woods that surround the temple complex, staring wide-eyed at the ruins of her home. The obsidian fae have just attacked, employing magics so powerful that they can destroy a goddess's warded temple. Max told me about this too.

She drops to her knees and sobs. "They're dead. They're all dead. I could've saved those poor souls if I'd freed them. Why didn't I do it?" She shoves her hands into her hair, knotting her fingers in it and tugging hard. "I wanted to do it, but I was afraid of being alone. What does that say about me? Oversoul, please, *you must destroy me.*"

Please? Speaking that word in the Unseen usually triggers a debt, but I don't know if anyone can indebt themselves to the Oversoul. Max told me it's like God in the mortal world.

After this moment, Hathor found Max and helped him gain entry into the palace of the obsidian fae. She was, in Max's own words, instrumental in helping him and Harper destroy Talos, the king of the obsidian fae. His death triggered the destruction of his entire tribe. It caused Harper's death too, but she came back to life, though she's now something more than human.

Hathor's tears have stopped flowing, and she sniffles. "You're right. I deserve to suffer endlessly. A quick death is not for me."

I'm yanked through the vortex, spinning and flailing, and dumped on the ground flat on my face. In the mud, naturally. But I'm holding the harpy talon tight in my hand. Janus must've finished his time-travel plans for me, and Ennea's spell did the rest, bringing me to this place in the mortal world. I push onto my knees, and with a flourish of power, eliminate the mud on my body. Wherever I am, it's nighttime here. I see a house in front of me and a wooden fence on three sides. Lights glow inside the house, but I have no idea where I am. Not Phoenix, that's for sure. A big oak tree looms over the house, and Arizona doesn't have those.

The back door bursts open—and Larissa runs out.

No time to wonder what's going on. I race toward Larissa, catching her mid-step and lifting her feet off the ground.

She yelps and beats her fists on my chest until she finally realizes it's me. "Travis? How did you—"

Another figure rushes out of the house. It's one of the vampires.

"Wait," Larissa says. "Don't whisk us away yet. Cyneric needs help."

"You're on a first-name basis with the bloodsucking fiend?"

"No. I'm on a first-name basis with the confused vampire who just got radically remade without his consent." She thumps my chest. "Put me down. We can't leave yet."

I set her down.

The vampire snarls, then lets out an ear-piercing bellow. And he runs straight for me, fangs bared.

Screw helping the vamp. I grab Larissa, teleporting us away.

Chapter Twenty-Six

WE TOUCH DOWN IN THE SUITE WHERE TRAVIS HAD HIDDEN OUT BEfore bounty hunters, gods, and vampires came after us. He flops onto the bed on his back, his legs hanging over the end and his feet on the floor. I flop down beside him, though I'm on my side with one elbow holding me up.

"I told you not to do that," I say. "We need to help Cyneric."

"He's a ruddy vampire, and he was about to try getting a blood donation from one of us. The kind of donation that's not voluntary."

"I think he would've stopped if I told him to."

"You think?" Travis casts me a sidelong look, his mouth crimped and his brows lowered. "That's not very comforting. I wasn't going to stick around and find out if he'd stop."

"Guess you're right." I roll onto my back. "But I feel oddly bad for him. He's confused and has no one to keep him company. Cyneric kept saying he wants to protect me, but then he tried to bite me."

"He tried—" Travis springs into a sitting position and squints at me. "I stand by my decision to whisk you the hell away from there."

"I know, you're right. But as a formerly evil person, I kind of identify with Cyneric."

"We can talk about that later. At least the three sex gods aren't after you anymore." He turns partway toward me. "Janus sent me on a time-travel adventure, complete with nauseating vortexes and gut-wrenching replays of my past—and yours."

"Mine?" I jerk upright, eyes wide, though I'm afraid to ask the obvious question. *Suck it up, girl.* "What did you see about me?"

"Your pain. You were torn, struggling to accept that you don't want to hurt anyone anymore. I heard you begging the Oversoul to destroy you, and I felt your anguish when you realized none of those people would've died in your temple if you'd set them free earlier, the way you'd wanted to."

"I was a coward. If I'd listened to myself and freed them—"

"They still might've died. You can't keep torturing yourself over mistakes that are in the past." He clasps my hands in his. "Neither of us can do that anymore. You are not Hathor, and I am not Sheriff Travis Blackwell. We're different now. We can't erase our mistakes, but we can do our damnedest to be good people."

"But I was completely evil."

"No, you weren't." He leans closer, splaying a hand on my cheek. "Max never escaped from you. I know you released him every time."

"But I kept capturing and ensorcelling him."

"You were conflicted. Those gods abused you, and so you became an abuser too. It's a well-known psychological model." He moves his thumb over my lips when I try to speak. "I'm not excusing anything you did. I'm saying I understand. Let's both forgive ourselves."

Should I do that? Don't I owe my victims some kind of justice? But justice and retribution aren't the same thing. I can never atone for what I did in the past, especially not for the deaths of all those innocent people. But justice isn't about atonement. It's about making sure every offender gets the punishment they deserve—no more, no less.

"Yes, we should forgive ourselves," I say. "But in my case, the Four Winds will decide what justice looks like. They will mete out my punishment, and I trust them to make a wise and fair choice."

And yes, I mean that. I feel at peace now, as if I've given up a pointless battle that had no winners or losers.

Travis pulls me into his arms. "You're an amazing woman. Whatever happens, I want you to know that I don't regret one second of the time I've spent with you."

"Neither do I."

He combs his fingers through my hair. "I love you, Larissa."

"I love you too, Travis."

A figure appears ten feet from the foot of the bed.

Travis jerks, and I yelp.

Cyneric stares at us. "Here to protect you. Save you."

He thinks he needs to rescue me from Travis. Cyneric did see the incubus whisk me away.

"I don't want to be saved," I tell the vampire. "Travis is my friend, not my enemy."

"But he took you."

"You were about to attack him, so he took us both away."

The vampire's gaze flits between me and Travis, and his brows furrow. "You want him?"

"Yes. I love him."

Cyneric crumples to his knees, then lists sideways, his fall checked only by his hand that he plants on the floor. "But I—You are—Who am I to serve now?"

"No one," Travis says. "You're free."

The vampire shakes his head. "I served Eros, not willingly. Then the goddess freed me, and now I serve her, but she does not want me."

I'm not a goddess anymore. As an elemental, he should be able to sense that I'm mortal now, but he thinks he needs to serve me. I never told him any such thing.

"You have never served me," I tell Cyneric. "Why do you think you need to?"

"Because you saved me."

I aim a confused look at Travis, who seems equally baffled. "I didn't save you, Cyneric. And I have never told you to protect me."

"The temple—" He slaps a hand on the side of his head and scrunches up his face. "Your temple. Your energy."

"Ohhhh," Travis says, "I get it."

I frown at him. "Glad one of us does. Care to enlighten me?"

"Cyneric here, and all his mates, were changed while inside your temple complex. The residual energies from your long-dead worshipers empowered you and me so we could survive. What if those energies also seeped into the vamps while Eros was making them pretty?"

My first impulse is to tell him that's baloney. But I take a moment to consider the idea, and little by little, I realize he might be right. The residual magics prevented gods from teleporting out of the temple precinct. They could come in, but they couldn't get out, not that way. They could've walked out, I'm sure. Maybe the magics also affected the vampires, and since it was a temple dedicated to Hathor, Cyneric latched on to me as the object of his obsession.

"I think you're right," I tell Travis. "He was affected by the energies in the temple. Which probably means his buddies were too."

"Great," Travis groans. "More vamps who adore you will be stopping by for a chat and a glass of my blood. How did he find you, though?"

"My magics—or rather, Hathor's magics are infused into him. He sniffed me out the supernatural way."

"But if they're Hathor's magics, and you are human now, then how could that work?"

"I probably have something of the goddess I used to be still inside me. The Four Winds haven't announced their decision yet, so they probably wouldn't have stripped all the magics out of me until they do that."

"You didn't mention that until now?"

"Just occurred to me."

Travis sighs, eying the vampire slumped on the floor. "What should we do with him? And his mates, if they turn up."

"Don't know. We can't do this alone, though."

He lays a hand on my thigh. "Don't worry. We've got family."

"I was created, not born, so I can't have parents or siblings."

"Not talking about Eros. I mean my friends, human and elemental. After everything we've been through together, we're like a family."

"They hate me, rightfully."

"No, they don't. Not even Max feels that way anymore." Travis squeezes my thigh. "Besides, once they get to know the new you, they won't worry about who you used to be. It'll take time, but you can do it."

"Do what?"

"Show them who you really are." He winks. "Larissa the badass maid with a sword."

Cyneric disappears.

"Where'd he go?" I ask.

"Guess he's gone off to sulk about his goddess not wanting him."

"Let's get moving. We need to find him." I hesitate as a question surfaces in my mind. "What happened to our endued swords?"

"Not sure. Things got rather confused when Janus sent me on a roller-coaster ride through time."

"Guess it doesn't matter right now. Finding Cyneric is more important."

"Can't we take a break first? Time-traveling really takes it out of me." He skates his hand up my inner thigh, his fingers grazing my groin and making me suck in a breath. "I'm hungry, Larissa."

"And I want to feed you. But my bladder has other ideas." I get up, then lean in to kiss him. "Just give me a minute. Then I'll strip for you."

"You know exactly how to make me ravenous for you." He hooks his thumb inside my waistband, tugging me closer, and slips his other hand under my shirt. "Let me devour you first. Promise you'll be glad you did."

"Mm, maybe I could wait a few minutes."

He unzips my jeans and drags them down along with my panties, letting them fall down to my knees. I spread my legs as far as I can, all but begging him to consume me, and he does. Travis pushes his mouth between my folds, lavishing his tongue over my flesh until I'm rocking my hips into him and grasping his head.

But damn, I really need to pee.

He pulls my clit into his mouth and suckles it.

I come so quickly that I barely notice my body tightening, and a soft cry is the only sound I can make. Pleasure fires down my nerves, stealing my breath and weakening my knees, but Travis holds me up with his hands under my bottom and keeps devouring me until the last wave of my climax subsides.

Then he flips us both onto the bed, with him on top. "This time, I plan on taking you hard and wild."

"I'd love that, really I would." I grimace. "But I seriously need to relieve my bladder."

He sighs and rolls onto his back. "Go on, but make it quick. I'm starving, and every second I'm not fucking you, I'm wasting away even more."

I sweep my gaze over his naked, muscular body, only now realizing he's ditched his clothes. "Yeah, sure. You're wasting away."

The insatiable incubus slaps my ass as I jump off the bed.

I pause just as I've shut the bathroom door behind me, needing a moment to take in the luxury of this room. Shiny silver fixtures adorn the double sinks and the spacious, multi-head shower. Oh, are those fancy little soaps? They're shaped like geese, I think. And ooh, the towels look divine. I rub my cheek against one, and yes, I was right. Sooo soft and thick. Maybe I wouldn't mind squatting in a luxury hotel for a while. I know the mattress is lush too, just right for a round of mind-blowing sex with my incubus lover.

After making my bladder happy, I wash my hands in the sink, mostly so I can try the fancy soap. It leaves my hands feeling silky. Yeah, I could handle hiding out here for a few days—or months.

I hear a noise out in the bedroom, like a grunt or a stifled shout.

What was that? I'm drying my hands, but I stop to listen.

Another sound. Gurgling? Thumping?

Every hair on my body stiffens and tingles. Something isn't right. I tear the door open and race into the bedroom, freezing halfway to the bed because my mind can't comprehend what I'm seeing.

The vampire Cyneric has his mouth on Travis's throat and his fangs sunk into the flesh. I can see Cyneric swallowing again and again as he guzzles the life out of Travis and blood dribbles down the salamander's chest.

"No!" I scream as I throw myself at Cyneric, leaping onto his back so I can lock my arms around his throat in a choke hold. "Get off him! Stop, Cyneric, now!"

The vampire keeps drinking, and the wet sucking sound as he drains Travis makes my stomach heave. I just stop myself from vomiting. I'm not strong enough to drag a vampire off of his prey. What happened to those swords we had? I'd dropped mine right before Cyneric took me, but I don't know where Travis's sword is.

Cyneric shakes me off, sending me flying.

Luckily, I crash onto the soft bed. And I see a weapon. It's a letter opener on the table beside the bed. I snatch it up and throw myself at the vampire again, this time jamming the letter opener into his neck. He rips his mouth away from Travis's throat and howls in pain.

Then he disappears.

And Travis collapses to the floor on his side, his eyes closed. Blood gushes from his neck where the vampire had ripped his teeth out of Travis's flesh.

I made it worse when I tried to help. He's dying, and it's my fault. I drop to my knees and wrestle with his big body until I get his head on my lap. While I stroke his cheek and tears blur my vision, I hug him to me. "I'm sorry. This is my fault, because I wanted to help that fucking vampire. I should've killed him."

He cracks his eyes open. "Not dead yet."

Though his voice is weak, I nearly collapse with relief when he speaks to me.

"You're alive." I burst into tears and pepper kisses over his face. "But you're still bleeding and—"

"Shh. It takes an endued weapon to kill me."

"Even if you never stop bleeding?"

"Not sure. Sew it up."

"How?" I can't stop staring at the blood gushing from his throat. Even if I somehow find something that will let me sew up his wound, I'm not sure I could do that right. And that's a gaping wound, not a couple of puncture marks. I don't think he realizes what Cyneric has done to him.

"Sewing kit...in the...bathroom."

Though I don't want to leave him, I heave myself off the floor. But I just stare down at him. Can't move. Can't think. Where's the bathroom? I stumble around to face the doorway I'd come out of a moment ago. I need to go in there. My heart is pounding so fast I feel like I might pass out, and a cold sweat chills my skin. *Go get the damn sewing kit.*

I start for the bathroom and make it halfway there before I stop. Why am I trying to sew him up? I should call his friends. Tris, the leprechaun, is the guardian of a healing vortex. I whirl around and rush back to Travis. "Can you conjure your phone? I can get help that way."

"Maybe..." His voice is slurred, and his whole face contorts with pain as he tries to do what I asked.

A cell phone appears, lying on his chest.

I almost can't see through the haze of tears in my eyes, but I manage to scroll through his contacts list, with my fingers trembling, though it takes me several tries before I find and dial the right number. I choke back a sob when Lindsey answers.

"Travis?"

"No, it's Larissa. A vampire ripped Travis's throat open and—"

"Hold on. Nevan! Get Tris!" She listens while her husband calls out to her, but I can't hear what he says. "Where are you, Larissa?"

"Don't know. An unfinished luxury hotel somewhere near Phoenix, I think."

Travis rasps, "Firebird of the Desert."

"I heard that," Lindsey says. "Try to stop the bleeding, and Tris will be there ASAP."

"He told me to sew it up, but I don't know how."

"Grab a towel, fold it up, and press it into the wound as hard as you can."

"Okay." While clutching the phone to my ear, I sprint into the bathroom to get a towel, then return to Travis and follow Lindsey's instructions. "It's not working."

"Give it a minute," she says. "Luckily, Max was here, so Nevan told him to get Tris. Then Max will come get Travis and bring him to the vortex."

Thank the stars. Maybe they can save him. No, not maybe. They *will* do it.

Max appears beside me. "Bloody hell."

I glance up at him. "Take him, quick."

He kneels and slaps a clear patch of something that looks like plastic onto Travis's throat. The material shimmers as it seals the wound, and even I can feel the magic emanating from it. "Tris gave me this. It should stem the bleeding long enough for me to get him to the vortex. Tris is stuffing copper down his throat as we speak."

Because he's a copper fae, and they feed on copper to fuel the healing vortexes.

I feel numb, as if I'm watching events unfold from a distance.

Max struggles to get Travis to his feet, lashing an arm around his waist to keep him upright.

Cyneric appears in front of us, only inches away. And he grips a sword with both hands.

That's Travis's new endued sword.

"Get out of here!" I scream at Max and Travis.

But it's too late. Cyneric thrusts the sword straight at Travis's chest.

I hurl my body into its path, not thinking about the consequences, only knowing that I cannot let Travis die. The blade punches through my chest and out the other side.

The world seems to fade away as I fall to the floor.

And Travis roars.

CHAPTER TWENTY-SEVEN

Travis

LARISSA IS LYING ON THE FLOOR WITH A SWORD RUN THROUGH HER, the hilt flush with her chest and most of its length sticking out of her back. My roar still echoes in the room because I'm still raging at the blood-sucking bastard who just murdered Larissa. No, she's not dead. I can see she's still breathing, but that won't last long.

I'm half-dead myself. Cold, weak, shaky.

Whatever the elemental version of adrenaline is, that hormone fires an electric surge down my veins and pumps me up with a burst of energy and power that I know won't last long. I have one chance to skewer the bastard.

"No!" Max shouts as I conjure the sword out of Larissa's chest and into my hand. "She'll bleed more, Travis."

Though I hear his words, they sound like meaningless gibberish. All I can focus on is Cyneric, who's standing there stone-still, his face blank, his attention zeroed in on Larissa and the red stain swiftly expanding across her chest. I hurtle my body straight at the vampire, plunging the blade into his heart. Or that's what I meant to do.

But Cyneric is gone.

Max picks up Larissa, cradling her in one arm while he lashes the other around me. "We're going to the fucking vortex, you bloody idiot."

We land there a split second later. Tris is already waiting inside the healing vortex, surrounded by the natural-stone benches that encircle it.

Tris sees us, and his face blanches. "I thought it was just him, not both of them. Don't know if I've got the power for a double healing."

Max lets go of me and sets Larissa on the ground. He vanishes for a moment, while Tris tells me where to lie down and he positions Larissa in the proper place. Blood is oozing out underneath the patch Max had put on my neck. I feel weaker every second, but I will not pass out until I know Larissa has been healed.

"Do her first," I say. "Please."

"You shouldn't have said that," the leprechaun whines. "Now you owe me. I had to pull in a sliver of the Unseen to get enough power from the vortex."

"Don't care. Just heal her."

Max reappears, holding an armload of copper ore from the rock shop. "Shove this down your throat, Tris."

"No," I snarl, "heal her first."

"You bloody-minded—"

"Do it!" I roar, summoning every last ounce of energy inside me to accomplish the feat.

Tris kneels beside Larissa. "Okay-okay, calm down. I'm doing it."

He'll save her, I know he will. That's what Tris does. I don't care what happens to me as long as she survives. While Tris begins the process, I grow cold and numb. Black spots appear in my vision, and my ears ring.

Then I pass out.

Sometime later, I wake up and find myself staring at the sky, but I see solid rock encircling it like I'm gazing up a tunnel. Is that the "light" people say they go into during near-death experiences? I don't feel like I'm moving toward it, though. The light stays stationary, and I don't remember anyone claiming the tunnel they went through was made of stone. Jagged stone. And I'm pretty sure I'm lying on a sofa or a bed or something.

What happened? My memories are hazy, but I recall blood. Lots of blood.

I try to raise my head, but things start to sway around me, and I drop back onto whatever surface I've wound up lying on.

"Whoa there, cowboy," a female voice says, and a hand settles on my shoulder, urging me to stay down. "You lost an insane amount of blood, and even with the healing vortex and even though you're a wicked-strong elemental, you'll still need time to recover."

Blood. Yes, I remember that. Fangs too. Sharp ones that tore through my flesh.

Cyneric.

I bolt upright, which makes my head throb, but I don't care. "Where's Larissa?"

Harper is sitting on the bed beside me, as if she's been watching over me while I lay unconscious. "One thing at a time."

"There is only one thing, so fucking tell me where she is."

"Jeez, you used to be so polite, following Max around like a lost puppy."

"Where is—"

Harper throws her hands up. "I surrender. Now quit snarling at me and I'll explain. You won't like it, though."

Max wanders out of the kitchen and halts halfway to the bed. "You'd better not be trying it on with my wife. If you're hungry, go shag a nymph."

"Not hungry," I growl. "I'm extremely annoyed. Will one of you tell me what I want to know?"

Max saunters up to the bed, tilting his head back to gaze up at the hole in the mountain. "How do you like our new window?"

I leap off the bed, dragging the fur blanket with me, and only then do I realize I'm stark naked. Who cares? I'm getting more annoyed every second that no one tells me what's going on.

Harper eyes me up and down, her lips kinking up on one side. "Wow, I had no idea you were so—"

"Tall?" Max says while seeming almost as irritated as I am.

"Uh-huh." Harper points toward a table, where my clothes are neatly folded. "Better get dressed. I don't want to be responsible for my husband tossing you into a volcano."

Max rolls his eyes. "I only did that with your silly little firearm."

"And my knife." She sighs with mock wistfulness. "I loved that dagger."

I've just gotten my clothes on, and I'm feeling no less irritated. I want to punch a hole in the mountain like Setesh did, or knock down a forest by punching the trees with my bare fist, or maybe hurl Max up that tunnel the god wanker created. "Someone had better tell me—"

"All right, all right," Max says. "Harper, you tell him."

"Your chivalry never ceases to amaze me."

"He'll be less…infuriated if a woman tells him."

"Oh, so it's sexism." Harper winks at her husband, then looks at me and squares her shoulders. "The Four Winds took her."

"What?" I shout. "And you let them?"

"Not sure you really get what the Four Winds are. Max will explain."

"They're the balancing power in the Unseen," he says. "That means they can tell the rest of what to go do with ourselves. We can't demand they explain their actions. They appeared in our living room, what's left of it, and whisked Hathor away."

"Her name is Larissa," I snarl.

Max raises his hands, palms out. "Take it easy, mate. I'm on your side, and shockingly, I'm on hers too."

"Brilliant. You've been to their temple, so take me there."

Max glances at Harper. "When did he start using words like 'brilliant'?"

I stomp my foot so hard that bits of stone flake off the walls. "Take me to their temple. *Now.* No more delay tactics."

Max winces. "You figured out we were delaying, eh? Told Harper it wouldn't work."

Harper falls backward onto the bed. "Just take him there, Max, before he destroys what's left of our home."

"Our *lair.* That's the correct term in the Unseen." He slaps a hand on my shoulder. "Here we go."

We've touched down on the side of a craggy, barren mountain surrounded by other similar peaks. It's nighttime, but the glow of two moons shines down on the mountain, though thick fog masks the summit, rotating slowly around a rectangular shape higher up the mountain.

"This is it," Max says. "The Temple of the Four Winds. No idea if they'll let you in."

"You can go back to Harper. I appreciate you bringing me here."

He pats my shoulder and vanishes.

Only those who are worthy will be admitted to the temple. Have I earned that designation? I'll find out soon enough. Lindsey told me once that the Four Winds are avatars and guardians of immense power, but I'm still not clear on what that means. They can do whatever they want whenever they want, to whoever they want. I guess that's what it means.

A gust of wind blusters around me, dispelling the fog and revealing the structure within it. A steep set of steps leads up to a portico with columns so high that I feel like an ant crawling up the Eiffel Tower. The building seems to be made of white stone that glistens faintly, as if it has diamond dust sprinkled on it. I sense the unmistakable aura of power that surrounds and infuses this place, making it feel like the temple of beings so awesome that no one can comprehend their nature. And I mean "awesome" in its truest definition—something of immense and incomprehensible power.

I hike up the steps and onto the portico, but a pair of massive wooden doors bar my way. Worthy or not? I'm about to find out.

The doors grind open, the noise rattling every bone in my body.

No going back now. I cross the threshold and enter the temple. Since nothing zaps me or shreds me into molecules that drift away on the breeze, I decide I must've been deemed worthy—at least for the moment. Glancing around, I can't judge the dimensions of this building. It seems to stretch on forever in every direction, disappearing into a fog like the one that shrouds the outside of the structure. I don't pay much attention to the carvings high up on the walls, but something does command my attention. I feel phantom fingers, borne of wind, exploring me. If there are going to be anal probes, I'll give these Wind beings a piece of my mind. But nothing dives that deep into me. It's more like they want to test my flesh to make sure I'm not trying to deceive them.

All right, I'm terrified right now. Not ashamed to admit it.

Four beings appear in front of me. They wear long white robes that graze the floor but leave their heads and arms exposed, and all of them sport white hair. I decide two of the beings are women and two are men, but honestly, I wouldn't sign an affidavit testifying to that. Their pale skin and glossy black eyes are…extremely unsettling.

I raise a hand to wave at them. "Hello."

Maybe that was a stupid thing to do, but I couldn't think of a more appropriate greeting. I've never met balancing powers before.

One of the beings that seems to be female floats closer to me. "Travis Blackwell, salamander and hero of the Unseen, why have you come to us?"

Hero? Me? I never expected to hear any of these beings refer to me that way.

"I'm here to stand up for Larissa," I say. "To testify on her behalf."

"You refer to Hathor, the depraved goddess."

"No, I'm talking about Larissa, the woman I love who used to be Hathor. She's not anymore."

The female being tips her head to one side, then the other. "Shall we allow this one to testify?"

Behind her, three beings nod their heads solemnly.

"Miriella," a male says, "should not the god undergoing judgment be present during this creature's testimony?"

"Indeed she should, Javren." Miriella shuts her eyes. "It is done."

Larissa has just appeared beside me, ten feet from where I stand. She gives me a shaky smile, and I swear I can feel her anxiety. How long has she been here, waiting for their judgment? Max and Harper said the Four Winds took her, but I hadn't gotten the chance to ask when that happened.

"Are you okay?" Larissa asks, her worried gaze aimed at me.

"Yes, I'm all healed up. What about you?"

"Same."

Miriella extends an arm toward me, her palm up. "Testify, salamander."

I scratch the back of my neck while I try to think of what to say. Sure, I'd volunteered to do this, but now I can't figure out where to start. What if I say the wrong thing and these beings destroy Larissa? *Suck it up and start talking.* I take a deep breath, and I do it.

"You stripped Hathor's powers and made her mortal," I begin, "and you left her to figure out how to survive on her own. She did that, and more. The goddess who ensorcelled countless beings became Larissa, a normal woman working a crap job for crap wages, without complaining or getting bitter about her lot in life. Not only that, but she also watched out for a six-year-old girl whose prostitute mother neglected her. Never once did Larissa hurt anyone. She found her inner strength and learned to live without minions to do her bidding, but she also found out what it means to be human. She is not the spoiled goddess you knew. Larissa is a good person with a good heart."

"We have seen this," Miriella says. "But she abused her power for thousands of years."

"Eros, Setesh, and Kamadeva abused *her* for thousands of years. I'm not saying that absolves her of the bad things she did, but it does help explain her behavior." I roll my shoulders back and force myself to look into the eerie black eyes of Miriella. "She has changed. I swear on my life that she's a different person now."

Miriella tips her head left and right, studying me with those shiny, fathomless eyes. "Why would you wager your immortal existence on her?"

"Because I love her. Because she deserves a second chance, not as a goddess, but as the woman she has become."

"We shall take your testimony into consideration as we deliberate her fate." Miriella floats backward to rejoin her mates. "Remain where you are."

The Four Winds turn to face each other, forming a tight circle as they speak in hushed tones. Their words sound like gibberish, but I suppose it's a language only they know. Or maybe it's the same language spoken during the forging process. I don't know, and honestly, I don't care. I want to move toward Larissa and hold her close, but Miriella cautioned us to stay where we are. I don't know if she meant "remain in the exact same spot," but I've decided it's best to stay rooted right here until they've finished deliberating. This really is a trial, isn't it? The Four Winds are the judges and the jury.

At last, they stop talking and face us.

Miriella glides toward us, still hovering above the stone floor. "We have but three choices when it comes to judging Larissa née Hathor—mortality, destruction, or imprisonment.»

My mouth has gone dry, my throat tight. I resist the need to clench my fists and force myself to wait patiently for their decision. When I glance sideways at Larissa, she's biting her lip and not blinking.

"Travis Blackwell, your testimony has moved us," Miriella says. "Therefore, mortality shall be her punishment. Her powers will be permanently stripped, and from this moment forward, Larissa will be human. This means she will be vulnerable to the same maladies as any mortal and will die as any mortal would, when her natural life has reached its conclusion. You will outlive her, and while she must age, you will not."

The thought of going on with my life after she dies, of spending eternity without her... Could I move on after that? No, I couldn't.

"I don't want to live forever without her," I say. "Make me human too."

"We anticipated that response, but we cannot return you to what you once were, not so soon after the forging." Miriella floats even closer, her black eyes fixed on me with disquieting intensity. "Here is what we offer. You may become mortal, but not human. You shall remain a salamander but live a natural, mortal life span. You shall remain difficult to kill, but it will not take an endued weapon to slay you."

"Don't care. I want to be with her, whatever the cost."

"No," Larissa says, "I won't let you do that. You should forget about me."

"It's my choice. I'd rather have eighty years by your side than eternity without you."

She rushes up to me, clutching my arm. "But you won't be able to have children. A hybrid pregnancy between a mortal and an elemental is too dangerous."

"There are other ways to have a family. I know of a little girl who needs a home."

Larissa smiles. "Dani."

Miriella rushes backward and raises her arms. "Let it be done."

"Excuse me?" I say. "Let what be done?"

"What you have requested and what we have decided. May your new life be blessed."

A flash of white light blinds me, and I blink furiously while the black spots left behind by the flash gradually fade away. "Larissa? Where are you?"

"Right beside you." Her hand clasps mine. "It's over."

My vision returns to normal, and I see the Four Winds hovering in front of us.

"I know it's not my place to ask," I say, "but what have you done with the three gods who wreaked havoc on the mortal world?"

Miriella's lips curl up a touch at the corners, though it's not quite a smile. "We have devised a revolutionary punishment for them, inspired by the success of Larissa's transformation. The gods will be stripped of their powers and their immortality, and their memories shall be erased. With a clean slate before them, the gods will be deposited into the mortal world to live as humans."

"Will you be dropping them off naked and alone?"

"Naked, yes. But each will have an elemental guardian to secretly observe their progress. If at any time we feel one of them is a danger to the mortal world, we shall destroy him."

"Sounds like a plan. What about the vampires?"

"They have been returned to the Unseen, and Janus will not allow any of them to pass through a portal. They are essentially quarantined here." She lifts her chin, doing that almost-smiling thing again. "We have decided to attempt to rehabilitate the vampires, and a trio of beings have agreed to oversee the project. Maximus, Harper, and Triskaideka volunteered for the task."

I should probably be surprised by that, but I'm not. My mates are some of the best people in the multiverse. Of course they want to help the vampires who have been thrust into a new existence with no one to guide them. Maybe they can become trustworthy allies, or maybe they'll need to be destroyed later. At least now they have the chance to prove their worth.

"What about Cyneric?" I ask. "He tried to kill me and Larissa."

"We leave his fate up to the two of you."

I glance at Larissa, and I know how she feels about it. Does Cyneric deserve a second chance? If Larissa does, then maybe we should cut the vampire some slack too. One last chance. "Let him go with the others and do that rehab thing. But if he so much as bares his fangs at me or Larissa or any of our friends, I'll slice his head off with an endued sword."

Miriella nods. "It shall be done."

I pull Larissa snugly against me.

"We wish you well," Miriella says, "Travis Blackwell and Larissa Robustelli. Enjoy the gifts we have given you."

The temple vanishes, and we're now standing inside a house I don't recognize.

Larissa runs to a window, peering out into the sunlit world. She looks at me and smiles. "We're in Phoenix."

"But whose house is this?"

I notice papers on the coffee table, though the rest of this living room seems devoid of any personal items. Wandering over to the table, I pick up the papers and flip through them. "Someone bought us a house. Here's the deed with our names on it."

"Who would do that? Your friends?"

"There's a note, and it's signed TFW."

Larissa rushes over to me, her face alight with excitement. "TFW? That has to mean The Four Winds."

"They have money to buy us a house?"

She shrugs. "They are beings of immense power."

I pick up a document that includes several pieces of paper stapled together. "These papers... We've adopted Dani."

Larissa shrieks and throws her arms around my neck, wrapping her legs around me too. She covers my face with kisses, then grins at me. "We're going to be a family."

"There's one more thing I need to do." Peeling her away from my body, I set her down and drop to one knee. "Larissa, will you marry me?"

She shrieks again and throws herself at me again, bowling us both over.

That's all the answer I need.

Chapter Twenty-Eight

Larissa
Six Weeks Later

Turns out an elemental can get married in Las Vegas—provided the Four Winds give him all the documents any mortal would have. We didn't need to hop on a plane, though. Travis whisked me and Dani away to one of those get-hitched-quick chapels on the Vegas Strip, and our friends joined us there. Max and Travis helped ferry Lindsey, Nevan, and baby Liam to the big event, though Harper can teleport on her own. Tris, Ennea, and Bob joined the party too.

A former goddess wed a mortal incubus in Las Vegas. It seems appropriate somehow.

Fate played a hand in our happy ending, but I also know the Four Winds gave it a boost. Not long after those beings issued their decision, I realized something very important. For two years, I'd assumed that when the Four Winds dumped me in Phoenix, they'd chosen that location at random. Only after I met Travis and he took me to his makeshift lair in a vacant luxury hotel did I understand. That hotel is called the Firebird of the Desert. In ancient mythology, the phoenix was a bird that set itself on fire so it could be reborn from the ashes. It's a bird of fire—a firebird. Myths all over the world speak of the phoenix and similar creatures, but only in the aftermath of my transformation did I fully understand. I'd been sent to the City of Phoenix on purpose, so I could burn away the old me, Hathor, and be reborn as Larissa.

The ashes of my past have blown away on the wind.

I know Travis feels the same way, since I told him about my revelation. He was a phoenix too, literally destroyed by the scalding heat of the forging and reborn from the remnants as a creature of fire. That's why we belong together, and why the Four Winds set us both on our separate paths that converged in the one place where we belonged.

The city of the firebird.

Today, five weeks after vowing to love Travis until the day I die, the gang has gathered in our backyard with the two kiddies for a barbecue. Our house lies in the desert, but Tris knows a nymph who transformed our barren yard into a lush landscape with palm trees, flowering bushes, and grass. We don't need to worry about how to keep the greenery green since the nymph connected it to an eternal spring, the kind of thing only elementals can tap into, so we never need to buy a sprinkler.

And I do not get jealous when Travis lets slip that he "shagged" that nymph several times. It happened ages ago, and I'm totally secure in my relationship with my husband. He knows I used to have sex with anybody and everybody, so I can't get upset about his past liaisons. Nothing matters now except the present and every moment to come.

I'm currently stretched out on a lawn chair enjoying the sunshine—until a shadow falls over me.

"Party's winding down," Travis says, kneeling beside me as I open my eyes to gaze at my smokin' hot sex god of a husband. "Dani wants to sleep over with Max and Harper. I said it would be okay."

"Sure. She loves watching Max conjure flowers one at a time."

"He'll be a great dad."

I sit up straight, leaning toward Travis. "Dad? Is there some secret news I haven't heard?"

"Mm-hm." He slants closer until his lips graze my ear. "Harper's pregnant."

Though I want to shriek, I restrain myself. It sounds like they haven't told everyone yet. "That's wonderful. I'm so happy for them. Can I help arrange the baby shower?"

My husband smiles. "I'm sure Lindsey and Ennea would love the help."

"Well, those two did find me the perfect wedding dress."

"Sure did." He nuzzles my neck. "Couldn't wait to take that dress off you, though."

I see Max across the yard just as he looks at me. The incubus smirks and announces, "Time to go, people. Travis and Larissa need to…wash the dishes."

Naturally, he's using "dishes" as a euphemism for sex. And oh yes, I need to get my husband naked right now.

Dani trots over to say goodbye, kissing me and Travis on the cheek. Then she and our guests disappear.

Except for one. Tris ambles over to us, hands stuffed into his jeans pockets, shoulders hunched. Though he'd once been a scrawny guy who looked like a teenager, Triskaideka the leprechaun has since transformed into a muscular hottie just like his friends Travis and Max. Tris has kept his red hair, but his freckles have mostly faded. Just like with Travis, Tris's change also affected his voice. He's lost his Bronx accent in favor of a general American one.

"Go away," my husband tells the leprechaun. "We're going to shag, and no, you can't watch."

Tris wrinkles his nose. "Don't want to. Got a thing to talk to you about, though."

"A thing?" Travis scrunches his eyebrows. "What are you on about?"

"You, uh, owe me one. Said the P-word back when—Well, you remember what happened."

When we both lay dying, Travis had begged Tris to "please" heal me first. That incurred a small magical debt between them.

"I get it," I say. "You want to call in Travis's debt."

"Yeah, but not for anything bad. Just need a little help."

My husband squints at his friend. "What sort of help?"

"Finding the right girl for me. A few pointers, that's all I need."

"Pointers?" With a resigned sigh, Travis nods. "All right, fine, I'll help. But not tonight."

"Sure, later. That's cool."

Grinning, Tris vanishes.

Travis teleports us straight into our bedroom. And of course, we both arrive at our destination naked.

"Crawl under the covers," he murmurs into my ear, "and close your eyes."

I obey my husband, but only because the way he whispered that command in his hot incubus voice makes me instantly wet for him.

Flames erupt from Travis's body, then snuff out. A cute little red salamander now sits on the floor beside the bed. I've always thought it was weird that an incubus, a being who feeds on sex, can turn into such an adorable and tiny creature.

He crawls up the bedpost and under the covers.

Tiny salamander feet skitter up my calf, making me giggle. I toss the covers off so I can watch Travis hop over my kneecap and walk up my thigh until he reaches my hip. He stretches out his little salamander neck, sniffing the hairs on my mound. His tiny red lips curve into a smile, and his eyes drift half-closed. Then he scampers up my tummy to leap onto my breast.

And I giggle again.

The salamander emits a tiny burst of flame as Travis shifts into human form—his body stretched out over mine and his hard cock nestled inside me.

"No foreplay?" I ask. "Guess you're already taking me for granted."

"That will never happen." He rolls his hips into me, and I gasp. "This is how I worship my goddess, Larissa the badass god slayer."

"I didn't slay Eros. I wounded him."

"He was on the ground, whimpering and whining, with blood pouring out of—"

"Yuck. Don't talk about blood when we're having sex."

"Sorry." He flips us over, positioning me on top of him while keeping his cock buried inside me. "Let me apologize by letting you take control of me."

"Hmm, that's an interesting idea."

"Do anything you want to me."

"Conjure me a scarf, please."

He flourishes his hand, producing a silky blue scarf.

I push up to sit astride him, which sinks his length deeper inside my body. I shiver a little because it feels so damn good. Then I drag the scarf over my shoulder, down to my breasts, and let the fabric flutter onto his belly.

He sucks in a breath. "Larissa…"

"Shh." I lean over to thread the scarf through the rails on the headboard, tying one end of the scarf to his left wrist, then the other to his right wrist. "You're at my mercy now."

We both know he could snap that scarf with barely a flick of his wrist, but that's not the point. He wants me to take control and make him go off like a supernova. And by the stars, I want that too.

I pinch his nipples between my teeth, one at a time, loving the way he growls and arches his back. His erection has gotten even stiffer, and the heat of it drives me crazy with the need to fuck him until we both scream. So I lift my body until only the head of his cock remains inside me, then I slam down onto him and start rocking my hips wildly, too starved for him to think or to care about anything except our bodies joined and writhing. He lunges his hips up every time I slam down onto him, and my breasts bounce. He tries to surge upward and latch onto my nipple, but the scarf restrains him, so he locks both legs around me and pulls me down until his mouth can reach my aching peak. He suckles it fiercely, grunting and growling while we both climb higher and higher toward the climax that will devastate us.

He thrusts like a mad man, while I cling to him and cry out. The slapping of our flesh echoes in the room, and sweat glistens on our bodies.

"Travis!" I shout, clawing my nails on his chest.

"Fuck," he snarls, then shreds the scarf with one swift tug, sending fragments flying.

In an instant, we move from the bed to the wall, with Travis pinning my body there while he pounds into me and his eyes swirl like a tornado, the brilliant colors colliding and separating in rhythm with our lovemaking. He thrusts into me so powerfully that I can't hold back anymore. I come with a hoarse scream, clutching him with my arms and legs, digging my nails into his back and gritting my teeth while my body squeezes his length over and over. He punches into me even harder, even deeper, as his release explodes inside me—and I come again with even more strength.

By the time our cries have faded away, we're both struggling to catch our breath. Sweat slicks our bodies, but Travis whisks us straight into the shower with the water already running, tuned to the perfect temperature.

And he's still buried inside me. His cock has softened, but I know it won't stay that way for long.

"Let's get dirtier before we get clean," he murmurs into my ear. "Promise I'll rub you down after."

"That would involve getting dirty again."

"Exactly." He nibbles on my earlobe. "Dani's with Max and Harper. We've got all night to do anything and everything you want."

"Already have everything." I lean my head back against the tile wall, letting the water drizzle down my skin. Not even a hot shower steams me up half as well as Travis does. "What was that you said about getting dirty again?"

He smiles in the sizzling way that always means he's about to fly me to the stars and back without moving one inch.

We do spend all night enjoying each other, with breaks to feed each other decadent desserts. Maybe I was created tens of thousands of years ago, but I never really lived until I became a mortal. Until I met a sexy, sarcastic incubus who made me so mad even while I sensed, deep down, that he might be the only one for me. Sure, our life together will probably involve the occasional world-ending peril, but with our extended family, we'll get through it all.

Hey, I wouldn't want life to get boring.

ANNA DURAND IS A BESTSELLING, MULTI-AWARD-WINNING AUTHOR OF contemporary and paranormal romance. Her books have earned bestseller status on every major retailer and wonderful reviews from readers around the world. But that's the boring spiel. Here are the really cool things you want to know about Anna!

Born on Lackland Air Force Base in Texas, Anna grew up moving here, there, and everywhere thanks to her dad's job as an instructor pilot. She's lived in Texas (twice), Mississippi, California (twice), Michigan (twice), and Alaska—and now Ohio.

As for her writing, Anna has always made up stories in her head, but she didn't write them down until her teen years. Those first awful books went into the trash can a few years later, though she learned a lot from those stories. Eventually, she would pen her first romance novel, the paranormal romance *Willpower*, and she's never looked back since.

Want even more details about Anna? Get access to her extended bio when you subscribe to her newsletter and download the free bonus ebook, *Hot Scots Confidential*. You'll also get hot deleted scenes, character interviews, fun facts, and more! Plus you'll receive the short story *Tempted by a Kiss* and mutliple bonus chapters in both ebook and audiobook formats.

VISIT ANNADURAND.COM TO SIGN UP.